Jigsaw

Janet E Sahafi

*For Marian ~
from one writer to
another ~ enjoy!*

J E Sahafi

POOLBEG

*All characters in this publication are fictitious and
any resemblance to real persons, living or dead, is
purely coincidental.*

Published 1999 by
Poolbeg Press Ltd
123 Baldoyle Industrial Estate
Dublin 13, Ireland

© Janet E Sahafi 1999

The moral right of the author has been asserted.

The Arts Council
An Chomhairle Ealaíoı
A catalogue record for this book is available from the British Library.

ISBN 1 85371 862 9

Cover photography by Attard
Cover design by Artmark
Set by Poolbeg Group Services Ltd in Berkeley 10.5/14
Printed by The Guernsey Press Ltd,
Vale, Guernsey, Channel Islands.

A Note on the Author

Janet E Sahafi is an addictions counsellor and psychodramatist who has presented Healing Workshops and retreats throughout the US, in Ireland and in Israel. She has also worked as a professional actor and yoga instructor. She has a Master of Science Degree in Education (as a literature major) and has taught in colleges of the State University of New York.

In 1991 she took a leap of faith by leaving her teaching work and psychotherapy practice and coming to Ireland to write. Her play "The Unravelling" was performed at the Beckett Theatre, Trinity College, in 1996. *Healing the Past*, on spiritual healing through psychodrama, was published by Poolbeg in 1997. *Jigsaw* is her first novel.

She currently divides her time between Ireland and the US. She loves dancing, the sea and Donegal – especially the Grianán of Aileach.

For Kate Cruise O'Brien
My Mentor, Midwife and Muse

A big thank you to all those who have supported me through this endeavor, especially my friends, my father and other family members. I also want to express my gratitude to Coleman for the use of his computer in the final edit of this project.

My only wish is that Kate Cruise O'Brien could be here now to help celebrate the publication of this novel which she really called into being. Her belief in my writing gave me the confidence to follow my dream. Gaye Shortland has been a wonderful friend and of great assistance in Kate's absence in guiding this work to completion.

I'd also like to acknowledge Maeve Binchy for the encouragement she's given me and all aspiring authors, by her admission of occasions of self-doubt that still arise even after becoming a successful author and her insistence on the need to be determined, persistent and positive.

Lastly, but most importantly, I thank my Creator for calling me to Ireland and giving me the time, courage and creative energy to write this novel. It has been healing, challenging and exciting.

Prologue

Pick up stix. Throw them up in the air and see where they land. Jigsaw puzzle. Match the colors and the shapes. Try to find where the pieces fit. Square peg in a round hole won't fit no matter how hard it's pushed.

Bits and pieces. People, places, things. Colliding, bumping up against her, shattering her sense of reality over and over again. Each person a larger-than-life puzzle piece, a player. Or places: houses, towns, geographical areas she was dropped into and then uprooted from. Things: things of big consequence or small, tiny as ant-hills. Who knows what will make the difference in a person's life – make one a prince, or a pauper, or a drama queen? Somebody's idea of a joke no doubt, a hat trick to deceive the heart, confuse the mind. Pieces with the answers written on them are buried in a dust-bowl of dreams but their outlines linger to haunt her waking hours.

While dancing with ghosts whose stories are told, she speaks her truth to you. Walk with her. Experience her as she moves through the maze and tries to put her life together, to make it all fit.

In the beginning there's a pile of jigsaw pieces and nothing makes much sense. As she fits each piece in place a picture begins to emerge, as through a glass darkly. But, when she comes face to face with the image, will it hold the answer that she is seeking?

Grammaw

Armored tank. Defended. More than defended – barricaded to the max! Twelve gores of boring beige material carefully cut, patiently matched. She'd make the bodice later – first worry about the skirt of the dress that could house all five of her grandchildren within its waist.

Oh, the threat of that waist!

"You'll be the one, Genelle. You'll be the one that ends up like me!"

She must have heard me coming down the steps from our utility room. I stop in the basement hallway outside her apartment door that stands slightly open, while wafting aromas of freshly popped corn and melted butter entice me in. Laughingly, I discount her statement to cover up the murky possibility of truth.

"No, no Grammaw, that's not possible," I say, confidently striding to the stove, grabbing a bowl and scooping a good-size helping of this evening's nirvana. "I have a twenty-one-inch waist."

The voice of doom continues from the big-armed, stuffed rocking-chair. "When I was nineteen, I had a nineteen-inch waist. I'm tellin' you, you're gonna end up just like me."

Lonely, bitter, sarcastic, battle-axe, intelligent but who cares, two hundred and eighty pounds, wrapping ace bandages around her swollen ankles and legs. How could they hold up all that weight day after day? Is that what you had in mind for your life, Genelle? No, thank you.

"You know what puzzles me, Mom?" I know she hears me, but she doesn't even pause as she empties the dishwasher. "How does Grammaw stay so heavy? I mean, she doesn't eat any more than we do."

Mom leans against the sink for a minute, looking out of the window. It's Pennsylvania not Oklahoma. She looks at trees, lots of them. The hillside sloping down to the stream in our backyard on the Mainline. Then softly she looks at me. She's tired. "Watch what she eats when the table is cleared," she says.

Hmmmn.

Carcasses cleaned as if by a bird of prey. Bowls scraped onto a dirty plate, "No need throwin' this out." Pieces of cake or pie wrapped up in napkins to "save" for us, but they disappear down the stairs to Grammaw's apartment.

"What was it like when you got married, Grammaw? Were you scared on your wedding night?" I ask.

"Hush, child. What made you think of such a thing!" She always talks to me like I'm ten, not eighteen.

She falls silent. Is she remembering?

❖ ❖ ❖ ❖

Oklahoma, 1906.

Standing.

She was still standing there close to the bedroom door.

"How long are you going to stay over there, Annie? Come warm me in the bed." Joseph had been waiting a long time for this night. Now she was his. He shouldn't have to wait any more.

Annie twisted the ribbon laced through the yoke of her camisole. She had been almost an hour undressing. Slowly taking down her hair and brushing it, unlacing her boots, corset, hooped skirt, slips, and putting them away. He lay in the bed watching. She was thinking of the wedding. It had been acceptable. Everyone invited had come. All said she had married a good man – loyal, hardworking. The children in the lane next to the dry-goods store would have to stop their chiding chant *"Ole Maid Annie, smart as a penny, still can't catch herself a man!"* No doubt they had heard the gossip in their kitchens and put it to their own tune. She had finally stilled all the wagging tongues. But now, what to do?

She scrunched up her shoulders and wrung her hands, looking at him in the bed. How am I ever to get through this? While Joseph was courting her, she had allowed him a few kisses, had tried to soften her lips to feel something – some sensation. But, there was nothing, only a tightness in the pit of her stomach. She tolerated his kisses. He had been her only suitor. Others had been scared off by her learning. But Joseph had a quick wit and a twinkle in his eye. He was intent upon having her – learning and all. And she had accepted the proposal, figuring she could manoeuvre the man, still get a job teaching somewhere, cook him his meals, and just do the household chores. That should be good enough. But the bedroom she had blanked out of her mind. She hadn't wanted to think about it. Now he was expecting her to lie next to him.

She summoned her courage. "He can try what he likes, but he'll never get the best of me," she thought to herself. "I'll out-wait him, out-think him, out-smart him on every score. Joseph Butler won't have his way with me just because I wear his ring or carry his name."

5

It took two months of marriage before Annie allowed Joseph to undo the drawstring of her bloomers and enter her. She felt only pain. Pain and annoyance. She hated the sweat of him dropping onto her nightgown and the smell of him filling up the bed. She got up afterwards and opened the window wide, grumbling to herself. Went to the woodstove and got the kettle, taking care to wash herself and make some bleach-water for the gown and the bloomers and the sheets. She made him get up, go out and pump some more water to soak them. While he was outside, she got fresh nightclothes, stripped the bed, and used cloth bandages to keep any more of her blood from staining the spare set of sheets.

She'd done her duty. He could say no more. But she hated him for it. She hated his long lanky body on top of her. She felt like she would be crushed by it. She would refuse this again and again. Under her armor, padding began to grow. Layers and layers of you-can't-reach-me-I-won't-feel-you fat started to fill in around the bones and balloon the thick skin outwards.

❖ ❖ ❖ ❖

"Well, did you think Granpaw was handsome?"

She pauses too long. My eighteen-year-old curiosity is getting to her. "He was all right, Genelle."

I study the pictures in the old frames that hang in the sitting-room of her basement apartment in our house on the Mainline, just outside of Philadelphia. Her waist does look small, and she was sort of pretty then too. She looked like such a lady. Funny clothes though. Skirts to the ground and high-collared starched blouses. "What's this picture of you with a bunch of other girls?" I shout in to her. She is in her bedroom getting dressed for church.

"Oh, that's from Valparaiso Teachers' College. Those are my classmates for the two years I was there."

I stare at Granpaw's picture. His eyes look like glass marbles of the palest blue. He looks a bit scary. A bit like a corpse with its eyes open.

"That's how I remember Granpaw, bald like this picture. Was he bald like that when you met him?"

"My, you're full of questions today." She is in the room now adjusting her belt. She has to make all her own clothes and belts because nothing sold in the stores is big enough to go around her. "No. He had a great shock of jet-black hair. That picture was taken years later."

I stare at his photo again. His eyes seem so frozen and fearful. No emotion in the face. Wherever he was hiding, it was down deep – to the outside world nobody was home.

Did she do this to him?

A stubborn woman can wear a man down. A bitter woman can wear a man away.

❖ ❖ ❖ ❖

Annie stood at the window in the kitchen of the farmhouse, looking out across the Oklahoma plain. Not even a tree to break the monotony of the horizon. The air was thick and still with the dark yellow light that comes before a storm. Even the chickens were hushed. She'd almost finished her chores. There'd be no getting on supper now with the storm coming. Doreen was working on her sums in the front room. Dirk had gone out to help his father get the animals penned up before it hit. Winona was outside. She was playing in the mud puddle around the hand-pump, making pies. God bless that child.

7

The house could catch on fire and she'd make sure and get her rag-doll and kitten out safely. Annie's back hurt from the work and the weight and the resentments she carried around in her gut like chunks of anthracite.

She went out into the yard to get in the clothes off the line before the twister hit. She was slow and deliberate. Part of her couldn't care less if it hit the little house directly and killed the whole lot of them. At least it would be over, this dull monotonous drudgery. She was sick of it.

It had been years since anything more than a superficial word had passed between herself and Joseph. She knew that Winona at age eight was getting too big to sleep in between them any more. She wanted to ignore that fact. But the squirming body and accidental kicks at night from the lengthening limbs of her youngest child were disturbing her own sleep these days. She couldn't bear the thought of Joseph's rough, clay-stained hands on her own starched nightgown again.

She didn't want any more children. She didn't want any more of him.

"That's it," she said to herself, putting the last of the wooden pegs in the cloth bag. "Clinton can give up the day-bed and take the cot from the shed for himself when he's home on the weekends. I'll move the day-bed into the sittin'-room and Joseph will sleep in there, and that's that!" She held the stiff shirts and denims in her big arms and was aware of the smell of the morning's sunshine still lingering on them, even with the storm about to break.

Dust began to kick up and blow around her. "Come on inside, Winona." Little mother with straggly light-brown hair looked up from her mud-pies. "Come on now. We've got to get those muddy hands washed quick, and get down in the root cellar with your Doreen. Twister's on its way."

Annie had seen them come, seen them go. Butcher's place

8

was flattened. Jason's homestead lost in one a few years back. The outbuildings as well. First year her family was in Oklahoma they survived two twisters. Bernadette Maura Russell, fiery Irishwoman, loved Annie's brothers but gave her only daughter the back of the wooden spoon, or the kick under the table or the handle of the broom. Sometimes even she didn't know why.

One time Annie had fled screaming back into the covered wagon that had carried them from Idaho into the Indian Territory of Oklahoma. Annie's dad was building a place for them, but in the meantime the wagon was still home for the eight of them. Yes, screaming Annie had come scrambling up the front of the buckboard, grabbing the canvas to hoist herself inside. Her fear was yelping out of her while the words whirled around in her head – *Red squirrel, never saw one before, just staring at it, Mama, and it flew at me! Flew at me! Out of the tree, came flying, almost landed on top of me, teeth, scary little teeth. I saw them, tiny pinned-back ears* – slobbering Annie was. Through tears she glimpsed the broom-handle come at her before she could even get the terrifying picture of what had happened out of her mind and into words rather than sound. Raging mother smacked her about her legs and buttocks, clipping her elbow then shoulder with the wooden pole as Annie got rigid like iron under the blows. The terror left. Numbness. Hardness growing in the seven-year-old body. Growing. Making leathery skin. One of too many beatings. Layers of armor beginning to form as she criss-crossed her arms over her crown, with her hands covering her ears against her mother's yelling, while protecting her head from the blows.

"Thankless child! Always lookin' for attention, screechin' like a banshee. Give you somethin' to screech about, you little wench. You'll stay in the wagon and learn what's good for you!"

Blows and torrents of words over the years intended to

break, subdue, shame into submission, only made her tough and determined. Annie went to Valparaiso long before most women got educated, and she became a teacher.

❖ ❖ ❖ ❖

Grammaw Annie sent my first reader to me in Philadelphia when I was sick in bed for a year at age six and missed out on first grade. I sat on my bed. I liked feeling the handmade cloth cover of maroon fabric. Looked at the letters made just for me. Drew them in a copybook my mom got for me. No sums, just letters. Then words. Some pictures pasted in the book. Stories. Simple stories I then taught myself to read.

First letter I wrote was to Grammaw. She was still out in Oklahoma where I'd left her and Granpaw. Didn't want to go. Didn't want to leave Granpaw. Didn't want to leave my dog Chippy, or the swing Granpaw had made me, or the only home I knew. Mainly, I didn't want to leave Granpaw.

❖ ❖ ❖ ❖

"This is your daddy."

I stare at them. I think I know Mommy a bit from her smell and I think I remember her voice. But this tall man that she bends to lift me up to I don't know at all. Grammaw stops Mommy's reaching arms with a left hand and scoops me up herself.

"Now Winona, you know you shouldn't be bendin' and liftin'."

I want to get down. I squirm my three-and-a-half-year-old body against the huge tree-trunk of a woman that is my Grammaw. I pat the back of her neck, my finger in my mouth. Sun's bright and hot. I frown against it, squinting to see my Mommy-just-come-back and the Daddy-with-her.

10

"Ellie, take your finger out of your mouth," Mommy says. I do know that voice.

I pat Grammaw's neck harder and turn her face to mine. "I want my granpaw. Where's Granpaw? I want to get down," I whimper.

"Now, now child." I watch my new white shoes meet hard-packed red soil as I'm lowered. Mommy takes my hand. Hers feels nice and soft. She fixes a bow in my blonde curls. Her face close up smells like the flowers.

The car is big and black and it is hot as I lean my back against the fender and hold Chippy tightly. Mommy kneels beside me. They snap the Brownie.

"Winona, you make sure and write regular now."

"I will, Mama."

"And Raymond, you make sure she takes care of herself and doesn't work too hard. We don't want to hear she's sick again."

He sticks out his hand. Grammaw's big, fleshy arm moves to shoo a fly, then shakes his hand strongly.

The car feels hot inside to me. Through the window I watch for my granpaw. Grammaw's big body blocks the view of the barn-door. I push my nose and fingers against the glass.

"Sit down, honey. Your daddy's going to start the car now."

"I'm hot, Mommy."

"It'll be cool when we start to move."

The back seat of the car is as big as the day-bed. The gray fuzzy material scratches and tickles my bare legs in a way I don't like. I look at the blue and white striped dress Mommy has put on me. I like it. I reach to feel the ruffles on the edge of my new panties. I think of Granpaw and start to whimper again.

"I want to say bye-bye to Granpaw. Where is he, Mommy?"

"That's a good question," Raymond says roughly. "Does that man have no manners at all?"

I start to cry.

"Hush now, Ellie. Don't cry. We're going to our new home. Your daddy's taking us to Pennsylvania. You'll like it there."

"Will Granpaw be there?"

Raymond starts the engine and makes it roar. It sounds angry. I feel scared.

"Granpaw and Grammaw will come and visit us there lots. You'll see." Mommy's hand pats my knee and then the shoulder of my-daddy-Raymond. She gives me a pink hankie to blow my nose.

"But if Granpaw wants me to come and see him, can I?"

"Sure, honey. Sure," she promises.

She promises.

The car lurches forward. I scoot my knees over the scratchy stuff on the seat to look out of the sedan's back window, straining for a glimpse of the one I knew most, loved best, but see only Grammaw, handkerchief in hand, other arm behind her back. Waving hankie. Waving hanging flesh where the big dress sleeve is scrunched from her uplifted arm.

I feel sick in my tummy as I start to cry again. I watch the farmhouse and Grammaw get smaller and smaller. Never see Granpaw.

※ ※ ※ ※

Inside the barn, Joseph Butler stuck the pitchfork forcefully into the hay. Pitching it into the loft. Stabbing the pile, using his strength to throw huge bunches of it. He knew his little Ellie was leaving him. Sweat mixed with the tears running down his face. Stabbing, hoisting, throwing hay. Silent.

The house was empty again. Only her and him left. She set her jaw. She'd be gone soon enough. Tomorrow would be here and she'd be gone the eighty miles back to Tyler, back to the regular routine of weekly teaching away and coming back on the weekends. "He'll get over Ellie leaving." She blew her nose then went into the kitchen. The apple-pie she'd baked for lunch lay on the table half-finished. She sat down and had a bite.

❖ ❖ ❖ ❖

Upstate New York, 1976.

I'm standing by the barstool, trying to make a decision, wanting what is in all those colored bottles on the other side of the counter. I'm like a kid in a candy store with Big Daddy dripping money into my palm.

"What'll it be, sugar? What's going to make you happy tonight? Come on, let me buy you a drink."

Will I have a Black Russian or a Grasshopper? No, get a White Russian. The cream will get the double shot down faster and maybe he'll buy you another one before he even gets you out on the dance floor (or into his car).

Carlos Ramirez, get out of my head with your persuasive Puerto Rican pirana eyes. I didn't "ask for it"! I was a naive little schoolgirl, just happened to have an above-average thirst. I didn't know the code, the game, or the city. I stuck my fingers into your neck, trying to choke you off of me, silently screaming for help.

Look, Genelle. It's not him. It's not Puerto Rico. You're not drinking Cuba Libres, and you're not eighteen any more. Joe's Disco is starting to fill up. I think of my sleeping children. They should be fine on their own for a few hours. "All I want to do is dance. I'm only gonna drink water tonight," I have pledged to myself. "Just need to get out and dance. I'll only have a drink if somebody offers to buy me one."

13

Ladies' Night at Joe's. Anyone want to place bets on the water?

"I'll take a White Russian," I say with the taste already in my mouth. After a few swallows, I glance sideways at my benefactor. Not bad. Nice chocolate-colored skin and I like the silk shirt. Disco Dan? Could be. Sweep me off my feet!

I know how to have fun. Not like Grammaw.

She's the one buried out in Oklahoma, buried in the dust-bowl of dreams that happened too late when nobody, hardly even her sweet Winona, cared. No fun in that.

Grammaw. A gray-haired woman in a graduation cap and gown. I had the photo but didn't have a clue what it meant to her to go back to school and graduate from the University at age sixty-four. Years of doing the washing on a scrub-board, washing work-clothes, play-clothes, hand-sewn denim. All of it stained by the red clay of the Oklahoma soil, ground so poor that not much would grow unless you broke your back working at it, and even then there was no guarantee. Why else would they give it to the Indians?

Cut off your nose to spite your face, that's my Grammaw for you. Show you how to get things done. Show you how things should be run. Show you how to wield an axe. Carrie Nation. Chop up the counter of a bar for the Women's Temperance League. Chop off relations with your own son, Clinton, cause he won't give up the "demon drink". Chop off Granpaw's vitals. Castrate and cast aside the man who wanted to love you, and stride the wind, strong mountain of a woman. Alone. Lonely. Longing.

No matter how armored the tank, thick the skin, fat-insulated the emotions, inside a seven-year-old little girl cries, powerless. Powerless as she watches her youngest child – sweet, good, gentle Winona – die. And that one. That one she

14

couldn't dominate. That Jew-boy Raymond, put her out at age seventy-four. Threw her out of the little downstairs apartment in Pennsylvania. Put a stop to her cutting tongue, her challenges, her control of his children.

Grammaw shrank. She shrivelled. Retreated back to Oklahoma.

I brought my young children to visit an old woman lying in a bed, white and gray. Bonnet like a young girl would wear was tied about her head as she slept and stirred in dreams. Then, only then, crying softly, she told me of the beatings she received as a child, the kicks in the back and behind the knees. Armor Falling Off. "Just let me die in peace," she prayed. "It should have been me; it should have been me, not your mother. It should have been me die back then, not my Winona."

Raymond

Broad shoulders. Broad enough to carry a chip on them the size of a city block – a South Philly block. It's the home of oil refineries, rough neighborhoods, air that looks dingy yellow and smells bad enough to make you want to hold your breath driving through it in the hot summertime with the windows all rolled up. And even then, can't get through it quick enough – South Philadelphia. His hometown.

He was the kick-the-dog-kid, the scapegoat. The never-do anything-right, won't-amount-to-anything, nothing-but-trouble-to-his-folks (but his mom never completely gave up on him) son. The originator of the "I'll-show-you-you're-gonna-be-the-sorry-one" attitude.

Raymond had speed, looks, and a taste for the big time. Risk-taker, crap-shooter, smooth-talker. Dropped out of school at fifteen and hustled quick money on the streets. Left home at seventeen after taking someone else's car and going for a joy-ride. One more notch on the belt of narrow escapes from the law; the police were coming in the front door of his folk's flat and he went out the back and just kept going.

Run, run, fast as you can. You can't catch Raymond, he's

the gingerbread man. Shot some fast craps in a back alley and hopped a train south.

What's the plan, Stan? Raymond always had to have a plan, a scheme, always had to prove himself right.

"Right. Right, here's the plan – let's see, I'll keep going south, yeah South Carolina. That's it. I'll go to Camp Lejune and join the Marines. They're drafting people left and right. I'll go blow up some Nazis and come back a hero! They'll be sorry for all they said about me. I'll come back with ribbons. They'll have a parade." He rested his head back against the train seat. All the cars were packed. Late arrivals sitting on their baggage in the aisles. Sardines stuffed in a can, some wearing army khakis, others bell-bottom sailor whites, flirting with the girls in the flowy, flowery, flimsy dresses. It was hot, but he didn't mind it. He made himself at home and dreamed a little dream of Raymond the war hero.

The train had a layover in Washington DC for the connection to South Carolina. He saw a girl walking down the platform in a red straight skirt. She looked good to him. Real good. He couldn't see her face, but her back drew his gaze like a magnet. Lovely rounded bottom like two large ripe red fruit bigger than life saying, "I'm the best there is and I'm fresh and ready for picking." She was talking to a friend, but he didn't let that stop him. He was on his way to the Marines to be a hero but didn't let that stop him either. No, what stopped him in his tracks was her legs and the way she looked in that straight skirt and heels. He went right up to her and stuck out his hand. "Raymond Stone's the name, wheel of fortune's my game. *Ooh ooh*, today looks like my lucky day."

Winona blushed and continued to talk to her girlfriend. He's tall and handsome, she thought, but he sure is full of himself.

"Say, could you two spare ten minutes to have a soda with

a guy on his way to die for his country?" What's a slight exaggeration if it gets you in the door?

Ten minutes. Ten days. Two weeks. Raymond put the Marines on hold and started slinging ham and eggs in a diner in DC. He was bound and determined to make this girl his for keeps. She had a helluva great job in a big office building and was making lots of money. She cooked and sewed her own clothes. Lots of gals could do that. But boy, could she dance!

Glen Echo Park – out on the dance floor on a late May night – warm and sultry on the outskirts of Washington DC – the end of the trolley line. Glenn Miller had them in the mood and Raymond sang his heart out, danced his shoes off, and asked her to marry him. Must have been a heat wave on. Check the stats.

Winona was flushed and struggled to keep her feet on the ground and her knees together. He was slick and a bit of a show-off that's for sure, but he was crazy about her, and every time she heard his voice her heart just pounded so loud she thought they'd be likely to hear it clear back in Oklahoma.

He lied about his age, his schooling, and his surname. Never mentioned his scrapes with the law. Never mentioned his religion.

Raymond listened to the operator putting through his collect call to Philadelphia. He was on a payphone in the lobby of the Ambassador Hotel. He could see the glass door to the hotel's coffee shop from where he was standing. He had just landed a job there to be in their front window and make doughnuts. Of course he'd never made a doughnut in his life. He lied to them. Made up a story about having been an experienced baker in Philly and had given them fake references. What could be so hard about it anyway? You just punch a hole in the centre of some dough and throw it in some grease. Piece of cake.

He heard his mother's worried voice accept the telephone charges. "Raymond? Raymond is that you?"

"Mom, yeah. Yeah, it's me? Listen, I'm in Washinton DC and I've met this wonderful girl. We're getting married. She's a dream, Mom." Raymond felt good. He felt like a million bucks. Winona had finally said "yes" to him. "It's all set, Mom. We're just saving money to go out to Oklahoma to meet her folks and tie the knot."

His mother's voice sounded like it was across an ocean, lots of static on the line. "Raymond, Raymond. What are you saying? What is this? We've been so worried about you! Why haven't you phoned? Your father almost had a heart attack when he realised you were really gone. And I, well, I haven't slept once since you dissappeared. How could you do that to us. And now you ring up and say you're getting married? *Oi gevalt!* You're trying to kill both of us, aren't you!"

"Come on, Mom. Don't yell at me. You're always yelling. And you know, if I was there right now Dad would just be throwing me out. I'm making something of myself here. I'm working. Working in the Ambassador Hotel. How do you like that? Nice, huh? And I'm stuck on this girl, Mom. She's great."

"Well, you hardly know her. Don't do something foolish, make a mistake you'll be sorry about for the rest of your life. You don't even know what kind of family she comes from!"

"They're farmers, Mom. I told you. From Oklahoma, 'salt of the earth' you know. And she's got a good job here. She's smart."

"Farmers? Oklahoma? I don't like the sounds of this. Is she a *shichsala*? Raymond, what are you doing? You're not thinking of marrying a Gentile, are you? Oh my God, you are! Listen, I'm getting on the train in the morning and coming down."

"It's no use, Mom. I've made up my mind. She's the one for

me. She doesn't have to be Jewish to believe in God, you know!"

"What a way to speak to your mother. *Haltz schmal und sagst nicht!* This is the beginning of the end of you. Mark my words. Where are you living? Tell me right this minute, Raymond! I'm coming down there tommorrow."

"Got to go, Mom. I'll be late for work. Don't come down here. Don't try to stop me. I know what I want and I'm going for it. If you try to stop me, if you do, I'll never speak to you again."

"But, Raymond. Listen to me, I'm your mother, I – "

"Bye Mom." Raymond put the phone down with authority, strode out of the hotel and headed uptown. Massachusetts Avenue and 17th Street – got to be a crap game around here somewhere. He felt big. His palm was itching. He felt lucky.

✜ ✤ ✛ ✤

Raymond knocked on the door harder. "Please Winona, let me in, talk to me. Look, I can explain." He could hear her sobbing. "It was a sure thing, baby. The guy told me it was a sure thing. He practically guaranteed it! You don't think I would have gambled your pay-check on a long shot, do you? Honey, please. I'm begging you, give me another chance!"

Basement apartments in Washington DC were the only hope of a bit of cool air in June of 1940. He kept banging on the door. She thought he might knock it down if he kept at it. On the bed, Winona cried because she couldn't help loving him, because she hated what he did to her, because she wanted to open the door, because life was so much easier on the farm out in Oklahoma in her own little world. If she could get him out of the city, she thought, he'd be OK. They'd be all right. "Oh God, why'd you make me love him so?" she whispered to the wall.

Two weeks later they were on their way to Bushmills, Oklahoma so Raymond could ask Winona's parents for permission to marry their daughter. Raymond sat scrunched up in the back seat of the Studebaker, all six foot four inches of him. Oklahoma dirt roads. Beads of sweat met for worried debate on his high forehead, as the two in summer hats and upswept hair chattered away in the front seat. They laughed a lot, Winona and her sister. He figured that was a good sign.

"God, this country is flat! No buildings, no trees. What do you do for fun out here?" he asked. More laughter. Lots of teeth. Doreen sure had a big set of teeth on her. Nobody answered his question. A few trees surprised the horizon on the right-hand side of the road. Doreen started slowing the car down as a small farmhouse came into view.

"Oh, look at that, Winona," she said with relief. "Mama's sitting out on the porch waiting for you. See, everything's gonna be all right, didn't I tell you?"

The three women stood around the Studebaker watching the lanky long-limbed eighteen-year-old Raymond climb out of the back seat trying to look the man. Quietly, out the side of the farmhouse, Joseph Butler pushed the wooden handle of the hand-pump up and down filling the pail to wash the farmyard off his hands. He took his bandanna out of the back pocket of his overalls and submerged it in the cool freshly pumped water. He doubled the faded red cloth and wrung it out. He wiped his face and neck slowly. He was tired. He looked out the back of the place and squinted at the sinking sun. "Nope," he decided, "can't say I'm wantin' to rest my bones across from some good-for-nothin' city-boy when there's still work to be done." He tied the damp bandanna around his neck and headed back out into the field.

Raymond tried. He schemed, he boasted, he bragged. He and

Winona attempted to raise chickens. Doreen taught him how to drive a car. That was after he assured her he already knew how to and landed the Studebaker in a deep ditch which Jansen's tractor had to pull them out of. Winona's father and Raymond never did get on. Raymond couldn't figure out the solemn, silent man who was more comfortable walking miles without a word than talking about the news or races or cars.

Winona's mother gave Raymond all the rope he needed. Her father just walked away. Raymond pitched hay with hayfever riddling his sinuses, rode horses bareback because he was too proud to ask someone to show him how to put on a saddle. He almost got himself killed when a horse he was riding to help move some cattle got spooked and took off at a full gallop. Raymond was bounced off the mare's back but held on to the mane for dear life. When Winona's cousins found him, the mare was pawing the ground and staring right into the ghostly white face of Raymond – nose to nose they were. His ankles were around the bay's shoulders and his hands still gripping her mane. He was terrified to let go and hit the ground for fear the horse would trample him. That was the deciding episode in "Raymond Conquers the West".

Raymond never did get Winona's folks to give their permission for the marriage. So they eloped. The army seemed like the only way to save face. Rather die on a battlefield than in a cow pasture. Finally he might even get a decent card-game going.

⊞ ⊠ ⊞ ⊠

Raymond. Raymond. Raymond. Crazy kid in a man's body. Army tried but didn't break him. Spent most of his time in the brig or the army hospital. Still had a knack for getting into trouble or getting hurt doing something cocky. But he loved his Winona. She never stopped loving him either. He was going to prove to the world she hadn't made a mistake putting her trust in him. And now that he had them back in Philly, he was doing it. No more craps, horses or cards.

Raymond. Did the jitterbug with his eight-year-old daughter. Raced the twelve-year-old boys around the block of row houses in West Philly now. A bit more class. Worked ten and twelve-hour days finishing patios, shovelling concrete, working his way through the muck to the ladder he hoped was there. Taught himself as he went along. Lightning learning by the seat of the pants had been his chance at holding on to her and making his way in the world. She might be three years older than him, but he was a fast learner. She had set him on the straight and narrow.

Would it last? What were the odds?

Winner takes all.

⚜ ⚜ ⚜ ⚜

My father's hand on the knob of the heavy oak door, a working-man's hand with the concrete washed off, still graying in the tiny lines around the ends of the long fleshy fingers. Door closes, shutting out the view of the light green Renault backing out of our driveway. It's the Thanksgiving holidays. The smell of burning leaves is in the afternoon air, and there is a chance of frost. Quan's worries had been unfounded. Everyone had been so nice. Really made him feel comfortable on his overnight stay with us.

Mom, pale, stands between my father and myself in the foyer of our home. She looks tired. I turn to go down the hall to my room. His hand moves off the knob to grip my shoulder tightly. Voice harsh and challenging, "Not so fast! You're not going anywhere right now."

"Dad, you're hurting me, let go!"

23

"Raymond, let me handle this," my mother pleads.

"No. You had your way up to now. We kept it nice and civilised while Charlie Chan was here. But it's my time now and she's gonna listen to me!"

Shock sets me down trembling on the moss-green sectional sofa, in the living-room of our nice suburban home outside Philadelphia, the "City of Brotherly Love". And now, it begins: "Life According to Raymond." Take 592. Mom sitting quietly in the armchair nods on cue whenever he looks at her. She's like a funny bobbing plastic toy on the dashboard of a stranger's car; head separate from body, resting on a spring. Maybe he was right. Maybe "she didn't know anything about anything", only how to nod as the car hit a bump or stopped too quickly.

"Is this what they're teaching you in that college I'm breaking my back to send you to? How to ruin your life? Huh? What the hell is going on in that stupid excuse of a mind of yours? Get this straight right now, Genelle, you're not to see him ever again!"

"But Dad, I love him!"

Sarcastic laugh curls his lip. "You don't know what love is. You can't love him. For Godsakes, he's Chinese! He's a different race! What do you think you're doing? Huh? Do you think I've worked my ass off day and night and built this house in a high-class neighborhood for you to bring a Chinaman home? Well? Look at me when I talk to you! What the hell can you be thinking of? I hope to God none of the neighbors saw him!"

I can't believe he's saying this! I want to shout at him, but I can't get my mouth opened. It's glued shut. He can't mean what he is saying? He can't forbid me to see Quan. He followed his heart, why can't I? And does he really think these neighbors accept us? That's a laugh! We don't fit in

24

here. The Mainliners dismantle the Alkis family over their cocktails. Our money's the wrong color, Dad. No matter how hard you work and how much you earn, face it – Jew money doesn't wash in the WASP world. It doesn't matter that Mom's Christian. Nothing matters to them. They're a bunch of snobs. That's all.

Scream at him, Genelle. Scream bloody murder!

I can't say a word to him. I hate myself. I just stare at the cleft in his chin. The top of my head wants to explode and fill the room with fire and smoke, so I can escape out the front door. I hate him. Hate the day I was born.

Damn it, don't make me hurt Quan.

I want a drink. Can't drink here! What the hell do we have a bar in this house for if nobody is allowed to drink in this family!

Dad's fist pounding on the table makes the ashtray nobody uses and the dish shaped like Oklahoma jump up and down in fear. His face is contorted as he spits out his words, spewing venom all over the blonde-mahogany coffee table. "Do as I say and take care of it yourself or I'll take care of it for you! You're not to see that slanty-eyed Chinaman again, understand? Answer me, Goddam it!"

Green bottles and brown ones and clear ones with orangey-brown or golden forbidden liquid in them that froths if I swish the bottle from side to side. Did that once at thirteen. Climbed over the top of the counter and slid the left cabinet door open a bit. That was before they got the locks on the cabinet doors. Swished one of them all right. Thought that Mom was down in Grammaw's apartment. But her voice calling me from the kitchen surprised me and sent me scrambling back over the formica countertop too soon to get to touch any more of those magic bottles.

"What are you making, Dad?"

"They're called Moscow Mules."

Copper mugs chilled in the freezer, filled with ginger beer and vodka with a squeeze of lime. Raymond prided himself on making a good drink. Never took a drop himself. His Lithuanian Grandad would be the only falling-down-drunk in the Alkis family. He'd make sure of it. At least that was his plan.

"Can I have a taste? Just a little taste, can I?" I was pushing it today. It was hot, middle of July, hadn't I just turned fifteen? Sweat ran down the copper barrel mugs – them mules were working hard carrying their pay-load. Ginger beer lived in green bottles. Limes smelled clean and tangy. Angry back turned as he brought the mule train to the visitors.

Mesmerised by the green.

Green syrup ran down the sides of vanilla ice cream. My eight-year-old eyes watch it run.

"I want that, Mommy."

"Okay, doll, if you clean your plate."

I know that the tingly, fuzzy, funny feeling I love is from that green stuff. A vanilla cone doesn't make my tummy warm and cheeks hot.

Mommy's hand takes mine and pulls me gently from the glass cabinet where the desserts are displayed.

"Daddy, I like this place. They have that green and white dessert. I'm gonna clean my plate. I won't spill the water. I promise." When that sweet green stuff was around, I didn't muss my dress, drop the fork, pick at my food, or knock over my glass.

"One *crème de menthe parfait* for the little lady, please."

Daddy's hand opened wide, gesturing in my direction, like a magic wand.

✠ ✿ ✣ ✤

"Fourth platoon all present and accounted for. Left face, right face, about face. *Hut, two, three, four.*" Trembling and proud I march in place. Five, no six-and-a-half, maybe seven. "Lift those knees up higher, soldier."

"Please count slower, Daddy, my legs are hurting."

"Tenshun."

Click my Buster Brown shoes tightly at the heels, and make my salute almost perfect. Repeat. "Fourth Platoon all present and accounted for," with lips stretched tightly, chin pressed back and my little jaw clamped.

"At ease, soldier."

"Yes, sir." Are my feet in the right place, not too wide apart? Will I pass inspection and get to go to the park and climb the monkey bars? I stand "at ease" in Mommy and Daddy's room. It is dark green like the woods behind our row house where the crazy man lives with no clothes on, Mommy says. I only peek in the woods sometimes, but I don't go inside where the trees are close together, too scary.

His big hand rests on my head for a moment.

Seven-year-old tries to weigh the pressure of the hand. "Did I pass inspection, Daddy?"

Be the boy, be the girl. Tell me what to do and I'll turn inside out for you, Daddy. You're so big and strong. I love it when you rub my legs and sing to me. They hurt so bad. I don't know why. Aren't I better? Can't I go out and play with the other kids? Why do you call me Irene, Daddy, when you sing me goodnight? Don't you know my name? *"The girl that*

27

I marry will have to be as soft and as pink as a nursery . . . "
Will you marry me when I'm big, Daddy – if I'm soft and pink?
Twirl me around again, Daddy. Catch me in your arms as we
dance. I think everybody is looking at us and smiling – even
the band. I'm the luckiest eight-year-old in the world. My new
dress has light-blue and white ruffles. It spreads out like the
ocean when you spin me around.

Quan

Little boy with eyes that couldn't lie about where he'd come from but could stare clean through the truth to the daydream the Tooth Fairy left. Still holding on to his stuffed-soft-bear-of-a-pal, Cuddles. He was eight waving goodbye to his mother as she headed back to Hong Kong and the rich tailor she had taken up with to take away the pain of her husband's death.

Lost lamb in Uncle Sam's land of the living, passed from aunt to aunt, and then to Uncle Wang at twelve who pronounced him "home". Quan's only sibling, sister Luanh, came later in sullen silence from the school she had been boarded in. Quan stared at her across the small kitchen table that was covered by a worn thin flowery oilcloth with red scalloped edges which matched the lantern's shade. Stared at her almond eyes, hoping to find a reflection of himself there. Or something else familiar. Something of the small woman that was his mother with a tight black bun at the nape of her neck above the mandarin collar of the black-on-black brocade dress she lived in and left in. No map back to her was found.

At thirteen, Quan was told he was to be a dentist. He must forget the baseball he threw at the circle drawn on the back wall of the garden. Pitching was for dreamers. One in a million chance to make good. Dentists had dignity and cash to spare. "Put your nose in those books and prove me right," his uncle said. A Chinaman is nothing if he doesn't use his brains.

Bridge over the River Kwai to a back alley in Chinatown USA (even in Washington DC) where the boys in the black silk jackets with the red dragons on them broke Quan's glasses, took his wallet, and threw him and his books into the puddle of stagnant garbage-growing black inky water. No lotus blossoms here. He learned to be fast on his feet, keep his glasses in his pocket, and take the long way home.

His first love was the Chinese siren in the red low-cut dress with the *fe ne* on Uncle's pin-up calendar in the back of the laundry. Her picture spoke to him. Steam rising from the big irons, smell of damp cotton, soap and starch sickeningly sweet when mixed with the sweat of those who labored over the baskets and baskets of shirts, blouses, sheets and fine tablecloths. Steam rising, caressing her, licking the lipstick on her mouth, her eyes peering out through the foggy mist to say, *"December's full moon is for you, Quan – only you"*. At fourteen, he was hers. At fifteen, he was Suzie Wong's, but a half a year later even Nancy Kwan's looks were not enough. He wanted to hold the real thing. Kiss real lips. Taste the promise his daydreams advertised.

He met Charlotte. At the Chinese church with her four sisters. She giggled with them as he went by, but her eyes were not laughing. They were challenging him to turn around and select her out of the garden of lilies tittering in Sunday's breeze.

Walking her home from school gave him a chance to see her pinch-me-pink lipstick up close and count her teeth when she smiled. He would make a good dentist.

Though he carried his books with him to her house, to the library with her, back and forth to school as he walked her, they were opened less and less and the thrill of touching the round softness of a female filled his thoughts and the space between them.

Wang didn't tolerate this for long. As soon as the grade report showed a lapse in Quan's conscientious concentration, Charlotte's parents received a phone call and the bud was plucked off the stem before it began to open.

Quan studied three and a half hours a night and worked for the laundry at the cash register two hours each evening and all day Saturday. Once a week he was allowed to go out with friends to the movies or a dance, but Uncle's curfew was tight and that left only Sunday, which was a day of worship and rest. Charlotte's eyes had found another suitor and Quan no longer looked her way in school or in church.

The sexual energy that was burning to find an outlet exploded into rock and roll. He was permitted to watch thirty minutes of television a day. For him that was a trip to heaven called *American Bandstand*. 1958 and don't be late. Turn it on and turn it up. Do the slop and the stroll, and don't stop till you get it out. Twist and shout!

So what if Charlotte Woo was out the window? Blonde-haired, blue-eyed Justine Correlli of *American Bandstand* took her place. In his dreams, he slow-danced her off of the television screen and into soft curtains of satin that matched the sky of her eyes. She swooned as he kissed her.

He dazzled them at the dances. The girls all thought he was great as he romanced them around the floor, but his heart belonged to Justine. Between the last bell of the school day and the ring of the laundry's cash register, there were thirty minutes of pure bliss. Of doing the jive, the "cha-lypso," and the slow, slow moves while he imagined Justine's curves pressed up against his body – the body of a sixteen-year-old that was ready for action.

"Hold my hand now, Ellie," says Mom, in a flowered print maternity blouse, as she crosses the street with me. I am her seven-year-old little Goldilocks. It is early autumn and the few trees that struggle to maintain their dignity among the concrete, asphalt, and row-to-row brick houses of Overbrook Park, West Philadelphia, have turned their perfunctory yellow and brown. No maples here to blow their red trumpet triumphantly.

Mommy's hand feels good but I'm not a baby any more. I'm in school now. The baby's coming. That's what Daddy says. Every day. "Let's listen to the baby in Mommy's big belly." I don't hear anything. I try. I feel it move under my head as I rest on Mommy's lap sometimes. It feels weird, like a kitty or something – not like me. The spare room has a cot in it now for when the baby comes.

Mommy says I can look at some new shoes today if I eat my lunch good. My legs are hurting again.

"Are we almost there, Mommy? I'm tired. My legs are tired."

"Be a good girl, Ellie. Be the big girl now. We have only a few more blocks to go. I really fancy some different food and a good long walk today. You can have my chicken pieces if you don't complain any more."

I bite my lip and walk. I don't want to cry. But I don't want the "charley-horse" to come behind my knees again. Daddy rubs my legs and sings to me at night when they hurt. That helps. But after he's gone, when it's dark and I close my eyes tight to try and sleep, it feels like something is sticking pins and needles in my legs and I cry. Just to myself. Quietly. Can't get out of bed. It's dark in the hallway and that's where the

32

boogie man hides at night. Mommy and Daddy are downstairs in the back of the house. I hear the television sounds.

I'm glad the bad man with the long needle doesn't come to my room any more. He made me cry all the time, poking my arm, making blood come out. Mommy said it would make me better. Why was she so scared and hiding her face against my closet door? Why did she let him do that to me, hurt me like that? I never ate the lollipops he left me.

"One chicken chow mein, yes?"

I look at the strange face on the woman. It's different. Like a mask. She doesn't look at me but goes away and comes back with a plate of steamy gooey stuff that has a handful of thin white things on top for Mommy. Oh, "chicken pieces". I get them on my plate with curly crackers out of the bowl.

"Who's that man staring at us? Look, Mommy! He's so old. Why is he looking at us?"

"Don't point, Ellie. That's not polite. He's not looking at us. He's just daydreaming. He doesn't even see us, I don't think."

His face is strange too like the woman's and all scrinched up. His eyes are hard to see in the wrinkly skin. He scares me. He is staring at me. I don't think he likes me.

I eat everything on my plate. I get to look at new shoes.

"Can't I have the brown and white saddles, Mommy? All the kids have shoes like that."

"No, honey. You know you have to wear the special shoes with the wedges and arch supports. They don't come in that style."

No more red Buster Browns either. Just these ugly black or dark brown shoes that look like something my Daddy would wear and cover with concrete. They're so yucky-looking. I hate them. And they're so heavy. They make my legs tired just going up the stairs. "Please, Mommy," I beg. She pats my head and talks to the salesman.

I look through the window of the magic machine in the shoe shop – Florascope – even the name is magic. I see my green feet. They don't have any skin and are just bones wiggling inside the shell of the ugly shoes' shape.

"Is that what you look like when you're dead, Mommy? Does all the skin go away like this when the big black box closes you inside?"

❖ ❖ ❖ ❖

Mommy's in the spare room holding a dark yellow paper in her hand. She doesn't hear me come in. I stand in the corner by the door and watch her cry. I feel scared. Mommy falls into the big old chair by the window and gasps for air.

"Mommy," somebody inside me says because I'm afraid to talk to her. I never saw Mommy cry before. Her face looks wrong, not like always. She looks up at me and squeezes the yellow paper against her tummy. She cries out to me but I don't move. I've forgotten how.

"It's Granpaw . . . Ellie, your granpaw is dead." She drops her head into her hands and shakes it from side to side. "Oh God, I can't believe it! It can't be true. He can't be dead!"

Water is filling up my eyes now too. Granpaw!

She reads the telegram again. I'm too frightened to cry. I look at the fish bowl on the bookshelf beside me. It's on the lower shelf so I can reach it. Even though I'm only four about to be five, I can feed my beautiful Goldie. I blink my eyes and stare at my pretty beauty Goldie. A tear squeezes out of my eye and runs down my cheek. My hand wipes it away. Goldie's bulging eyes stare back at me. He's floating on his side. Is that what "dead" is?

I keep staring at it. My lips make bubbles with the water in my mouth as I watch and wait for Goldie to move. He doesn't. I don't look at Mommy. I want to.

She comes across the room to me. She gets on her knees and presses me tight against her bony body. Her ear and cheek are wet against my face. She holds me tight. "We're goin' home, Ellie. We're goin' to leave Philadelphia tonight for Oklahoma, honey. Don't worry. It'll be all right. We'll get there as quick as we can."

She promises.

Mommy doesn't see Goldie, but I do. His eyes don't blink. "Dead"? I tap the glass with little fingers.

Cousin Joanie plays on the floor with her doll. Her brother is squirming under the eyes of his father, Uncle Clinton, whose glare glues him to the chair in spite of himself. Mommy's inside the bedroom with Grammaw and Aunt Doreen. I sit on the day-bed and wait. Wait for Granpaw. "We're going to go see him," Mommy said. I fix my socks again and wait.

Screaming – shrill screams – high-pitched shrieks from the bedroom. Uncle Clinton moves to the door as he points his finger at the boy in the chair, nailing him to the spot. "For God sakes," he yells in through the door. "Get her under control. She's scaring these kids half to death!"

I am afraid of the sounds. But I try to be good and wait.

"I did it, Clinton!" It's Grammaw's voice screaming. "It was my fault! Oh God help me! If only I hadn't left him all alone. Oh God, forgive me." Bellowing like a beached whale or a wounded elephant hiding in the deep cave of a room full of agony, Grammaw shrieks all the louder.

Clinton braces himself against the doorjamb, impatient and disgusted, frustrated and hot. "Mama, you didn't kill him. He was old and tired. His heart just plain stopped! Now pull yourself together. I've had about as much of this as I can take in this heat. I'm goin' into town." He slams the door as he goes out.

Wailing continues. Aunt Doreen's voice tries to hush Grammaw. Mom comes to the doorway and calls after my uncle desperately. "Clinton! Come on back. Don't you go. She needs you." The truck door is slammed. The engine starts. Mom stands at the screen-door, helpless for a moment. Then shouts "OK, go on and run away! But don't you come back here drunk, Clinton Butler! Just don't hurt her like that. She can't take much more."

The dust from the Oklahoma dirt road kicks up and fills the doorway as Clinton's pickup heads out. Mommy hangs her head as she moves back towards the bedroom. Halfway there, she turns and stops for a moment to look at me. She bursts out crying and dashes in to see Grammaw for a moment and then comes out and takes me firmly by the hand, grabs her hat and purse, and out the door we go.

She takes me to see Granpaw three times that day. I ask to go back again. The last time I try to climb up into the coffin to lie next to him. She has to pick me up in her arms to pull me away.

I know the truth.

He's in there hiding. He's mad at me and keeping his eyes shut, pretending he's sleeping. But if I get next to him, lie real close to him, he'll put his arm around me like he always does and take me with him.

"I want to go. Granpaw, don't go away mad without me to heaven. I want to go with you." Clutching the side of the black shiny box as I put my knee up over the edge onto the soft creamy satin.

Mommy won't take me back there again. "Gettin' dark," she says.

"Tell me, who d'ya love?"

"You, Granpaw!"

His heart stopped. They said it was broken. I know the truth. I don't say anything.

They bury him the next day. They don't let us kids go to the funeral. "Funerals are only for adults. Children don't belong there." That's what Uncle Clinton says to us next day. He is gray around the eyes and looks sick.

I stamp and pout and beg, but Mommy says no. She wants me to go. I know she does. She knows Granpaw wants me there. "It wouldn't be fair to your cousins if you went and they weren't allowed to go, so you be a good girl and stay over with cousin Joanie and Gerry. The neighbor lady will mind you and make you all a nice cake," Mommy says.

I don't want a cake. I want my granpaw.

I wear my nice yellow dress and act as grown-up as I can – funeral-ready I am, but get sent away anyway.

Chocolate cake on a paper plate in my hand has no bites out of it as cousin Gerry turns the garden hose on and blows the plate out of my hand with the force of the water, drowning me, drenching me in tears.

I'm crying, wet from head to toe. That horrible crying when my body shakes and chest pushes in on itself in quick jerky movements with so little sound.

I hate them. I hate them all. I want my granpaw. I don't care what names you call me, Gerry. I'm not a baby. I'm the one he loved, not Grammaw. I'm the one.

Mommy lied! We came back too late. I asked. She promised we'd go back. Granpaw, please.

✠ ❖ ✢ ❖

High school graduation. Charlotte was at the top of her class. How'd she do that? Quan never saw her studying in the

37

library. She always had some creep hanging around her, drooling on her every word.

Quan was jealous. He had studied, read, worked his ass off and had at best only a once-a-week social life and still he had ended up third in his graduating class. Wang was satisfied for the moment. Acceptance for the freshman year at George Washington University as a science major was good enough for a would-be dentist. But Quan wasn't happy. Charlotte had received a full Merit Scholarship and added financial support from the Chinese community church, while Uncle Wang's wallet sang a tune that sounded like a combination of "Nobody Knows the Trouble I've Seen" and "The Tennessee Waltz". The pressure was on before classes even began. Quan had to get only A's or Uncle would pull the plug on the funds and Quan would be listening to the laundry's steam irons non-stop.

Charlotte had decided to live at home and go to Catholic University. Quan spent every spare moment at Charlotte's house over that summer under the pretense of chatting up her younger sister, Cheryl. He lapped up her mother's attention and delicious cooking and eyeballed every boy that waltzed Charlotte out of the door. He was hoping to discover the magic in her home that gave her the edge over him. It couldn't be her brains. She couldn't really be that much smarter than him without even studying, could she? He never could get her to even have any kind of serious conversation with him to try and match wits.

"It must be her mother," he told himself. "Her father's just like Uncle Wang – worrisome, weary, working too much. But Charlotte's mom, she's like a butterfly who makes you smile when you look at her. She flits around the kitchen, setting down goodies for you and chatting for a moment and then flitting off to see what other bit of loving she can do."

Her touch was soft and maternal as she doted on Quan. He was a sweetheart all right – a lovely boy who needed a proper home. Born in the Year of the Horse, he had much to offer her daughter. She had her eye on him for Charlotte and was always sending the younger sister, Cheryl, off on errands and praising Charlotte to Quan. All of this was to no avail because Charlotte herself wouldn't give him the time of day.

Charlotte's basic attitude: Quan move out of the way, you're just cluttering up our kitchen or front room. Her "Are you still here?" in stinging sarcastic tones hurt him, and he struggled to stay and not run out. If her mother was a butterfly, she was a hornet delivering her poisonous stabs word after word: "Don't you have a home to go to?" or, in a snide remark to Cheryl, "Don't you get sick of him around all the time? He's so boring."

Autumn came. Quan said goodbye to Cheryl and Charlotte's mom, and the back of Charlotte's head as she watched television.

"Well, I'm off tomorrow to GW. Uncle wants me to stay in the dorms and make the most of the university's labs. I'll be able to work in them after class and in the evenings if I'm on campus. Uncle feels I'll be able to study easier without the distractions of the laundry, I guess."

Guess again. Wang wanted Quan away from Charlotte's house and the temptation of the trap he was sure was being laid for his nephew there. Plenty of time for marriage after. Finish school first or end up folding shirts.

Charlotte's mother hugged him and asked him not to forget them. "Visit whenever you're home. We enjoy having you here." Her eyes were moist, Cheryl's were already distracted, and Charlotte's never even turned around. He was out the door tucking in his back pocket the memory of received bits of mothering. He went home to pack his bags.

❖ ❖ ❖ ❖

Washington, DC 1961.

Quan came into the "mixer" with his friend Roy and his roommate Bob. He was a sophomore now, on the prowl with his buddies to look over Glebe Hall's fresh selection of coeds. Orientation week was the time to squeeze in there fast and grab a good one before the classes started and the girls got smart to the rules and the lay of the land. He was wearing his black satin vest with the solid gold back that looked flashy as he turned and twirled on the dance floor.

He saw her right away, over by the soda table. Nice and tall with that wavy blonde hair. He hoped her eyes were blue. "Bet she can boogie," Quan thought to himself. "She can't even stand still pouring her soda she wants to dance so bad."

He was sexy, solid and strong, and he flashed his winning boyish grin at the girl he was doing the twist with, but his body was talking to the one sipping Pepsi in the corner.

Be cool, Quan. Play it right. Let her wait. Make her want you before you even say hello.

It didn't take much. I was primed for the touch. Virgins, he and I, playing in the park, kissing in the dark, rubbing forbidden parts up against each other. Tempting fate and each other by sneaking into places where the rules were against it in spades just for the thrill of it – to kiss in an off-limits space made the taste of our lips even sweeter.

Kissing Quan was like drinking a cool glass of spring water while the dew was still on the roses. His lips were soft and fresh. He smelled clean like ivory soap. His skin was like cream-colored silk. We spent hours mouth-to-mouth and more, exploring like two trying-to-be-grown-up little kids

40

playing doctor, finding out what felt good, what smelled good, resting in each other's arms, drinking beer, listening to Chet Baker's velvet lovemaking to his horn, "My old Flame".

In a house, in his car, in the dorm, always going too far but not far enough to quench the fire, release, find peace – but what did we know? Only the build-up that wanted to explode, the ecstacy of going still higher, not being able to stand being touched any more because it felt so good and might burst. Not knowing the bursting was what was meant to happen. Innocent bliss. Not knowing. Just loving every minute of it and every inch of each other. Not wanting it to end. Hours parked in Rock Creek Park listening to the rain beat on the roof of his old Renault, dreaming his hand was a dove resting on my breast.

✠ ✦ ✢ ✖

The car's engine had died again. I loved having an important job to do – steer, pop the clutch when he shouted "Now" and feel the exhilaration of the motor igniting and the car beginning again. Starting over. Responding. Quan seemed to know about everything. He'd tackle the light green machine with his tool box and it would work again. He knew when a push would do or when it was tool-box time. He had rigged up a radio for the car in a cigar box and used his famous "alligator clips" to get it going.

We were almost to the Mainline. The green machine, Quan and me. The day before Thanksgiving. He'd stay over on his way to New Jersey for turkey with Luanh. She had married an Italian man there. Photos fanned out before me to prove how beautiful Eurasian kids were could not be denied. "Our children will be beautiful too. We'll make wonderful children together – the most beautiful kids in the world," he said. "Did you tell your folks about me?"

"Sure. They know I'm crazy about you. That's why they said you could stay over at the house tonight. You can sleep in our den. It's got a big sofa bed. You'll love it."

"No. I mean did you tell them about *me*?" Quan asked.

"What do you mean? That you're studying to be a dentist and a year ahead of me in college?"

"Come on, Genelle. You know what I'm getting at. Did you tell them I'm Chinese?"

I stare at him in disbelief. Kiss his cheek, his ear, his hand on the steering wheel. Silly boy!

"Is that what's got you nervous? Got you in shades? Hey, my parents don't care if you're Chinese. They don't have a prejudice bone in their bodies. We've always had black people in and out of our home. Dad's Jewish for God's sake and Mom's southern Methodist. They had so many battles to fight themselves, they aren't prejudiced at all. Is that why you're hiding behind sunglasses all of a sudden? And here I thought you were just trying to look cool for me."

I laugh – he doesn't.

"You didn't tell them, did you?"

"No, Quan. It didn't even occur to me to tell them and they never asked. I mean they know your name. Now stop worrying. They'll love you. I love you. I think you're great!"

✥ ✥ ✥ ✥

Three months later, February 1962.

My head is spinning and I am seeing blotches of darkness and light. I feel like I am burning up with fever, and I can't stop shaking. Oh Quan, I wish you were still here by my side.

I open the drawer of the hospital table beside my bed and look at the presents he brought me today. The chocolates, the toy model of his Renault to build as I recoup from my surgery, and the four ounces of Johnny Walker Red in the glass jelly-jar. I pull the covers up over my head and try to stay warm. Sipping the scotch helps for a little while. Quan's fabulous face swims before me. What a love to surprise me like that today. I chuckle as my teeth chatter. Mom was pretty surprised too.

They were just sitting me up on the side of the bed for me to try walking with the crutches for the first time after my leg was operated on, when he walked through the doors of the hospital ward with flowers in his hand and that million-dollar I-love-you-with-all-my-heart-forever-and-ever-and-ever-and-ever smile. Bet every one of the ladies in the room wished he was their sweetheart!

It had taken him five and a half hours in the cold, icy, stormy February weather to drive up to Philadelphia in his old Renault, that now had no heat, to surprise me! Brought me presents, my books and assignments from all my professors, and his love. Mom didn't even thank him. She just stared at him. It was shock, I guess. She must have thought I'd listened to the Thanksgiving Day lecture from Dad and had broken up with Quan. Well, I tried feebly to end things and failed. At least I had learned not to mention his name to them again. But my time with Quan had become even more precious to me. His kindness and respect I treasured. Laying next to him in the place off-campus he now rented, I felt safe. Even when he wanted to enter me in the most loving, gentle way, he listened to me and held himself back. We were brother and sister, best friends and lovers. My heart couldn't stop loving him, though I knew I was disappointing my parents and that hurt.

Quan only could stay in the hospital with me for a couple of hours. He was broke, and Mom didn't offer him a place to stay or anything. Besides he had to get back to Washington DC for his own classes in the morning. Mom didn't really speak to me after he left. Just gathered her magazines, gave me a faint kiss on the cheek and left too.

The chills set in then. My temperature spiked.

Sound of curtain-rings being pulled across metal. Angry scraping of steel on steel. My bed is suddenly enclosed in a muslin cloud by a mad man – a wild man. Who let him in here? Get him away from me. He's roaring and shouting at me. He's wearing my father's face but it's twisted in a grotesque expression. The nurses must have seen him come into the ward. They must have told him "We just started the antibiotics for your daughter, she's very ill". He hears only his own rage rattling the bottom of the metal bed.

"You little brat, how could you! I know what you've been up to. You think you're ever going back to Washington DC? Hah!" The muslin clouds shook with the waving of his fists and the bellowing of his breath. "I've had a private investigator following you all over Washington DC, you whore! You're never leaving home again! And you can forget about your Chinaman – you'll never see him again, I'll make sure of that!"

"Daddy, please. Please. I love him. Don't, Daddy." My heart will explode through the top of my head any minute. The water is streaming from my armpits. "I'm sick, Daddy. Please. Please don't yell. I feel like I'm going to faint!"

Why don't the nurses come? Why don't they stop him? Why don't they help me? He is yelling at the top of his lungs. I can't see his face any more for the white and black spots before my eyes. My head is pounding and I'm shaking so badly the bed is squeaking. My ears start ringing.

"Is this how you show your respect to your parents? You

ungrateful little brat! You're disgusting! Disgusting! Do you hear me? You've hurt your mother so badly, I don't know if she'll *ever* get over it. This is the thanks we get for all the sacrifices we've made. Sick? Ha! You know nothing about it yet! You'll see just how miserable I can make your life. You just wait and see!"

He storms out through the clouds of muslin surrounding the bed like lightning after thunder. It's a long time after he's gone that the nurses finally open the curtains. I've stopped weeping and am choking and vomiting now. The chills have become more terrible. I'm burning up. They give me an injection and cover me up with more blankets. Late that night as I am still crying silently into my pillow, the elderly black woman in the bed next to mine speaks to me. She has waited until they turned the lights out in the ward. She speaks quietly, in a whisper. "Don't you worry, honey. Don't you fret. Stop your crying, darlin'. That boy loves you and you love him. Any fool can see it. You'll get better, you'll see. Don't you cry no more. You'll get better and be able to walk again and they won't be able to keep you from him. You rest now, honey. You jes' rest. He's downright handsome, that boy. And good, too. Yes, he's a fine young man. Go sleep now, sugar, go sleep."

✠ ❖ ✢ ✸

Quan held the letter in his hand. He read it again. Golden skin turned pale. He would be late to physics. Set his jaw. Swallowed tears. Quickly walked to class. Denied the reality he had been afraid of all along. Respected her parents and didn't phone. Believed she would return.

"A horse and a sheep are an unlucky match in the Year of the Tiger. Anyone will tell you."

45

"I don't care, Uncle. I want to marry her. That's old-fashioned anyway. Who believes that stuff? This is America not Manchuria!"

"The stars don't lie and they don't change. You have no business thinking of marriage with two more years of university and then dental school. So forget her!"

He turned his back on Quan and moved through the beaded curtains in the kitchen doorway back into the laundry to count his money and put it in the safe. Wang considered phoning Charlotte's mother, Mrs Woo. Perhaps it was time to arrange a marriage contract for Charlotte to Quan. He could do it in secret so the bonds would be set. It was all right for Luanh to have married an Italian and be working in a pizza restaurant, but Quan carried the family name. He must stay where he belonged. Be a dentist, not a white woman's tool.

Quan worked, he watched, and he waited. He blocked out the letter, the sadness and fears, even the plans. Physics. Organic Chemistry. Comparative Anatomy. It didn't matter when, but he was certain she would appear again like the new moon after the darkness turns on its side. When she did, the dream would wake up and remember.

Spring returned and brought Genelle with the cherry-blossoms. They walked the lover's lane around the tidal basin in the night with floodlights making the blossoms shimmer in delight, showering their sweetness over them as they walked beneath the boughs. Mounted the steps and witnessed Lincoln emerge in the night, surrounded by light, like some great giant that could save them and set them free, but he looked tired to them. Their embrace was a long night filled with sadness. Longing and fear squeezed the joy from their eyes slowly, even as they watched and wanted it to be otherwise.

Genelle tried to drink her father's threats and contempt away, to drown them out, but they remained carved deeply into her heart. Guilty was the verdict.

✠ ❖ ✠ ◈

I know the truth. Quan, I'll only bring you sadness. I'm no good. I'll hurt you even more. I don't want *your* heart to stop. You're too good, too kind. A porcelain doll, I am not strong enough. I want to turn my back on them but I can't. Words in my head, never said.

I look at Quan's beautiful face. It is May. Glen Echo Amusement Park. Happened once, couldn't happen again. Exams are coming but just for tonight we don't care. He is my best friend. My brother. My still-virgin lover. We walk in silence holding hands. His hands. Have I mentioned his hands? I can't describe them well. It is hard to explain. It brings back tears. They are dry and soft at the same time. They are too old for him. They look like they have worked for fifty years taking things apart and putting them back together, making them work, and yet they are so clean. Always clean. Those hands.

It is quiet. Why has the music stopped? Where have the people gone? Only the man by the ring-toss booth moves around inside whistling to himself softly. Quan stands still. Strange light like we're on a stage but the theatre is empty. Under the lights he tells me he loves me. He asks me to be his wife.

Sweet smell of cotton candy in the air. Quan holds me to him as I cry. He knows the answer won't change, won't be spoken, can't be said. He just holds me. He has his white baseball jacket on with the red stripe around the sleeves. He wipes my eyes with his handkerchief.

"Come on," he says. "Dry your eyes now and let's get a picture together before we leave."

We sit in the little booth where you get four pictures for twenty-five cents. May 1962. We kiss and kiss as the camera clicks and the lights flash and the salt of our tears flavors our lips.

The Mainline

Straight line. Line them up and take the photos. Debutantes only. The rest of the riff-raff have no place at the Mainline's perfectly laid table. Etiquette above all, but pour another drink quickly before the children get home.

Home? Manor! Mansions. Stone upon stone graciously laid. Stucco and timber Tudors or castle-like Grays, several storeys. Take your pick. As long as you have the right kind of money and name you're very welcome.

We didn't have either.

We were the nightmares invading the Mainliners' waking hours. The Alkis, Berini, O'Grady, Rosenberg families. We were the ethnic invaders that spilled over the Mainline's long established White Anglo-Saxon Protestant boundaries. The nouveau riche and the self-made men arrived on this wide strip of land that struck through the heart of Montgomery county, Pennsylvania.

"Raymond Alkis makes it big and moves to the Mainline," read the headline in my father's mind. Built his own home, a ranch house on three acres of land in the shadow of the Davies' and the Shackelton's walled mansions.

Ah, the Mainline. Landed aristocracy. *La crème de la*

crème. Cricket. Bailey, Banks, and Biddle. Land, money and power. They could turn up their nose or offer a cold shoulder or be graciously condescending whichever way the wind blew. The Debs delighted in their difference with an effortless air of superiority that must have been in-bred. It had to be in the veins. Blue-blood must know its own, instinctively.

I hated it. I was eleven when we moved out of Overbrook Park, West Philadelphia, and our home which looked the same as every other one on the block. We were part of a connected row of look-alike houses that stretched for a mile or more. Moved from the comfort of sameness into The House That Raymond Built, that stuck out like a sore thumb amongst the mansions it neighbored. It never was home to me. I loved the new house Dad had built. I just hated the Mainline.

My first day at my new school. *"Genelle, you smell!"* *"Smelly Ellie!"* Children could be so kind on the Mainline. Next-door neighbor walked me to school, seemed like a friend, but threw my books on the ground when the kids made fun of his "funny-looking girlfriend" in the pink leather jacket. An eleven-year-old's prize possession. I had begged Mom for it that spring – a powder-pink, pastel, soft smooth leather. All the kids had leather jackets in Robert Lewis Elementary School, Overbrook Park, West Philadelphia. Not one hung on the hooks in the cloakrooms of Penn Valley Elementary School except mine. Mainliners wore Pendleton jumpers or blazers, Blackwatch or Windsor tartan skirts, knee socks and penny loafers. I was out of my depth. The whole family was. Let's face it, Alkis wasn't Hollingsworth or Rawling. Mom's Protestant blood wasn't rich enough, blue enough, to earn us even a corner of respectability here. Farm-girl from Oklahoma might be a good seamstress or pie-maker, but the breeding was lacking. And she didn't even drink! Who could be "social" with her? Really.

50

It's not hard to figure out when you're not wanted. A few years of banging your head against a stone wall and you get it.

The light bulb goes on. No matter how talented, smart, pretty, witty – no matter how hard I tried, they didn't want to like me.

There's the line, the main line, and you can't cross over it. You may think you can, but you can't. So just give up.

The confusing part was how I was treated outside of school. Surrounded by boys in the mansions, I had no female playmates except one girl who was three years younger than myself. I never saw her in school. She disappeared. It was like she didn't exist for me to relate to except inside the walls of her mansion. She never came to my house to play. Her brother, who was my age, was friendly enough at their house, but would not speak to me in school. If any boy showed an interest in me in the classroom or cafeteria, they were shamed by the rest and had to attack me on the sports field to prove that contempt was the feeling truly in their hearts for me. My shins were black and blue even when the soccer ball came nowhere near me. The girls just giggled at me, put tacks on my chair, or made fun of my hair – unruly, thick, naturally curly frizz. "That's Jew-hair, you know," I heard one of them say. I wanted their hair – straight and brown or sandy-blonde, soft and shiny, and always neat even when the rain poured down.

Painful times. My body didn't grow the same as the other girls in my class. I grew tall and they grew round. Gym class. I hated it. Mandatory showers. Open display of blossoming breasts and dark pubic hair. I wanted to run and hide my too tall, too small, unhairy form. Studied the pale peach fuzz that grew on me that no one could see because it was too fine, too light. Horrible gym uniforms that never fit my body right. At night I would cry. Didn't belong. It couldn't be they were wrong. They were so sure of themselves. It had to be me.

51

Uprooted. Transplanted again. I wasn't faring as well as the roses Mom planted when we moved, but then they hadn't been moved as many times. Eleven years had already brought five times for me to move house. But now, we had finally "arrived". Moved into the beautiful stone ranchhouse Dad had built, proud that he had finally "made it". Finally got to the top. They couldn't keep him from buying a lot and building on the Mainline, Alkis or not.

Dad even built a swimming pool in the back garden for parties and friends. Who had friends? Invite anyone, they'll come be your friend on *June 16th, 2-5pm, for a pool party. RSVP.* Love to splash water in your face for fun, race you to the end of the pool and back.

Got to go. Don't know you any more. You bore me.

Score one for the Mainliners. I was gored again. Takes a while to learn not to go for the red flag, not to try to connect or fit in, not to care.

❖ ❖ ❖ ❖

New York, 1979. Upstate. I think I know the score.

Black and white checkered bathroom tiles, grayed, lined and cracked in places. Grouting loose. Blood-drops on a seam where black rests next to white and has done so for thirty years.

Main-lining. They say it's the best. Better than all the rest of the ways you can use "stuff" because it's there in a hurry. Hits the heart – *Smack* – and the instant feeling of sweet-baby-love-it's-OK-again warm all over, like a hot flush of well-being flooding through, washing out the pain, hitting the stomach right after the heart. Too warm for a minute, sick at his stomach. Throwing up into the toilet bowl. Heaving the

52

Twinkies and coffee that was lunch, dinner, and breakfast for him.

Pay dirt! This is good stuff. Nice and sick for a few minutes then the doorway to heaven opens and the music swims in and he's wrapped in the womb of the lady he loves. Spoon and works slide to the floor. Mainliner he never was, but is. *They shoot horses, don't they?*

Daniel. He was last in the chain of lovers that began with the end of my marriage.

I knock on the bathroom door. "Daniel? Daniel are you all right? Are you sick again?"

"I'm all right, baby. I'm good," he murmured.

"What?" I was scared. His voice was muffled.

He raised his head slowly. He was into a good nod. He cleared his throat, made the effort to come up for air. "Yeah, baby. Yeah," he said a bit louder. "I'm OK now. I just need to lie down. Got a headache. I'm gonna lie down. Come get me in an hour and we'll go for a walk."

Walking on air, no ground under his feet, I held his hand and didn't know, didn't want to know. While my children fought over which show to watch on the TV, Daniel and I walked on the back roads Upstate New York and I thought I was finally home.

"How could you not know?" Tony asked me in his deep raspy voice. "For God sake, you're living with the man, Genelle. Don't you ever look at his arms? They must be well marked up. He's into some good stuff, that's all I can say. His pupils were pinned to the wall!"

I didn't want to believe Tony. But why would he lie to me? He was a recovering addict himself, had been in and out of prison like Daniel, but hadn't gotten high or drunk alcohol in four years now. He was a drug-abuse counsellor for a local migrant-worker program. I had met him through the clinic where I was working as a drug-abuse counsellor myself. Mostly I had worked with school kids who were experimenting with hash and alcohol.

The place where I worked believed that addiction was only a symptom of a deeper underlying psychological problem. Treat the underlying problem and the drug/alcohol abuse would go away and the person could use chemicals recreationally. This made sense to me. Our clients were wiser than us. A few were surprised to see me in Joe's Disco. One girl said to me, a bit self-consciously, "What are you doing here?"

"Ladies' Night," I answered. "Where else is there to be?"

I saw nothing strange in me being there. My client was hipper than me to what addiction was all about.

I study the scar that runs from the outside corner of Tony's left eye down his cheek almost to his chin. I wonder if he had received that on the street or in prison. He's looking at me, waiting for me to respond to what he has been saying.

"I don't want it to be true, Tony. Are you absolutely sure?" I asked him.

"Genelle, look. Who's kidding who here? You asked me to come out and talk to Dan, help him to get a job or something, right? I'm sitting here having lunch with the guy and he's fighting a nod right in front of me. And he knew I was on to him. That's how come he got up and went for a walk. He was afraid I'd bust him right then. If you doubt me, check his arms, Genelle. Check his eyes. And if you know what's good for you, chuck him out before he pulls you down with him. I mean it."

Another line to cross over. But where is it? Where is the invisible line between abuse and addiction? Hey, everyone knows addicts are strung out, stealing, robbing, hiding in doorways. I know the ring Aunt Doreen gave me for graduation is around here somewhere. I've just misplaced it.

Shotgun between Daniel's lips, smouldering joint filling his mouth with hot hashish smoke I suck out of his half-closed lips into my lungs. Mouth to mouth resuscitation. It can't be true. "I love you" till I'm blue in the face. How would I know with eyes like that? Big brown soft doe-eyes looking at me so seductively, sweetly singing your favorite song's lines as you strum my son's guitar and I mouth the words *"If I listened long enough to you, I'd find a way to believe that it's all true, knowin' that you lied straight-faced as I cried, still I'd look to find the reason to believe . . . "* How can I find the line Daniel's crossed over when I have lost sight of my own?

There they are. Not in a cluster but up his forearm. Dots connecting an invisible line that would appear on time as soon as he tied up his arm. I can see them now. Tiny dots of darkness that must follow the vein. Oh, Daniel, how can you do that to yourself? Stick a needle in your own arm. I want to throw up just thinking about it.

A little man with an ugly big hat and dark scruffy beard and moustache stood in the middle between me and the serenely sleeping Daniel, hands folded across his heart as in a coffin. Morpheus has him wrapped in sweet dreams I envy, but the price of the ticket has to be paid to the little bad man with the black bag and I don't want to wait in that line.

❖ ❖ ❖ ❖

I'm sixteen, running for the school's late bus. I'd been rehearsing for the school play. Theatrics are the only way to be noticed, recognised, when you had the wrong name, wrong looks, wrong money for the cliques. I'm good at it so the Mainline in-crowd include me on their party list if it is a big "do" and they need a bit of entertainment. Genelle would be swell. She's good for a laugh. Laughing at me even then as my books fly up in the air and I slide down the concrete steps in a spill-slide-fall that fractures my coccyx. Look it up. Never heard of it. But the tail-bone ain't funny when it's yours and it's injured. Can't sit, or stand, or lie down without pain.

Then the ringing starts. Two days after the fall, lying in bed, my ears start ringing and they won't stop. On the way to the bathroom, dizziness with blotches of light overcomes me and I feel as if I will faint.

What's happening to me? Can't stand up any more. No energy to eat. Listless. Going, going, gone to a hospital room. In the dark. Philadelphia again. Semi-private room. Whispers in the hallway outside of my door, often. They don't let me know what's going on. Don't tell me directly. Just let me read it in the terror of my mother's and father's faces. In their eyes the question is real, "Will she live?"

Dr Fitzgerald at the doorway talks to my parents with his back to me. Big barrel-chested man – "Best blood-man around" the nurses assured me; but he can't whisper quietly enough to keep me from hearing the newest news. "We don't know, we still don't know. We've run all the blood tests we can think of. The white cells are rampant and red blood count is going dangerously lower every day. We're doing a bone-marrow tap in the morning. If we don't find an answer there . . . well . . . I'm afraid we won't have much hope."

An Italian grandmother in the other bed of the hospital room, with sleeping pills filling her mouth with a cotton-wool tongue but not quite wanting to sleep yet, tries to explain the Virgin birth to save the soul of the young girl who must be very sick the way her family looks at her – poor thing. Isn't it a shame at sixteen. "You see-a, it can-a happen. Like-a cysts-a, you know-a, a growth, a lump-a, lump-a blood and skin-a. It

56

could-a happen, you see-a. Mary, she had-a something like-a that, and-a God-a touched it-a and-a it-a changed from-a cyst-a in-a her womb to a babino – you know-a little-a Jesus. For you-a for me-a, for you-a for me-a."

Frightening, sickening thought to go to sleep with – a bloody mass of skin and cysts to save me. Not possible. She's a bit crazy and scary how she talks to me without her teeth in the dark room.

Morning they come again to steal blood from my arm. Every time I panic. Remembering the man with the black bag that came every other day to my bedroom in the row house when I was little to stick that needle in my arm and take away my blood. He hurt me so badly. But this woman doesn't hurt me, why? I tell her that morning about the pain that happened to me with the needle as a child.

"Was he a little man with a dark moustache and beard?"

"He seemed big to me. I was so little, only five or six. But he did have a black curled-up moustache and a beard, and he carried a big ugly hat with him," I say.

She tells me she knew him. He had taught her how to draw blood. "He was a good teacher, but he wasn't a good technician because he was frightened himself. He didn't have the confidence he told us we must have. He used to say the veins would roll and sometimes cause pain for people because you couldn't hit the vein properly. But, I watched him and he was scared mostly. Especially with children. And he couldn't hold the needle right then. It must have been horrible for you," she says.

Strange, ten years later to have the nightmare experience explained. But I am still scared of the dark. She swabs the soft inner fold of my arm with the alcohol wipe and places a plaster over the most recent needle-hole.

They come later with the spike. It looks huge. It is a thick hollow needle. I'm terrified. Who are these people? Curtains are pulled around my hospital bed. Are they doctors, nurses? They have on the hospital white and green uniforms.

"What are you going to do with that?" I ask in a panic.

"Dr Fitzgerald has ordered a bone-marrow tap. We're going to put this spike down into your sternum and draw up some of the bone marrow in the centre of your breast bone. And hopefully we'll find out what's wrong with you then," the older of the two uniformed men says. "It won't take long. Just relax. It won't hurt. Honestly." I have heard those words before.

Panic sets in deeper. I want to see a face I know. I want to see my parents. Where is Dr Fitzgerald? It is all happening too fast. The nurse has unbuttoned my pyjama top and is spreading orange-brown stuff on the bone over my heart.

Oh, my God. Please help me. I'm going to die now. I grab the technician's hand holding the spike and try to stall her. I ask all kinds of questions trying to appear calm, trying to make them wait until, hopefully, somebody else appears to save me.

"You'll have to keep your hands away, Miss Alkis, and lay very still. Bill, you're going to have to hold her arms, I think."

"No. No! That's all right. I'll lay quiet. Please don't hold me down. Please. I'll lie still." Close my eyes, bite down hard, clench my fists. Hear the crunch-punch sound and feel the dull thud of pain as my chest bone is pierced. The pressure is fierce for a moment as I feel the marrow pulled up and out of me. Open my eyes and look at them working away as if I wasn't even there, only my empty body for them to pierce and leave plastered. Tidy up and they're gone. The ache in my heart bone is the dull steady pain of the wounded, the torn, the violated innocent that provides the answer they were searching for.

Diagnosis discovered. Something Latin. Two words.

Sounded serious. It was. The faces around my bed were. But a miracle drug – a new drug – had been shown quite effective in prolonging life for the sufferer from this disease in tests so far, they told me. They started me on the drug immediately.

Treat the body, forget the mind. And what could the spirit have to do with disease, anyway? Please be real. It's 1959. This was way before Louise Hay could say that this affliction was the result of a child giving up. Better to die than stand up for one's self. Anger and punishment turned inward. At five years old to six Genelle had almost died with it, but they called it something else – rheumatic fever then. Romantic fever. He loved her too much. Her heart murmured. His stopped. She remembered the verdict.

Dr Fitzgerald explains it all to me. All he feels I need to know, that is. Take this little white tablet, a magic wand of a pill, three times a day and you'll live. Without it, you'll die. Simple. Simple. Simple. Not much of a choice. "Don't drink alcohol. Don't smoke. That could kill you. Having children is very dangerous with this disease. Too risky to chance. You might not live through it. Come and see me every month, we'll test the blood, check for swelling, side effects, weight gain, weight loss. We'll find the right dosage. Just a matter of time. See you next month."

Not one person from my school rings me. Marvelous Mainline compassion. But who cares? With these tiny white tablets I can fly in the face of any disgrace they want to pin on me. In no time I'm back on my feet and in school taking on the whole lot of them. All my inhibitions seem to be gone and I don't care what I say to whom, or when. Talking back to the English teacher, laughing hysterically in history, flirting with Mr Carlson in Spanish, getting thrown out of chemistry lab for playing with the flame of the bunsen burner. Full-tilt boogie by the time I'm seventeen. They tell me I have a fatal disease and I feel invincible.

Even my father's stern looks or authoritative ultimatums have little effect on me for the moment. I'm a rebel expelled to the utility room for first fighting with father – bad example for younger sister and brother – or for hysterical laughter ending in tears for no apparent reason except "Pass me the peas, please, Winona," from Dad seems so funny, so seriously said like the politics of the country rest on them, or so it seems.

Under the influence? Over the line? They don't know what is happening to me and neither do I. But for the first time in my life, I don't care. I have some flare, some flash, some power it seems. I feel indestructible. Little white pills, I don't even know it is you making me feel so real, wild, and free.

I think it's just me – late to blossom but what a color!

Easter

Sunrise. Sunset. Services. *Seder.* Hide the *matzo.* *"Crucify him, crucify him!"* Mom's corsage. Grammaw's orchid. Wearing hat and gloves I hated. Who died? What's suffering got to do with a new outfit? Check the magazines. They're showing lilac and moss-green this spring. Match your shoes and bag. *Hallelujah! Mazeltov!*

Confusion reigned. Brushing younger sister's tangled hair, causing the shrieks because I was rushing – couldn't be late to church, in tears, on Easter. Hating having to go at fifteen. Couldn't even think about the words I was saying or singing because I was so angry at having to be "little-mother" and mind my sister and four-year-old brother squirming, poking, impatient at my side. Who could sit still for an hour in uncomfortable new fussy clothes, gloves, hat or little bow tie?

Two families. Two cultures trying to mix. The mingling of it all left me confused and bereft. Again there was nowhere I belonged. Rooted in No Man's Land. I hated my Jewish blood. Renounced it, rejected it. Everyone on the Mainline made fun of the Jews. They were lower than the Italians because "Jews are all crooked lawyers or moneylenders of the worst kind". A pound of flesh – you know the play! I begged Mom not to make me stay out of school on Jewish holidays as she said I had to in order to show some respect for my dad who was playing golf on the day. Never saw him set a foot in a temple.

I didn't want anybody to think I was Jewish. I said I was Polish – a Catholic Pole. I didn't think they had Protestants in Poland or I would have said I was a Protestant Pole. Alkis could be Polish instead of Lithuanian, I thought. Now Catholic wasn't Protestant, but they didn't kill Christ so they weren't contemptible worms, only statue-worshipping pagans to the Mainliners.

That's what I told them in school when they questioned my name as somebody always did – "Alkis, that's a Jew-name!"

"No. Alkis is Polish. Didn't you know? I'm a Catholic Pole. Don't you see my blonde hair? My grandmother from Poland has the same hair."

Anyway my mother was Protestant so I couldn't *really* be Jewish. That's what my Nana, Dad's Mom, explained. "You have Jewish blood, dear. But to be a real Jew, your mother has to be Jewish. That's how it goes in the Jewish religion. You see it's passed from the mother's side always to the children. So you, unfortunately or fortunately, take your pick, are a Gentile like your mother. Come help me put the little dishes for the meatballs on the table."

Seder. The Passover meal. I didn't know what it was about. We were never told. It was never explained. Like some big secret buried in the "Old Country". All of us crowded around the table in my Nana and Pop-Pop's small dining-room eating strange food we had only once a year. Chicken soup with matzo balls in it. Knishes. Potato and liver latkas – *yuck*. Roast lamb – *yum*. But the best was always the meatballs. I loved my Nana's sweet-and-sour meatballs. Always wanted more. Purple wine, Mogan David, stained the linen cloth if spilled, even a drop, so beware, be careful. Extra special cloth was old covering the table, felt so smooth under my ten-year-old hand. Felt the flowers shiny and soft, white-on-white. Big cloth serviettes like we never had at home. Pop-Pop held the matzo in the linen serviette. His eyes twinkled as he showed it to my cousins and me before he hid it. We closed our eyes tightly and didn't peek until he clapped his hands twice and then we opened them and ran to hunt. Dad looked like a little boy in his *yamaka*. But he couldn't hunt with us this game. Only the real kids got to look. Whoever found it got the prize – candy from Nana and a silver dollar from Pop-Pop. Baby sister, too small to play, filled my older too-big-to-play cousin's arms.

Nana was beautiful. Straight blonde hair swept up off her high Austrian forehead. She went to the hairdresser every week. Pop-Pop had a false tooth he'd stick out to scare us with and then make us laugh.

But always after the Seder supper, while the children watched the TV and the women cleared the table and washed the stacks and stacks of fine Austrian china, my father Raymond and his father would argue. It would start with a question about work, then a mild discussion would ensue. An accusation would be made, and then the voices would be raised. Heated words would fly, cursing, challenges, threats, shouts. Crazy Litvaks! My grandparents' little apartment would feel like it was going to explode. The walls shook as we cousins huddled against them pretending it wasn't happening. Uncle Reuben came in to talk to us and distract us from the roaring that his in-laws were making in the other room. Mom would get worried and leave the other women at the sink and go into the living-room to try and calm Dad down. She'd be told to leave and then Nana would come in. Then, they were all in there and at it. A free for all. Soon we'd be hurriedly handed our coats and rushed out the door as Nana chastised Pop-Pop for "not leaving well enough alone!"

Then, of course, there would be Nana's phone call when we arrived home to try and smooth things over between her son and his father. But every year it was the same. Every time they saw each other it ended the same. Even sometime on the phone, it would happen – *spark, crackle, pop, fire.*

Passover.

Matzahs were sent home with Mom, packed before the inevitable explosion, to mix with eggs and onions in Nana's recipe to give us fried breakfast a few days later. It was the frying in the chicken fat that made it taste so good, she said. Fried matzahs. I made them for my children years later. Fried matzahs, sweet and sour meatballs, and prockus – stuffed cabbage with delicious savoury tomato sauce. Nana's legacy.

Our Last Supper together I can't even remember, but the fights and the meatballs linger vivid in my mind.

Easter. Resurrection. Eggs. Colored eggs. Tatooed eggs. Blown-out eggs delicately painted. Smell of vinegar. Blue and red dye-stained fingers. Patience, patience – it takes time to turn the white shell to robin's-egg-blue. Daffodils, tulips and thick earth-shrouding packasandra hid the eggs so well if it was sunny. We'd never find them all in yard. Dad joined this hunt.

"Don't worry if you can't find them all, the bunnies will eat the ones you miss," he said. Feed the bunnies with soon-to-be rotten purple, yellow, orange, red and blue eggs.

Eat the bunnies. Oops, he lost his chocolate ears. Christ bleeding, dying or rising, had no meaning whatsoever in my mind. Heard the stories, saw the pictures, passed over me, I'd say it did all three of us children.

No religious instruction received. No confirmations, no Sunday School classes, no christenings or baptisms. Bargain made before wedding. Winona and Raymond sacrificed their beliefs for the freedom of the children to decide, and so

64

burned the barricades to the mixed-marriage. But we all could say the *Lord's Prayer* and *Glory be*, put in our two pence or twenty pence that Mom pressed into our hand and sing *"Praise God from whom all blessings flow . . . "* And the fear of God was firmly entrenched in us, Mom made sure of that, though we only witnessed Bible-pounding from the pulpit on our two or three visits to church a year.

Easter, Mother's Day and Christmas. On each occasion Raymond dutifully walked beside Winona, children in tow, and bowed his head when prayer was called for. Obligation fulfilled. No comment made.

✠ ✦ ✠ ✦

Still sick. Just six. Late springtime, almost summer. Window open. Kids playing in the alley behind our row house. I can't go out and play again today. It's been too long, can't count, since I was last outside with my friends playing hopscotch. Watch Cathy O'Neill playing on the swing set with her little brother in the garden plot beyond the alley. They're laughing. Rest my chin on my spread fingers stretched across the windowsill. Still in my jama-top. Bare bum. So quiet in the house. Mom washing clothes in the basement before she bakes a cake. Window open bringing in gentle breeze filled with late afternoon sun.

I want to play. I want to swing. Windowsill has old paint chips and flakes in it with some dirty-dirt. Knees on the cool painted wood of the window-seat covering my toy-box. Toes wiggle free over the edge of the window-seat. Don't feel sick in the sunshine. Feel like I could run and play if Mommy'd let me. Have to go to the loo. Have to make dumpety-doo. Don't want to leave Cathy. Wait some more. See what Cathy plays on next. The trapeze swing catches her eye and then her hand.

Black and white spotted cat crosses alley to bit of grassy patch along the fence. I love the trapeze swing. It's my favourite. Hanging upside down. She makes faces at her brother. Laughing. Giggling. Cat turns its back on me and watches Cathy through the fence. The movement of its back – it seems so smooth, like waves beginning in my belly, I don't stop them. Watching Cathy upside down, everything moving, opening, pushing, stretching, opening, feeling warmth as it passes out of me. Perfect purring animal. Naughty. Nasty and nice. Nice feeling body moving inside outside, finishing off with tinkle, closing up, dropping the ripe fruit. I giggle again. Cat's head swivels to see me in the window, rises unceremoniously, smells its work and moves away. I feel the warmth of my secret rising between my legs. Smell of animal mixes with breeze and sunshine feeling free like upside down on a trapeze in the breeze my bum, was like a teddy bear under a lemon-tree in a storybook smiling. Cathy swinging. Brother giggling. I laughing, feeling my little body's natural flow. Loving the secret of it. Cathy can't see me. Even the smell is mine alone. I know I'm naughty. This is "not-nice", but I like the feeling, Mommy in the kitchen making a cake, and Ellie quiet as a mouse – she must be reading her storybooks. Smile.

They're on the teeter-totter now and I'm a good girl. I'm getting the loo-roll for messy-mess. I carry the big lump carefully smiling to myself. Plop it in the toilet. Flush once. Use more paper to clean the mess. Flush again. Wet some paper and rub it good. No one knows but me. Nobody sees. Nobody knows but me curled back up in bed. Feeling safe. Feeling well. I'm hungry. Want some toast with purple jelly, and ginger ale.

Pink fuzzy slippers on my feet, in my robe, down to the kitchen.

"I'm hungry," I announce.

Mommy's eyes look at me full in the face. "Feeling better, sweetheart?" Now they narrow and look deeper, seeing me. See me different.

I feel hot in my face and squirmy inside. I look away from her and sit at the kitchen table.

"What have you done, Ellie? Have you been a bad girl? Did you do something wrong? Tell me. You can't fool me, Ellie."

I look at my hands. They look clean. I want to smell them and check but I don't. I just shake thick blonde curls side to side – "No, Mommy" – and wait. I feel bad. I want to cry. I don't because I'd have to tell then. I've been really bad I know for sure. I don't want spanking from Daddy when he comes home.

"Ellie, look at me. I can see you've done something wrong. Are you going to be a good girl now and tell me what it is?"

Mommy places toast on the table before me. Little dots of butter making tiny yellow puddles on the warm crunchy brown of the bread. I wish I was still hungry. I stick my finger in one of the little puddles and pull it back. It's dirty I know even though I remember washing up. I'm not hungry any more at all. I feel sick all over.

Mother, hands on her hips where the apron goes around her, doesn't need to point her finger at me. The words go in like an arrow all by themselves. Into my teddy bear in the woods now hiding, but arrow finds the mark anyway. "It doesn't matter Ellie, if you tell me or not. It doesn't matter if I can't find out. God sees everything you do. He saw what you did wrong and He will punish you!"

✠ ❖ ✠ ❖

Nailed to the cross. The Lily was white and pure. Delicate

67

yellows lines trumpeted out from the middle of it. Guilty. He loved you so much. He died because of you. Repent or get zapped. Punish yourself fast or be thrown into hell. Get out the hairshirt. There's no turning back.

❇ ❖ ❇ ❖

On the small balcony, we watched the procession of mourners passing through the tiny alley of the street a floor below us. They were carrying candles, wearing black mantillas. Wailing. Weeping. Men, women and children cried aloud. Aunt Doreen, my little cousins and I could see the streams of light coming down the mountain paths into this small Puerto Rican village in the valley of San German. *Sabado Negro.* Black Saturday.

Ten days visiting Aunt Doreen, dodging wild pigs in Boqueron, swimming in clear Caribbean water warm as a bathtub. Falling to sleep under the shroud of netting to keep the mosquitoes out. Trying to believe I wouldn't die from the noxious repellant Aunt Doreen insisted we wear day and night. Beautiful ring she bought me in San Turci, swirls of gold around cultured pearls too beautiful for me. Why me?

"You only graduate from secondary school once, Genelle. My post here at the Collegio won't be over until after summer school. I'll miss your birthday and your graduation. So wear the ring and think of me. OK?" It was packed away in its blue velvet box, safe in my suitcase that was ready to go that night. Susan, a fellow-student I had met on the plane coming over, was picking me up in a few hours and taking me to her host family's house. They'd bring us to the airport early on Easter morning.

Spring semester break in Puerto Rico for a Spanish major.

Best graduation gift Mom and Dad could have surprised me with. Now all I'd had to do was pass my exams!

The little village streets were filled six and seven deep and flowing like a human river of emotion. The life-size old carved wood statue of Mary was carried aloft through the streets as the procession made its way to San German's church.

"I want to go down there. I want to go to the church, Aunt Doreen. I've never seen anything like this, and I'll never have a chance again." My Aunt's three young boys begged her to go down also.

"No. You could get crushed in that crowd. You watch from here, Genelle. And boys, it's late enough. I want you to get to bed early. We have a lot of visiting to do tomorrow. Say goodbye to your cousin now, because she'll be leaving for Moca soon," my aunt said.

"Happy Easter." Hug. Kiss.

"Happy Easter."

"Nighty-night," young Robert said.

"It's not fair," muttered Edward. Aunt and cousins disappeared to back of house to brush teeth, wash faces, say prayers. I stared at the endless stream of faces lit by candles. There were tears on these faces. There was grief here, real grief. I didn't understand. It was only Easter.

Solemn dirges. *Ave Maria. Nuestro Señor. "La Iglesia habla por la gente lleno de la pena grava."*

I listened to the Mass broadcasted in Spanish over loudspeakers that crackled and sputtered with static over the crowded square filled with mourners overflowing the second oldest church in the western hemisphere. Overflowing even the Square and spilling into the *calles* surrounding it. I could see the edge of the crowd at the end of our street where it curved around to travel to the market square.

My aunt joined me quietly on the balcony. There were tears in my eyes. "I don't understand all this sadness." I said.

Doreen put her hand on my shoulder. "It's all show, Genelle. It's not real. Wait," she said calmly. "Wait until you see what happens next."

She was wrong of course. I had seen the tears. I had felt them. I knew those eyes filled with despair behind the flickering candle flames weren't lying. I waited.

The old church bells began to clang loudly. Cheers went up from the crowds. People started running through the streets shouting and laughing. Music seemed to burst into the air as every shut and darkened door was flung open, light pouring out into the streets.

I looked at my aunt in disbelief. "What's happening? I don't understand!"

She laughed and gave me a quick hug. "Christ has risen, Genelle! It's time to celebrate! They don't wait for tomorrow when they can party tonight. *Oiga! Oiga! Felicidad está aqui!*"

Susan rang the buzzer below. Bags were loaded into Mr and Mrs Ramirez' car. Hurried goodbyes and thanks were said as we parted and they carried me away into a night exploding with celebration.

"Una Cuba Libre para tu, niñita!" Mr Ramirez hands me my first drink. Susan smiles at me and winks. "It's a rum and coke," she says. "Isn't this great? I hate to think about leaving it all behind in the morning. I've had such a wonderful time."

"Well, I'm kind of glad to be going home," I said. "I mean it's beautiful here, but I miss stuff back in the States. It was getting kind of boring in San German with my aunt these last few days. Besides I can't wait to get back in school on Monday and show off my tan."

"Yeah. I guess it would have been boring to be here with

family. That's what's been so great about being with this Puerto Rican host family. We've had lots of parties and dancing. It's been fun. I love their rum and cokes too," Susan said.

"This does taste great, you're right about that. I've never had one before. Actually, I've never had a drink before. I mean, I had a sip of beer one time at a party a year ago and it was so bitter. I couldn't stand the taste. I actually wanted to spit it out. I gave the can to someone else. But this tastes sweet. I'm almost done with this one."

The pit of my stomach is warming nicely as I drain my glass and follow Susan out onto the patio. Any shyness I had in being in a stranger's home, with a girl that I had only sat next to on a plane before, has disappeared down my throat. Mr Ramirez hands me another drink as I move by him to go outside.

"*Muchas gracias*, Mr Ramirez. These are good," I say.

"Call me Carlos, *por favór*," he says and opens the screen-door for me. White teeth, gold around the edges of one. Laughter. Candles of citronella burn on wooden posts. Mostly men out here playing cards while a few women look on. Where has Susan gone?

He stands up. A tall young man. He looks away from the card-game into my eyes by chance and stumbles through the door of my heart by accident. Tall slim body. Darkly tanned skin. Eyes like a panther soothed by a full moon and full belly. "Chemón." His warm hand takes mine. I can't speak for a moment. My pounding heart repeats his name. Chemón, Chemón, Chemón.

He doesn't speak English. I don't know what the rum is saying. Rum running through my veins releasing any fear, releasing any guilt, releasing warmth into my lips that want to touch his.

71

My tongue feels a bit thick so laughter is easier than talking. Older men finish their card-game and watch us dance close. They whisper and wink at each other. I'm lost in a dreamland of forever.

Carlos in the doorway speaks rapidly, pleasantly to Chemón. I try to understand the words but they are too fast for my slowed brain. Chemón tells me he has to go into the village to get more coca-cola for Carlos. He'll be right back.

No. I want to go too. *"Yo voy tambien."* I reach for his hand. The watch on his wrist says one o'clock. *"Es damasiado tarde.* The shops are all closed."

"Yo voy a mi casa. No puede vas conmigo, querida," Chemón says.

"Si. Yo voy." I insist, not letting go of his hand.

Carlos tells me, "It's too dark on the road. There are no street lights here. This is the country. It's dangerous."

I squeeze Chemón's hand. "But I'm not afraid. There's the moon and Chemón will protect me." He smiles softly enjoying my trust and looks at Carlos who shakes his head "No".

The old men laugh. "There are giant frogs on the roads now and huge lizards here. Chemón would have to go too slow if he takes you to his house. Without you he can run, return fast. Right Chemón? Tell her about the lizards that bite, and the gigantic frogs with the big eyes, Chemón?"

His smile brings light into the pit of my belly. Such a warm mouth he gives me to kiss before he leaves. *"Yo voy rapidamente!"*

Carlos places a rum with a tad of coke in my hand as I watch Chemón disappear into the darkness beyond the patio.

Wet lips softly suck on my mouth. I open my closed eyes. I'm leaning on the makeshift bar inside the house. I see the face of Carlos whose lips I thought were Chemón's moving back from my opening eyes. I pick up my drink. It is light caramel in color. Bacardi. Pure Bacardi with a stick of banana in it. I drink some and look around. I'm all alone with the man of the house.

"Where did everybody go?" I ask.

"Home. *A ellas casas*," says Carlos with a shrug, finishing his drink.

"Where's Chemón?"

"Home."

"Where's Mrs Ramirez? Susan?" I am very confused. Where have I been? It seems like just a minute ago I was watching the boy of my seventeen-year-old dreams step off the patio and now I'm inside the house and everyone has disappeared except Carlos. I feel like I'm caught in some weird Twilight Zone experience.

"*Ellas? Están dormido.* They went to sleep a while ago."

"Is it that late?" I ask, drinking my rum, leaning on my elbow to stand up.

Carlos looks at his watch. "*Es solamente cinco, ahora.* Only five o'clock. The night is still young. *Está un* hour of darkness left before morning comes and we don't have to leave for the airport for a half an hour after that! Plenty of time for some more kisses." His hand slips from my waist moving down my hip. "*Dame un otro beso, hermosita.*"

I feel sick at my stomach as his mouth moves towards me. I struggle to push him away. I scan the room over his shoulder, dirty glasses and plates everywhere. Ashtrays and saucers with stubbed-out cigarettes. Carlos is drunk and so am I. I'm swaying, trying to push him away from me. What's happened here. What have I already done? Where did the four hours disappear to? The memory's blacked out. Did Chemón come back? My head feels so foggy. My eyelid is itching and so is my thigh and ankle. Carlos grabs my hand and starts

73

kissing it passionately. I pull away and stumble to the loo, then escape to the extra bed in Susan's room. Crawl under mosquito netting. Hear Susan's deep-sleep breathing as I lay my head down on the bed. The room spins me to sleep.

The trip to the airport is in silence. Sun is just rising over the sea as we travel down from the mountains and follow the coast road to the waiting plane. I doze between scratching massive mosquito bites on my left arm, ankles and thigh. My right eyelid is swollen with a bite and almost completely closed. My tongue feels swollen too. Susan is the only one who speaks in the awkwardness that envelopes the car.

I drift in and out of a drunken sleep on the six-hour flight and the three-and-a-half-hour bus trip to the Mainline. My eyelid is still swollen closed. Bus pulls into the Ardmore station. Anxious faces through the fogged-up bus window. Happy to see them. Happy to be home. Climb off the bus calling to them *"Mama, Papa – Mamacita, Papa mia.* It's good to be home! *A mi me gusta . . . "* Mainliners turn heads in shock. I fall into my mother's arms in the rum-reeking clothes of the night before.

Happy Easter.

I feel drunk for the next two days and I love it. Couldn't care less about the fighting behind my parents' closed bedroom door. Horrified looks they shoot back and forth at each other at the dinner table my first night back. So my speech is still slurred. So I don't have much of an appetite, just want to drink lots of soda. *"Mira, Mira. Policia!"* I say and double over in laughter. Nobody joines in. Old fuddy-duddies.

A fuzzy softness surrounding me at school. The rejection by the in-crowd, especially in the cafeteria at lunch-time, doesn't affect me for days. Everything is like underwater life according to ducks.

And surprise, surprise – I don't die. Don't end up in the hospital or miss a day of school even. So I figure those doctors are lying. Dr Fitzgerald with all those dire warnings, his bushy eyebrows knitted into a worried frown, had been just a put-on, a pact made with my folks to keep me away from that sweet-tasting, honey-colored liquid Puerto Rican gold – Rum!

❖ ❖ ❖ ❖

There is a sharp bend in the deserted road. It curves around to the left. Everything is dark dusky gray. Open sky. Country road. See it through the car window. Sudden blackness. Horrible sound. Not thunder, but loud – too loud to be safe. My eyes spring open, immediately wide awake, perspiring, panicky. Someone is going to die. I know it.

Sitting bolt upright in the bedroom of my parents' house. It's still my room even though I am living away at the university. Go back over every detail of the dream in my mind. I remember being, not in my physical body, but me none the less, in the back seat of a car where someone is lying down. Can see the back of the head of the man who is driving. It's not full daylight, in the dream it's dawn or dusk. There are mountains which the road snakes in and out of. The car speeds along. There it is. The bend in the road to the left. The car goes out of control. Careens off the roadway. Terrible sound. Extreme blackness. Then, everything is white and empty.

I feel completely powerless. Someone I know is going to die in a car crash and I don't have any idea of who to call or warn.

Splash water on my face. Look out the window of the bathroom. Talk to myself in the mirror. It's only a dream, Genelle. Forget it.

Breakfast. Lunch. Good Friday. Never can understand what's "good" about it.

Can't shake it off. Something's happened to Quan. That's the only explanation. It must be that. He's been in an accident.

Make an excuse to leave my parents' house. Go to the shopping mall. Mainliners pushing past me purchasing the finishing touches for their Easter outfits. Families must be decorated as well as eggs. Find a payphone. Call Quan's sister, Luanh. She assures me Quan is fine.

"He went with Vinny and the kids a few minutes ago to fly some Chinese kites he brought up with him," she said. "I thought you and Quan weren't seeing each other any more."

"Well, we're not going together. I mean we're both trying to get on with our lives. Luanh, it's hard to explain. I still love him a lot, and I just had this awful dream – a real nightmare. Please ask him to drive carefully going back to DC and have him call me next week and let me know he's back safely. I'm going back early, right after church on Easter. Listen, I'm sorry if I've disturbed you. Just promise me you'll warn Quan and ask him to be extra special careful. Please."

Darkness for two days. Steady driving rain. Edginess. Don't even help the young ones with dyeing the eggs. Want to leave. Don't want to wait. Want to go right now back to Washington and find out what's happened. Who died? This whole Easter vacation has been strange. Received a phone call from a man, a judge in a Pennsylvania talent competition I had been in during my senior year in high school. He now wants my permission to enter my name in the first step of the Miss America Pageant – the county competition. Bizarre. Me? Miss Montgomery County? What a joke. Represent the Mainline? I'm trying to forget I have ever lived here!

Mom is so excited at the offer. She had always competed in

the county fairs in Oklahoma. Snap the photo. Winona and her prize-winning apple-pie. Snap it again. Winona in her prize-winning Easter ensemble she designed and sewed herself. Oh, here's one of Winona at eleven with her prize-winning chickens she raised herself. Why not give it a try, Genelle? Find a drama coach when you're back in DC and have a go at it. Be good for a laugh.

Easter Sunday. Rain has stopped, but the sky is low dark gray. We sit in the stiff-backed pew, sermon settling over us like a shroud of words I barely hear but feel weighed down by. Still troubled by the nightmare. Listening. Not hearing any good news. Light coming in the stain-glass windows gets shut off by a sudden dark cloud. Lectern light makes a halo around the pastor as he speaks and gestures dramatically. "He's not dead. He has triumphed over death!" I try to focus on his face which blurs in the halo's brightness. "Death comes. No matter what your hopes and dreams are. No matter how important your work is. Death is inescapable . . . " A shudder starts at the nape of my neck and sends an icy streak of tingling whiteness down my spine and into my legs. Every inch of me is now listening to the voice speaking truth to me from the pulpit. "Yes, my friends, Death comes. Sometimes slowly, sometimes suddenly – but always it comes . . . "

Forget the victory. Forget the Salvation. The rest of the resurrection sermon flutters away from me on goose-down wings. I hear nothing more. I see the road winding to the left. Feel the speed of the car as it cuts through the dim light of the sun, distant from the horizon, still not scattering the darkness or being swallowed completely by it.

Uncomfortable in my own skin now. Feeling like I have spent too much time underwater with no clothes on. I pick up Barbara at Philadelphia's 30th Street Station. She has taken the train in from New Jersey. Load her suitcases into my Rambler station-wagon that used to be Mom's and we head south, back to George Washington University. After only a few minutes on the highway, I tell her about the dream. She lights a cigarette, her hand shaking.

"Who do you think it is?" she asks.

"I don't know. It's not Quan, anyway. I phoned his sister."

I drive on in silence, immersed in dread. We smoke a lot. Barbara is my best friend at GW. Quiet. Controlled. Shy. Dark eyes that burn a hole through the wall of your mind if you try to shut her out and she wanted in, or soft like a child's before crying. Barbara can drink. Almost as much as me. Our favourite hang-out is Mama's – an Italian restaurant just off Dupont Circle. Staffed by *latinos*. We practise our Spanish by flirting with the waiters. We do that whatever restaurant we go to – flirt with the waiters.

Barbara has been dating a Moslem pre-med student and part-time waiter, Ali. She is a Jewess who doesn't care which side of the bread you spread your butter on. She just listens, observes, smokes, and sometimes smiles. She balances my wildness and impulsiveness – calms me down and helps me sit still in the same place a bit easier. I meet Hikmet a week after Barbara met Ali. Both are friends and work at Blackie's Steakhouse. But Hikmet has dropped out of college, he's just into playing around. I'm not into anything serious with him. Still trying to get over Quan. Barbara is in love with Ali. He has a lovely sweet genuine manner, more preoccupied with his studies than looking for a sweetheart though.

We unload the car at the dorm. Go to dinner. We decide to try out a new place that we had often passed by but have never gone into. Need to take our minds off the eerie dream. I drive up and down the street that this little restaurant is on. Strange. It had been there just ten days ago. Now, we can't find it.

"This is really weird. I know it's here. I know it's on this street. Where did it go, Barbara?"

"I don't know. It definitely is on this street. I walked by it just two weeks ago but I don't see it either. Now *I've* got the chills, Genelle. Something is going on. It's like we're not meant to eat in that restaurant tonight. Let's go to Mama's and have a drink."

Stained red and white checkered tablecloth is like an old friend. The owner brings us our drinks. Slow night. A man gets up from a table way in the back where it is dark, lit only by candles. He comes towards us.

It's Domingo. He works sometimes as a waiter here but it must have been his night off.

"*Ola, amiga.* I saw you come in." He slides into the seat next to me. He looks terrible.

"*Como esta*, Domingo? What's wrong?" I ask.

He keeps shaking his head to choke back his tears. "*Que lastima.* It's so bad. They closed Blackie's down for the whole weekend! Everyone was too upset to work." He bursts into tears.

"Blackie's?" Barbara and I look at each other in dread.

"Who is it, Domingo? Who died?"

"You don't know him, Genelle. He never worked here. He's someone I worked with last year at my old job. He was a waiter in Blackie's and I was his busboy." He starts to cry again. "He was such a good man, so kind. Why'd he have to die? He was studying at the University. He was going to help his people."

I'm shaking him now. "Who? Who! Domingo, for God sake, what is his name?"

"Ali. His name was Ali. A Turkish student, he was."

"Oh my God. Oh my God," Barbara mumbles as she sits trembling. The cigarette in her hand shakes and her eyes stare

79

straight at me but don't see me at all. They are looking right through me to somewhere far away. Then her body begins to shake violently. I take hold of Barbara's arm, and speak softly and very slowly to Domingo. "Yes, Barbara and I knew him. You must tell us all you know. Everything. Please."

Dream come true. Blue.

Hikmet had been thrown from the car. Leg broken in three places, broken ribs, and one of his arms was broken. Ali had been driving. He was killed immediately.

Barbara and I are up all night. The funeral is in the morning. We go to the hospital early. Hikmet, wishing he was dead, lying alive, a mass of bandages and pain. The physical pain is nothing compared to the wishing he was dead. Three of his friends are with him. Two of them I know. One is a stranger. I'm introduced to Mesut who sits on the bed up near Hikmet's head, stroking him. He slides down to sit on the floor as Barbara and I move closer to share our grief with Hikmet. Barbara holds his hand and silently weeps. Hikmet doesn't want to look at me. I look down at Mesut on the floor leaning against the wall. His cream-colored jeans are dirty and he has an old zip-up black and pink jacket on with dragon designs. A red chiffon scarf is tied around his neck. He wears boots that are old and splitting at the sole. He stares at his hand then looks up at me. Like a gypsy he sits on the hospital floor, his dark eyes consumed with sadness. His softness repulses me.

We give him a lift to the cemetery. He is a directing major in the drama department at Howard University, he tells us. As we near the grave-site, I slow the car down to park. Before my car has come to a stop, Mesut jumps out of it.

Moslem men huddle together near the grave, arms around each other. Women with black scarves covering their heads stare at us and turn away. Lots of others. Domingo is there. I keep my arm around Barbara's shaking body.

As the casket is lowered into the ground the shouts ring out. Screams in words we cannot understand. Sound of unbearable pain. Hikmet is in a wheelchair and being restrained from throwing himself on the ground by two friends. Yells filling the air "Ali, Ali!"

As if to plunge himself into the grave with his friend, a young man throws himself on the ground and begins to roll towards the open grave. Three men grab him and pull him back. Another has to be restrained from trying to stop the cemetery workers from placing the dirt in the grave and covering the coffin. Mesut alternately weeping, wailing, tearing at his clothes and comforting Hikmet.

This is how it began between Mesut and me. The man I was to marry. Easter Monday. Tasting death's sting. No resurrection. Just a bad dream.

Winona

Perky. Pretty. Persistent. Honey-haired green-eyed farm girl with the get-up-and-go, was going . . . going . . . gone. Two hundred matched globes of light-beaming eyes followed the winding road from the church to the cemetery. Winona, won't you come out tonight, come out tonight, come out tonight, Winona, won't you come out tonight – nothin' will be right without you.

"They say she almost died at twenty-four. Just a miracle she lived another twenty years!" said the one under the black umbrella to the one under the navy umbrella in the crowd by the grave-site. "Pure miracle."

"Miracle-worker, you mean. That's what Winona was. Miracle-worker, plain and simple," the other mourner responded. "How she turned that Raymond around. He'd a been lost without her. She watched every penny, kept the books for him, minded the purse-strings. She knew how to stretch a dollar four-ways to sundown."

"Did you see him crying in the church," another said. "Poor man. Don't know if he'll make it through. And those poor children, the youngest ones just coming into their teens without a mother now. What a terrible loss."

A young Winona walked the floor of an Oklahoma farmhouse. Terrible pain in her lower back, crying baby in her arms. Back and forth across the back porch that had been screened in and converted to be the bedroom for her and the baby. Her brother Dirk was back from the war. He'd been injured in France and had settled into the box-room. There was no shifting him and all his books and machine gadgets that Winona's mother wouldn't let him clutter up the canning shed with. Besides, as colicky as this baby was, they needed to be in the back of the old farmhouse to let the others get their sleep.

"Hush now, little Ellie. Don't cry any more, please. What's the matter with you, honey? What's the matter, baby? Mommy wants to make it all better." Winona held the baby close and cried quietly herself. "Shhh. Shhh. Hush now. Everybody's sleeping. We need to sleep too, little darlin'." Baby wouldn't be stilled. Baby's tiny hands scratched baby's own cheek, trying to find mouth. Mouth was always open, gaping, gasping, crying. Winona ached for sleep. She knew something was wrong. This baby only slept when exhausted from crying and then it was a fitful sleep. She seemed hungry all the time but hardly wanted to suck any more. Winona's small breasts were full, dripping milk, when Genelle was a few days old but not any more. Over the past two weeks the pain in Winona's back was getting worse and worse, and her breasts didn't hurt any more from stretching bursting skin. Little Genelle was wanting more and more feedings and her crying hardly stopped.

She was her first child. Her lovely, little one. She wished Raymond was there to see and hold the baby. Wished he was there to take her in his arms too, and take away the pain with his kisses. But he was out west in California for basic training in the army. Preparing to go to war like all the young men.

How'd it all go wrong like this, she wondered. Where would the strength come from, with no sleep, to care for this crying child and cook the meals for her father and her brother now that her mother had left to work away for the week? Winona collapsed on the makeshift bed, holding her baby next to her, hoping for a moment's peace.

Something was wrong. Desperately wrong. Had been wrong for over a week since they came home from the hospital where the baby had been born. Only a day or two after they had arrived back at the farmhouse, the baby had become fussy and cranky.

"She just has wind," Winona's mother told her. "It'll pass." Days later, she added "That's one colicky baby, Winona. Make a compress for her tummy with some peppermint leaf tea. That should help."

But it was worse she had gotten not better. She was hungry all the time. Nothing helped.

※ ※ ※ ※

Pain in my belly. Screaming pain. Makes my tiny legs twitch and kick. Pull my knees up and down. Stuff my tiny fist into my gaping mouth. Feed me, someone feed me. I'm hungry, hungry, hungry. All empty inside of me feeding off my own cells, losing ground on living. Slipping away, maybe into the darkness of the big hole. Screaming. Crying. Gimme, gimme. Mommy, Mommy feed me, feed me. Body moves beside me. Lifts me up in arms again. See the teat. See it. Grab it with my gums and lips and suck. *SUCK HARD*. Whimper. Whimper. Body twists and turns to try and get a drop squeezed out. Suck. Sucking, sucking, sucking, nothing coming. Try harder!

84

Black hole sucks me into it. Gaping black hole in my belly getting larger. Crying out. Breast is changed. Suck some more. Is that a drop? Suck it harder. Nothing there. Own saliva not enough to feed my screaming cells. Give up. Stop trying. Stop sucking. Stop crying. Give up. No milk coming. No more strength. Go into the dark hole and sleep. Whimper, sleep. Stop moving so much. Stop crying. Stop sucking. Stop trying. It's over. Go away. Nothing here.

✠ ✦ ✢ ◈

Winona looked at the listless baby in the handmade cradle, asleep with her eyes half-opened and glassy. Not moving. Looking dead, but breathing. Winona, on her knees prayed the prayer of every mother, "God help this child. God help me. I don't know what to do." She begged and pleaded, holding her own head in her hands. Crying. Then a quiet came over her too. She stood up slowly, holding her lower back with her left hand, went to the kitchen and cranked the handle on the wooden telephone box.

The operator came on, "Hello. Butler's place? Hello?"

"Yes, Gert. It's me, Winona. Say can you ring Doc Stewart for me, see can he come out?"

"Sure. What happened? Did your Pa take a fall?" Gert asked over the crackling telephone connection.

"No. No, it's the baby. She's doing poorly. I'm worried how she's looking. Think she's taken a turn for the worse. Need to see if the doctor can stop out right away. Ring him for me, Gert. Please."

Doc Stewart wasn't long in assessing the problem. Winona's milk had dried up. He didn't know why it had happened so fast, just three weeks after the baby was born. But that was the problem. The baby wasn't colicky. She just wasn't getting any milk.

"Good thing you called me when you did, Winona. Another day and that little miss wouldn't have lived, I'm afraid. Now, you have your Pa get this formula filled right away and start that young one on it this evening. She'll be right as rain soon. You'll see. By the way, how's that back pain you had when you were pregnant? Gone now?"

"Well, it still bothers me a bit. I think it's just worry with the baby crying, me not sleeping, and carrying her a lot. It just nags at me a bit, but I'm sure it'll be all right real soon."

The doctor looked at Winona as she carried the baby on her hip and busied herself with tidying the breakfast dishes left by her brother and father. He closed up his black bag and placed a hand on her shoulder. "You mind yourself, young lady. You're the only Mama that young one has. You let me know if it keeps troubling you, you hear?"

Bottle-fed baby came back to life and thrived. Winona picked her up less and less as back hurt more and more, but baby Genelle grew anyway. Lifted her head and shoulders up in the Oklahoma sunlight streaming through the window spot-lighting her on the yellow blanket Grammaw had crocheted for her.

When the letter came from Raymond saying he had finished boot-camp and had saved enough from his army wages for them to have a place to stay out in California with him, Genelle was just a year old. Winona was delighted. She didn't even care if he'd won the money for their train ticket in a crap shoot – she was going. She needed him. She needed his arms around her. She was scared about how she would hide her pain from him, but she knew she would do it.

Holy hell was raised in the farmhouse about her going. "Traipsing half-cross the world with a little baby and not looking well yourself. He oughta come here and getcha if he was right, not send you a ticket!" her mother said. Her tirade lasted the whole afternoon. Her father just looked at the baby and shook his head. But Winona was going, there was no stopping her.

Raymond loved her, and loved the baby girl so small in his big hands. He couldn't do enough for them on his days off. He got an old beat-up jalopy with no brakes and got it in running condition so he could take them to the beach. Made a rocking horse for little Ellie who was sitting up now but not yet big enough for it, so he built a wooden wagon to pull her around in. He found an old buggy Winona could push the baby in and carry groceries back from the shop. He didn't notice the pain that flitted across her face as she bent to get food out of the oven, or how thin she was getting. He was too happy to have his family by his side. Each moment was precious with his time in the Pacific looming large upon the horizon.

Genelle was fifteen months old when Winona got on the bus and went secretly to see a doctor in Monterey, California. He sent her for X-rays. They confirmed his fears. He told her she had a large tumor on her fifth lumbar. "I'm afraid it's quite big," he said gravely. "We can't operate. It's intertwined around a few of the vertebrae, but the fifth is completely covered. No lifting or straining. You really should be in bed all the time. You must be in terrible pain. Let me give you something for it."

Winona would take nothing and told no one for a month. Then she took Genelle with her on the train up to Portland, Oregon, to visit her sister Doreen who had married and was living there at that time and going to graduate school.

It was a long trip. Winona was gone for five days. But she accomplished what she set out to do. The sisters cried over empty tea cups while the little blonde-haired toddler played with her Auntie's dominoes and the handmade cloth blocks her mother had brought with her.

"Promise me you'll take care of Ellie," Winona said pleadingly to her sister. "I need to know that. I'm writing it in my will, if you say 'Yes'. When I die, I need to know that you'll be there for her. You get along with Raymond okay. Better than him and Mama, anyway. I just need to know you'll always watch over Ellie and mind her like she was your own."

"Winona, now hush, please. You're not gonna go and die on us. That's just not going to happen. Jesus won't let it happen. Mama, Pa and I will see to that!" Doreen said with tears in her eyes.

"No. Now Doreen, you mustn't say anything to Mama or Pa, or Raymond for that matter. I don't want anybody to know. Raymond's going to get shipped overseas any time now with the war in the Pacific heating up, I don't want him worrying about us while he's over there getting shot at. And Mama wouldn't leave us rest for a moment if she knew what the doctor said. And I won't leave my husband now to go back out to Oklahoma. I won't! I don't know if I'll ever get to see him again after he leaves so I don't want to miss a second of being with him. You're not to breathe a word of this, you understand?"

Doreen was the older sister but she bowed to Winona's plea.

Agreement reached. Little girl lifted by Auntie's firm hands and placed on the train seat next to her mother. Big rubber balloon to blow up and put on a stick was placed in Genelle's hand. Auntie's parting gift. Tears and tissues, kisses blown at the window and waving hands. Train lurched forward and then set into regular rhythm down the track. Balloon smelled funny to Genelle. Like old tires. Genelle tried to blow it up. Her tummy hurt trying. Winona finished it and Genelle got sick all over the green and yellow ball on a stick that had to be taken to the little cubby toilet and washed. She didn't want it back and laid her head in her mother's lap. Slept the whole way home.

Raymond was shipped out a few weeks later. Joy disappeared. They returned to Oklahoma. Within a few weeks, Winona couldn't get out of bed the pain was so bad. Genelle watched her mother laying still under the covers. Genelle was quiet as a mouse.

✠ ❖ ✣ ❖

Everything changes from colorful to shades of gray. The house, the Oklahoma dirt, my Grammaw's apron, Aunt Doreen home from Washington standing in the doorway waving her hand above me – waving to the car disappearing from sight. All of it gray. Darker, lighter, shadowy or cold clear steel – gray all the same. Even the air seems dull and heavy. Gray.

Grammaw sitting on the chair outside in the yard. I lean against her great log of a leg and look at the saltine crackers with butter spread on them as they rest on her apron. I look up at her to ask if I can have some. My hand ready to pluck up the nearest one if she nods "yes". Her eyes watch the gray dust the car has left behind and she doesn't see me looking up at her.

Dead silence. Aunt Doreen goes inside the house. Granpaw moves away to wash his face with water he pumps. The splashing sound fills the air. There's so much quiet. Nobody breathes. I pat the wetness on Grammaw's cheek. She grabs the saltines and sets me on the chair and puts them in my hands, making cracker sandwiches of them. She says nothing. Climbs the two front steps slowly and disappears too.

Crackers taste yummy. I swing my legs a little. Feet don't touch the ground. Creamy butter on my lips, cracker crumbs on my summer frock Mommy made me. I can't remember her kiss goodbye. Don't think of her face even. Can't remember looking at the car. Don't know why I never cry. Only frown. Granpaw says "smile turned upside-down." Upside-down cake Grammaw makes with pineapple rings and cherries in the middle.

I don't even think about my mommy. It's so quiet. *Crunch, crunch* of the crackers. Why has everybody disappeared? Lick the gray butter and listen to the gray breeze now cutting through the one tree, cottonwood, near the house. Don't want to move. Don't wipe the butter off my face.

Even the littley kitten Granpaw gives me next morning is gray. Tiger-striped. So tiny and soft. So lov-il-lee. It's nose is wet and cool as it nuzzles my cheek and licks my chin. I giggle and lay on the day-bed next to my little Kitty-kit. Sometimes it cries. I'm its Mommy now. I give it a tiny bit of milk in a saucer. It likes it, makes it disappear. I give my littley-one more milk. I carry her in my frock to sit on the swing Granpaw hung for me in the cottonwood. I don't think of Mommy at all. I have my Kitty-kitty, soft and warm against my chest inside my pinafore. My pal.

I only cry when they want to take my kitty away. Aunt Doreen says, "Time to sleep. Put the kitty down, Ellie. It has to stay outside at night. She can't sleep with you." I won't put my Kitty down. I don't want to let her go.

Arguing in the hallway. Granpaw and Aunt Doreen.

Granpaw takes me by the hand. Makes a soft bed for Kitty putting clean rags in the old bread basket, and sets the bed on the stump by the side of the house. He takes the littley-one-so-soft from my hand and puts her in the basket.

"Nighty-night," I say.

Inside in the room empty of my mother's breathing, I lay on my cot by the big window screen that goes down to the floor. It is getting dark outside. I want my Kitty. I want something warm and close. Mommy's bed is cold. I feel the spread. Grammaw has it all made up. I start to whimper. Don't know why. I'm so small. Room's so big. I close my eyes and try to sleep. I hear my Kitty cry. I stop my whimpering and strain to listen. I'm sure I hear my Kitty cry.

"Go back to bed, Ellie," Grammaw says with a cross sound in her voice. The kitchen light hurts my eyes. I go back to my bed in the closed-in-porch that is where Mommy and me stay.

"You'll be sorry for what you've started with that child now, Joseph Butler. You couldn't leave things be, could you?" Grammaw says crossly to Granpaw. I can hear them plainly from my cot.

"The child needs somethin', Annie. Winona's gone. God knows when they'll let her out of that hospital over in Arkansas. You're leavin' tomorrow to go back to school for the week in Tyler, and Doreen's off to Oregon day after next. That child needs somethin' to take her mind off missin' her mama," Granpaw says. I hear him go into the front room where his day-bed is.

"You're spoilin' her, Joseph. Simple as that. But you can do what you want. I don't care any more."

I hear it again. It's closer this time. I scrunch up my eyes and peer out of the screen into the darkness. "Kitty-kit, is that you? P*sss. Psss. Psss.*"

"*Meow.*" The darkness moves. A shadow comes near the screen.

"Meow," so softly cried but I hear it and see her, my littley-Kit.

"Oh Kitty-Kit," I whisper and scratch the screen. She cries. I can't get out. She can't get in. I whimper. Try to tell her. Want to pat her. Want to touch her. My nose presses into the screen. My little fingers try to grip the mesh wall that is between us. My mouth makes little sounds to try and soothe us both.

"Meow. Meow." So wanting me, needing me, calling me.

"Kitty-kit. Littley Kitty-kit, *Meow, Meow,*" I whimper back.

Light over my cot comes on. I cover my eyes. Auntie Doreen lifts me away from the screen, gripping my arms tightly. I wriggle and struggle. "I want my kitty. She wants me," I cry.

"You both need your sleep or you'll both get sick. Now, stop this nonsense. If you stop talking to her, she'll go back into her own little bed your Granpaw made for her and sleep for the night. You're keeping her awake with your carry-on," she says. "No more of this now! You hear me?"

I close my eyes. Don't want to see Auntie's face. I want my mommy, not Aunt Doreen being mean, talking loud. I bury my head in the pillow so Kitty doesn't hear me cry and not go to sleep like Auntie says she needs to. After a little while I stop my crying and listen. I don't hear anything any more. No *meows.* No arguing in the kitchen. I'm too sleepy from crying to keep my eyes open and listen any more.

I wake up and see the early morning sunlight coming through the screen on the corner of Mommy's still empty bed. Everything is quiet.

I tip the little jug I can reach when I climb up on the chair by the kitchen table and fill my little saucer with milky-white. Around the corner of the house I go. I see Kitty in the basket.

I smile-happy, moving closer, minding not to spill the milk. I see Kitty in the basket, head turned funny, sticking out. Moving closer. I see Kitty in the basket eyes open not moving, not *meow*ing, not seeing me coming with my saucer. I see Kitty – somthing's wrong.

Milk splatters against my bare legs as saucer drops and breaks. Find Granpaw. Run find Granpaw. Find Granpaw now. "Come look at Kitty, Granpaw. Come look at Kitty, quick. She's not moving. Help her, Granpaw. Help her."

Granpaw's hand covers Kitty's head up with cloth of her bed. Granpaw's hand lifts me up. Holding me crying in my shaking body, choking sounds coming out.

More whispers. I can hear them. Auntie's voice. "She loved the poor thing to death. She handled it all day. Smothered it with love." Grammaw grumbling. "You had no business taking that kitten away from its mother. It needed to be in the barn to nurse, not with Ellie. Once she had her hands all over it you had to know the mother would stay away and this was bound to happen. Fine kettle of fish, Joseph. Hope you're satisfied."

Hang on tight. Don't let Granpaw go. Kitty-kit all gone. Others disappear. Don't let Granpaw go. Hang on his back while he digs the potatoes. Sit on his lap as he drives the tractor. Go with him to market. Sleep with him on the day-bed. Only way to stop the bad dream of Kitty's head turned funny with staring eyes. Don't let Granpaw disappear.

✠ ✥ ✠ ✥

Winona came back after two months in an Arkansas hospital. She was in a cast from her neck to hips. Tried but could do little. Weakening. Watching the mail for a bit of news from Raymond to nourish her will to live. Still hadn't written him the truth. Doc Stewart said nothing else could be done. "It's really only a matter of time, I'm afraid," he said quietly to Annie. What's the big secret? Everybody that saw her knew she was dying.

Genelle tried to get close and snuggle up, but the plaster wall encasing her mother shut her out. Only her mother's hands moving weakly but lovingly over her curls at night when she knelt by the side of her mother's bed made her smile. Otherwise Genelle stayed away to leave her mommy rest, and stuck to her Granpaw like glue.

This was what Raymond returned to. He had been through his own personal war over in the Pacific and was shipped stateside after a brief encounter with the powers that could not be shifted. He got a weekend pass to fly to Oklahoma to surprise his love who still imagined him on the other side of the world. One look at Winona wobbling around inside the plaster cast, wasted away to almost nothing, set him straight over the edge. A cyclone hit that farmhouse the likes of which no other twister before or since has done.

Winona fainted. Next thing she knew she was on a train with Raymond en route to the Mayo Clinic, a few states away to the North. Received some of the first ever radium treatment for cancer to be done in America. Test case that worked. Check the records. Winona Alkis – documented living proof that cancer was treatable.

"Miracle. Plain and simple." The girl wanted to survive, and that she did. Her back in a brace or corsetted, laced-up for support, she carried on against the odds.

Pregnant twice more when she was told never to try again. Both miscarried. But Winona and Raymond refused to listen to the harbingers of doom. Raymond always went for the long shots and Winona for the gray horse. After the miscarriages, two more children were born and no more attempted. Weakness wearing on her, but she struggled on without complaint.

She was always working or catching up. Doing, doing, done. Or resting. Resting. Sick a lot of the time. Migraines she couldn't fight her way through. And always, her back – she had to mind that back.

Genelle couldn't reach her either way. Genelle was in bed sick or her mother was in bed. Genelle was well, Winona was sick. Or she was sewing, cleaning, cooking, gardening, ironing. *A woman's work is never done,* until she's so sick she has to stop. Rest. Rest now to work tomorrow even harder.

✠ ✠ ✠ ✠

Mom's sick again. I bathe her belly with the steel ball in it where the ugly stitches are when I come home from school at almost ten years old. Bathe it every day with warm washcloths dipped in a metal bowl of warm water I get from the bathroom. Ugly scar wrinkles the skin like a strange animal carved with a knife into my mommy's belly. An animal with a steel ball for a head. I put the washcloth in the water, then wring it out. She puts it on her tummy covering up the metal ball. Don't want to touch her belly. Too ugly. Too yucky. Who hurt her like this? Will my belly look like this when I grow up?

"When the ball dissolves they'll take the stitches out," she tells me, her head propped on the pillow. Baby sister cries waking from her nap. Cleaning lady busy making supper-meal downstairs doesn't hear.

"I can do it. I can change the diaper. I can do it and not dirty the bed," I say.

"So proud of you, Ellie. You're my big girl. You're such a help." She pats my back and turns her head towards the

95

curtains that close out life beyond the window in Overbrook Park.

Tino is my first crush. The boy-next-door. I am nine, he is twelve. We go sledding in the winter. Daddy takes us and the dog down to the big hill in Overbrook Park. We build snowmen together. I watch him play badminton with his friend Richard in the summertime. I don't like his friend Richard. Tino acts different to me when Richard is around. I have my green shorts on and they are rolled up on my legs. It's roasting out. I have to get the birdie for them when it goes out of bounds. My job. Feel important. Then I hear them laughing as I bend over to pick the birdie up. What's so funny?

Brush dirt off birdie, frowning. Hand it back to Tino. Richard laughing hits it out of bounds again. On purpose. Into the bushes. They wait, smiling, for me to go fetch it back. It's in the tall grass. I look for it, my bum in the air. Then Tino's hand touches my bum and slides between my legs making me jump. He scares me. My bottom feels bad. I run into the house while they laugh. Tell Mommy.

"Change your clothes and wash your hands, then stay inside for now," she says. I go upstairs and hear her on the phone.

I hear Tino's Mom calling him to come home. Tino gets a licking. Tino doesn't talk to me. Won't play with me. Calls me scaredy-cat and stupid. I have my doll anyway, and my roller skates. Cathy O'Neill has moved away. I miss Tino. Want him back to play with. Wish Mommy didn't tell his mommy, then we'd still be friends. Frowning, hanging upside-down from the trapeze. Alone.

Soon I'm eleven. I play the dummy for newspaper bridge with Mommy. She's in her bed again. Sick or resting, can't tell which. Lay down next to her and read my book. Don't tell her what happened in school today. Couldn't. Couldn't tell her how Tommy and Peter trapped me in the classroom coat closet at lunch time. How Tommy held me down in the closet with Peter standing guard at the door watching in case the teacher or a stray student returned early. He was the look-out, while Tommy sat on my legs and threw my skirt up over my face, blinding me, muffling my cries for help, smothering me, holding my struggling body as he pushed his hands roughly up and down over my panties and then ripped them, all the time taunting me, saying "What's the matter, don't you like it Genelle? This is what you were asking for, isn't it? Twirling around before me. Smiling. Letting your skirt go up in class, dancing by me. This is what you wanted, isn't it? Stop your crying!"

I want to tell her. Can't. Feel ashamed. Feel bad. I liked Tommy before. Why'd he hurt me like he did? Why does he hate me so? I thought he liked me. I'm afraid to tell her. Can't trust her, I know. Can't trust her to see me, hear me, help me. She'll do what she wants to do, not what I ask, even if she promises. She'll do what she thinks is best. A mother always does.

✠ ❖ ✢ ✣

I look at photos of boyfriends with their arms around my mom before I'm even a dream in her heart.

"All the boys wanted to have a date with Winona. She loved to laugh and sing, had lots of friends, was full of life," my Aunt Doreen tells me.

I study the photos of Mom in her band uniform with flute in hand, of Mom by the Stuedebaker in a flowery dress. She grins showing shiny white teeth. Neat as a pin, soft as a pin-cushion.

I try to know the side of my mother which had been in hiding from me all my life by looking at photos after she is dead. The side that did the charcoal drawings hanging in our Mainline den, that designed the clothes and drew the sketches in the folder marked "OSU" at the back of her desk drawer next to the books for my father's business.

When I was younger and found the drawings and asked her about them, she flicked through them shaking her head and put them back, way back at the bottom of the pile of accounts and letters to write and bookkeeping records. She dismissed my question with a tired shrug. "Those were from a long time ago. Back when I was in school at Oklahoma State. Those drawings were just one of those things we had to do for class."

All I ever saw was Mom washing potatoes, sewing clothes, planting gardens she had no time to relax in and enjoy. She kept on smiling though. Smiled while she poured the concrete, laid the flagstone herself. Dad was too busy building roads to help with a few stone steps right then.

Mom worked like a mule. Carried the load. Met the strangers and made them friends. Coaxed Dad. Cajoled him. Manipulated him into being social for one night a month to get her out for two hours to laugh and breathe and feel like a person. Washed the concrete-loaded workpants on the Oklahoma wood and metal washboard in the Mainline utility-room sink. But it was all for love.

Lessons I have learned at my mother's knee. That's what love is all about. That's what a woman does. Sacrifices everything for the one she loves. I have watched. I have listened. I have learned.

In her nightgown in the utility room where the dog slept, the utility room of their beautiful new Mainline home, Winona stood. Water running in the sink. She picked up the ticks and threw them in the sink to drown them at 11:30 at night. They were coming out of the woodwork. She had to catch them, drown them, kill them while she could or they would overrun the house.

Raymond in bed sleeping, dreaming dreams of highways, bridges and tarmac. Winona, in her nightgown, battling blood-sucking insects. Pancake breasts with enlarged nipples visible through the filmy blue.

Genelle feared those breasts. Crone breasts Winona had at thirty-four-years old. Were they ever full, round, soft, nourishing? Genelle had always wanted nice round big ones like the curvy women had in her father's magazines that came in brown-paper wrappers through the mail. Genelle stole them away when no one was looking, to see what was so special about them. Women with beautiful skin and see-through clothes showing lovely full breasts and bums. Shame.

Raymond always told Winona it didn't matter about her breasts – she was beautiful inside and out, but still he looked forward to next month's issue, "for the interviews with influential people," he explained. Still he saved the pin-up calendar from the January issue in his sock drawer for the whole year. Genelle looked at the pictures. This was what men must like to look at, she thought.

In Overbrook Park the girls developed early. By ten years of age the breasts were budding, by eleven they were blooming. Genelle balled up tiny bits of tissue to try and make budding teats under her thin jumper. They wouldn't stay put. She gave up. Winona gave Genelle her first bra, a "trainer", at twelve. They had moved to the Mainline by then, and the torment of gym classes and showers had begun.

It is a warm July night and my face is flushed after my shower. I dress carefully. Now I'm not sure about my choice. Think maybe I should wear a different pair of shorts. These are a bit longer than the style. But I feel more comfortable in them than the mini-skorts everyone is wearing this summer on the Mainline. The blouse is new and I love the color. It's pastel pink and such a soft, pretty material.

I look at myself in the full-length mirror hung on the back of my bedroom door. I have that horrible sick feeling in my stomach all of a sudden. I hate my body. It's so ugly. Look at those bony knees! I turn sideways and try to stick out my chest. "It's no use, Genelle. Just face it. You just don't have it. You just make that obvious when you stick it out." Why couldn't I be built like my cousin Karen? She'd look great in this blouse. She'd look great in any blouse.

Mazeltov! I should be so lucky. My full-fledged Jewish cousin is blowing up like water balloons that know no limit. I get her hand-me-down clothes but the blood in my breasts comes from Mom's side not Dad's. For once I wish I was all Jewish. Don't look at me anyone. Shame.

I look in the mirror again. At least my breasts are soft and round, not flat and dry.

I hear Kelly's brother beep his horn for me. I run into the kitchen and give my mom a kiss goodbye.

"Have fun now, Genelle. don't forget to say goodbye to your father."

I go into the den timidly. Dad is in his contour recliner reading a book, relaxing after his dinner.

"Bye, Dad." I give him a quick peck on the forehead and turn to rush out.

"Goodbye? Wait a minute. Where are you going?"

"Oh, just over to Kelly's for the night. We're going to a fair."

"Well, wait a minute. Let me look at you before you run out of here." He pushes his recliner into an upright position and takes off his reading-glasses.

Military inspection at age eight I remember, front and centre, right face, left face, about face, *hut, two, three, four.* I hate having to stand before his scrutinizing eyes in my teens. I think of my friend Kelly and her brother in the car and try to stammer out excuses to get myself out the door, but it's too late.

"You can't go out of here like that," my father's voice booms. "Winona. Winona come in here," he shouts. My mother comes into the den, tea towel in hand. "You were going to let her go out of here like that? Look at that blouse. You can see right through it! Winona, have her put on an undershirt or something over that bra. I won't have my daughter walking around like a whore!"

"Daddy, Daddy, keep your voice down, please. My friends are in the car. Mom, tell him I don't wear undershirts any more. I'm too old. You don't wear undershirts over a bra, Daddy."

"Well, there must be something you wear. I don't want my daughter walking around in public in a blouse that you can see her bra-strap through."

"Yes, well, there are camisoles, Raymond," Mom said. "I'll see about getting her one tomorrow. You can put on a cardigan over the blouse for tonight, Genelle."

"But it's so hot. It's boiling, Mom."

"That's no good, Winona. See! She'll just get out the door and take it off. That's what we've got on our hands, Winona. A little slut. She doesn't care anything about modesty! You're going to let her go out and I bet you don't even really know where she's going."

Mom says nothing. I'm starting to cry. Stand up to him, for God's sake, Mom. Don't let him say those things about me. Defend me. Take my side for once!

I run out of the room. Mark is beeping the horn again as I run down the hallway to my room and throw myself on the bed. I hate my father! How could he be so crude?

"Right Dad – I'm a real slut. No guys even look at me! You really have something to worry about. I wish you did. I really wish you did!" I punch my pillow hard. Mom comes into the room.

"Genelle, honey. I poked my head out the front door and told Kelly you'd be right out. Now come on, go into the bathroom, and splash some cold water on your face. I'll pick out another blouse for you to wear."

"Oh Mom, I hate him so. Why does he have to be such a jerk? I was so excited about going to the fair. He's messed everything up!"

"Your father means well, Ellie. He's just worried about you and he doesn't understand a lot of things. Now hurry up and run into the bathroom."

The navy blouse Mom finds passes Dad's inspection and I leave the house finally. My eyes feel puffy and I don't want to look at anybody in the car for a while.

When Kelly gives me a poke and tries to get me to talk, I just mutter, "My dad, I hate him. He's a jerk," and stare out of the window.

A male voice from the back seat pipes up, "Hey, I've got a father from hell, too. Wanna beer?"

I shoot Kelly a look like who is that? – who else is in this car? Mark takes his hand off the steering wheel and changes the channel on the radio. "Genelle, don't pay him

102

any mind. That's my friend Gus. I've got to swing by and pick up Eddie too. Sorry your old man's bugging you. Don't let him get to you. Forget it and have a good time tonight at the fair."

"Yeah," Kelly says. "Come on, cheer up."

I turn around and take a look at the caped crusader in the back seat. Get on the bus, Gus – not bad. A grinning red-haired boy with a bottle of beer in his hand. *This Bud's for You* the sign over his head says. I make up my mind there and then that this is the night I will not disappoint dear old Dad. I'm marching right in and living up to his low expectations of me, *hut, two, three, four.*

"Hey, what are we waiting for?" I say. "Let's open a bottle now."

Kelly shoots me a sideways glare. "You don't even drink, Genelle. What are you talking about? Those six-packs are for Mark and his buddies. They're just doing us a favor and dropping us off at the fair."

"Hey, I don't mind letting you in on my share," Gus says stirring the pot. "I'll pop the cap on this one right now. Let the good times roll, babe."

I try to drink it. I hate the taste. Can't get it down. Feel like I won't keep it down. Rebel without the claws. I'll have to put the revenge on hold for the next opportunity. I'm just sweet sixteen for another couple of months. I'll show him in time. I will show him. Meanwhile pin the tail on the donkey, ride the Ferris wheel, the rollercoaster, and try to forget how I look and feel.

❖ ❖ ❖ ❖

Winona's stomach burned before, after, and during the meals. Why couldn't Genelle keep her teenage mouth shut, her opinions to herself? Why did she always have to rock the boat? Didn't she see how tired her father was, how hard he had worked all day?

Winona watched them battle and she felt powerless. The same way she felt when her own mother, who lived with them in the basement apartment, and her husband started arguing. Why did the fights always happen at mealtimes? She worked hard to make a nice meal and nobody seemed to care, to even notice.

After Genelle was gone away to college, Winona's migraines got worse. Then she had a hysterectomy. The doctors were taking women's insides out right and left in the 1960s. Don't want any more kids? Having painful periods? Easy answer – take out the plumbing, put you on a new wonderful tablet – pharmaceutical estrogen. Pain in the stomach? Must be stress. Take another tablet. Valium. Modern medicine. All the time Winona feared the worst. She dreaded to hear the word "tumor". Afraid that's what the headaches were from. But she never heard it. Never even was checked for it. She was given antacids and tranquilizers. There, there – stop your worrying. With "Mommy's Little Helper" – that sweet little yellow tablet, you'll be all right. Patted on the head by Doctor Perkins and sent home.

None of her family wanted to see it. None of the family wanted to open their eyes and challenge the doctor, get a second opinion. They all colluded with her fear of the truth and wore blinders. Didn't notice the weight dropping off her. Winona continued to push herself relentlessly.

Genelle had married Mesut now and had a baby girl of her own that was a year old when Winona met them for lunch one day. Three generations seated at the Clover Leaf Cafe's choice booth by the window that had a view of a pond.

Winona wanted to hold her granddaughter on her lap. She reached to lift her, stopping in mid-air. Instead she sank into the soft leather seat, looking almost defeated, whiter than the tablecloth.

"I'll be all right in a second, Genelle," she said. She saw the shocked look on Genelle's face and added quickly, "Lela's geting too heavy from Grammy, I guess. Now, let's have a look at that menu."

Winona said she was starving, but couldn't settle on what to order. When her cheese omelette sat on her plate with only two bites taken as she chattered away to her granddaughter Lela, Genelle felt she had to say something.

"Does Dad know how sick you are, Mom?"

"I'm okay. Just a little nauseous today. Must have a tummy bug. Dr Perkins says I'm fine. It's just stress," Winona says, putting a napkin over the uneaten omlette. "I guess I wasn't as hungry as I thought I was. Besides this omelette is huge."

Not as huge as Winona's denial was. And everyone continued to play along. They prayed in the quiet corners of their lives, but never admitted to each other that something was terribly wrong.

Winona and Raymond went to Paris for their twenty-fifth wedding anniversary a half a year after the incident in the Clover Leaf. Genelle minded her siblings while her parents were gone. They were only ten and twelve years old. Her parents had never had a honeymoon, never even had a holiday without the children in all of their twenty-five years together. Raymond had done fabulously well that year financially and told Winona to plan the holiday she had always dreamed of. She wanted to see Paris, to see the fashions and the shops, the Arc de Triomphe. So they went.

On the night of their anniversary, Raymond gave Winona a diamond ring – the ring he had never been able to afford to give her when he had asked her to marry him.

She looked at him. The finest French champagne in their glasses, candles on the table of the elegant restaurant in the fine hotel that they were spending the week in. Soft music playing. Everything was picture-perfect. Everything except Winona knowing she was lying. Lying like she had so many years ago when the tumor on her spine had almost killed her. But she knew that the pain in her stomach was too much for her to bear a second longer. She took Raymond's hand and squeezed it with the little strength she had and smiled. That sweet apple-pie, shiny white teeth, down-home smile. "I love you, Raymond. Always have." She lowered her eyes now. The pain shot through her again, almost immobilizing her. "You need to help me right now, Raymond honey . . . I'm sorry . . . I . . . " She gasped for breath and seemed to choke, trying to whisper the words and unable to. Clutching her stomach, she doubled over before him and he caught her before she hit the floor. In horror he carried her from the plush dining-room. Carried her in his arms like a bridegroom crossing the threshold. Carried her onto the elevator calling to the bell-captain to get a doctor – quick!

✠ ✠ ✠ ✠

I sit by my mom's hospital bed and look at the shell that she has become and wish it had been different, as I try to be sane, sweet and calm.

Mom tells me I look lovely today, really beautiful. She says the baby in my belly must be a baby boy because I look so pretty. The lipstick I put on before entering the hospital has worked. Mom is happy to see it, satisfied. I've done the right thing putting a wash of color on my mouth that is not wanting to be there again, not wanting to see my dying mother, a shrunken woman, even smaller than before.

I feed her. Feed my mother. Spooning bits of broth into her mouth. Brown broth, nothing but colored water with a strong, horrible smell. She's unable to move really, flat on her back. I crank up the bed. From off the piece of lambskin her head struggles forward a bit to meet the spoon I hold for her.

My father is in the hospital doorway, not wanting to look at this. Not wanting to see. Wanting to run away.

My spoon catches a dribble. Mom smiles like a baby. The baby kicks in my belly as I hold the spoon wanting to run away myself. Tear rolling down my cheek. I stop the next one from coming out of my eye. Be brave, be brave, carry on – pretend.

Isn't that all you ever taught me, Mom? Isn't that all you ever knew how to do? Look at the great deal it got you, Mom. Look at the great friggen deal! Forty-six-years old, in your prime of cancer, of dying, dying, but tenaciously holding on, trying to grip, grasp a drop – same as it always was, same as it always was. Me nursing you, Mom.

Remembering bathing your belly. I had come home from school and wanted what Cathy next door had – some chocolate-chip cookies and milk. Never mind. Bring up the basin of hot water – not too hot, get the washcloth from the bathroom. Look at the horrible scar on your belly.

Where were you ever? Where were you really? Just the tease of a taste, never milk, really milk, enough to drink. Always hungry, I was always sucking, always hoping you wouldn't be dry.

I struggle, Mom. I struggle still to find out all you never told me, showed me. Can't you see me, Mom? Couldn't you see what I needed? I didn't need you to dress me up and pretend I was some little doll to paint the mouth of and tilt forward to say "Mama" just like you. I didn't need you to stand in my bedroom when I was little and cringe against the back

107

wall while that horrible man stuck needles in my arm. For God's sake help me. Throw the bastard out. Make him stop hurting me. Stuff your prayers back down your throat. I don't need your punishing God. I need a woman who is vibrant and strong and self-loving and alive, not sinking into the grave from the very time I arrived on this earth. Leaving, always leaving me. Don't leave, Mom. For God's sake, I need you! It's you I've always needed.

My mother, Winona Alkis. So admired, so loved, so perfect – such a saint! Never raise your voice, never fight back. Love your man no matter what and set the table, light the fire, tend the garden, bake the pies, sew the graduation dress, pour the concrete, do it all, do it all, Mom. Do everything but don't rock the boat, don't be a passionate, powerful, out there woman. Don't defend yourself. Be a fool. Be a sexless fool held together with corset braces and string laces. I don't want to be a woman if it means being like you, dying here too soon, much too soon for me, Mom. I love you and needed your love. Look at me. I struggle inside this body of mine that you've taught me to hide. I rebel, fighting your fights, performing your scenes, dancing your dance that you have trained me to do. Mom. Mom don't go. I need you to see me. Listen, just listen.

I wipe the corner of her mouth with a napkin and she rests her head back against the lamb's-wool. How can I tell you, Mom? I'll never be good enough. I can't be a saint like you are. Mom don't go, please don't go. She sleeps and I still can't speak.

✠ ◈ ✠ ◈

Is it my fault? It's not yours, Mom. Your fault – God knows it could never be you, Mom, laying so sweet in the coffin. Church full. Choir singing "Somewhere my love". Dad crying like a baby. Then "In the garden" on the organ, the song you taught me to play on the piano.

Valium works. Seagrams Seven works. Cold and numb I look at my two-year-old daughter clinging to the curtain – one sock on, and one sock off. I lean back against the wall and turn my head. My hand rests on my belly. Baby hasn't moved for days now. Is it dead? Is it dead too? Come on, Genelle, turn inside out. Make a way to get through, up the years, to the place that can look at that strange statue of a woman stiffly standing against illness or lying down, resting. Carry on.

Mom, you've gone without ever answering the questions "Why?" "How come?" "How long?" Gone before I even know to ask. Gone, much too soon.

Mesut

Maverick. Mad dog in sheepskin. Master of the chess moves. Macho man in love-beads and sandals. Able to do backward somersaults for the crowd on the hard ground in the park. He didn't need a trampoline. He had a mind that could stop the world while he spun around. He had been a championship diver on the national Turkish swimming team in Ankara before the trouble had happened. He could have gone to the Olympics. Instead he went into the cavalry, like the father he hated. It was a well-calculated move to prove he was truly patriotic, was not a trouble-making dissident throwing rocks at buildings in the dark, passing out flyers in doorways to encourage the overthrow of the government. No. Better to don an army uniform and be sent to Turkey's Russian border to stare at the moonlight on the barren mountains, drink vodka straight from the bottle – everyone did there in that remote spot high above the narrow Coruh Valley – and kick the head of his horse when it disobeyed him. If he towed the line, made his moves carefully, he could get away with it all.

When Mesut was only five years old, his three-year-old sister,

Hatice, was found dead one morning in the family bed. All six of them shared the same bed in the winter to stay warm. His mother had wailed for weeks after it happened. Somehow Hatice had suffocated at the foot of the bed. The father blamed the mother. Mesut blamed the father for blaming the mother and making her cry more. A few months later, Mesut's father deserted the family.

When Mesut was twelve, he decided that his father, who saw him and his two older brothers only once a year on the Feast of Feasts, was dead. His father no longer existed as far as Mesut was concerned. He never spoke to his father or saw his father again. If Mesut's mother had word that the father was coming, Mesut disappeared for days.

He idolized his mother. She could do no wrong. She kept a perfect house, knitted the perfect jumpers, vests and socks, cooked the perfect meals, loved the perfect love, waved the perfect goodbye wave, tears held back in the eyes, as Mesut left Ankara to go to America.

Mesut was her baby, her youngest. She knew he had gotten into trouble. She didn't want to know what exactly had happened. She knew that he was wild, and too passionate about politics.

He had saved all his spare money from the four years in the cavalry. He deserved to follow his dream – the great dream. He would become a fabulous film director like Elia Kazan. Be rich and famous, known all over the world. And he would bring them, the whole family, to live in America. Mesut knew he would do it. He knew he was great. He wore his greatness like a cape of many colors. Anybody could see it. Anybody that had eyes. Surely he would be discovered by Hollywood, sought after by producers, make the epic film of all time.

But even deeper within him was the dream that he hadn't

111

even shared with his mother. The dream that he would be a star himself. On Broadway, like Brando. Then in Hollywood. An actor of international fame. A Moslem James Dean. The heart-throb of millions. He had the looks. A body that was agile, muscular and a face like Clark Gable without the funny ears. Mesut's ears were perfect. And he did have talent. He knew he had talent enough in his little finger to put others to shame. He'd do it. He'd make it happen. He knew it.

Twenty-four years old, with one suitcase in his hand, he arrived at La Guardia Airport in New York City ready to seek his fortune on Broadway with fifty dollars in his pocket and the address of the YMCA written in Turkish on a piece of paper stuck in the front of his Quran. It was 1960. Broadway must have trembled. Mesut Basharan had arrived.

Mesut had been shocked by his first night in the YMCA in downtown Manhattan. He prayed to Allah all night after one of the other men staying there put his hand on Mesut's bottom in the toilet and offered Mesut money to come to bed with him. Mesut was unnerved. Masturbation was a sin his older brother had carefully instructed him to avoid. Homosexuality was an insult to God as far as he was concerned. No self-respecting Moslem man would entertain such a thought. Mesut came from a country where heroin addicts were seen as traitors to their country and could be executed before a firing squad. Homosexuality was a curse worse than death to him. What sort of a country was he in now that on the first night such a thing should occur?

Mesut didn't sleep. He lay on the bed with his clothes on and his wallet in the sleeve of the jacket he kept on. Next day, he went to the embassy and asked for help – some temporary housing and the name of someone that could guide him.

Storming Broadway turned out to be a long walk off a

short pier. No equity card, no résumé, no education – no thank you! Actually the door slammed with just a look like "Are you crazy or what, don't waste my time!" Thank you's were never even mentioned. Time to regroup and make a plan. Mesut found the middle-eastern restaurants and made connection with students who were ambitious and knew the ropes. They helped Mesut get a scholarship to Howard University in Washington DC where he enrolled in the theatre department. He was learning the American way for all those who were born without money in their name – start at the bottom and work like a dog until you meet the right people and make the right impression and don't stop till you make it to the top.

He was a hard worker and he was talented. A good combination. He was bright and he perfected his English rapidly. Blackie's Steakhouse was the place he worked to pay for his flat and food. Mesut had a way with the European women he met. He melted them with his eyes and his quietly seductive way. American women were a challenge to him – bolder, stronger than he was used to. But he was a skilled manipulator. He knew how to sacrifice his pawns when necessary to get his bishop and knight into a commanding position of intimidation and surrender. The girls at Howard University were crazy about him, but he liked to see his swarthy hand on light skin rather than dark. He liked the blondes and the redheads that came into Blackie's.

Mesut had been living on Adams Mill Road right up the hill from the Washington zoo for over a year when he met Genelle. The stoop of his building was always filled with immigrants or students from all over the world. They sat by the light of the street lamp talking about their struggles or romanticizing their homeland.

It really wasn't an apartment he lived in. It was one room

with a tiny kitchen and shower. The room was always cluttered with books, clothes, magazines and newspapers strewn over the bed and the floor. The mess seemed to fill the gap of too much floor space and too little furniture. Besides the bed, Mesut had only a small bookcase and one rickety chair. The smell of this tiny apartment was amazing. The aroma was a strange combination of garlic and curry and the strong smell of Mesut's body – salty, spicy, sweet and pungent – very sensual.

Mesut loved the freedom he had found in America. He loved running down the streets singing whatever came into his head. Playing soccer with the young kids in the street on his way to the steakhouse. His clothes were his freedom flag. He loved rummaging through the charity shops and finding costumes to wear in the park or to class. Clothes were props to him. Playthings for the day.

✠ ✦ ✠ ✦

I'm nervous walking across the campus of Howard University in Washington DC. I haven't seen another white face since I parked the car in the visitor's lot. I know this was founded as an all-black university, but it's the 60s and I thought it was intergrated by now. I've got to be out of my mind doing this. I don't even want to be in the Miss America Pageant. But it would be a bit of a gas to see the faces of debutantes register shock at my photo in the Mainline Times if I was to win the competition for Miss Montgomery County. I see the Fine Arts building up ahead and continue to walk with an air of confidence covering up the fear that my blonde hair and white skin will be a red flag to some over-zealous Black Panther looking to make a name for himself within the party. Pure paranoia. Can't help it. I wish I had stopped at Mama's Restaurant and had a drink or two before I came over here to meet Mesut for my first session with him as my drama coach. I will next time if I have to come back. I clutch my copy of the script in my hand and act the part of Miss Cool-to-the-Core-slick-chick-don't-mess-with-me-I've-got -my-shades-on until I get inside the theatre where Mesut is waiting for me.

We go to a classroom with a large floor-space taped for a scene that is under production. I'm nervous. I have spoken to Mesut only once since I met him at Ali's funeral and that was on the phone. As he clears the stage of a few chairs and props from the previous class, I look at him more closely. He's wearing a long-sleeved black, red and tan plaid cotton shirt that's very wrinkled and fraying at the cuffs. It's half tucked in his pale green denim jeans that are faded and quite dirty. He has an orange chiffon scarf tied around his neck and is wearing beat-up black leather clogs on his sockless feet. The clogs make him appear taller than he is. I notice the denims are stretched out, but even so they hang very nicely over his well-formed bum. It's the only thing I find attractive about this man. That, and his eyes. His eyes remind me of something. Something from a long time ago. Something as familiar as my room growing up. Beautiful long lashes shouldn't be wasted on a man, and the large dark eyes, pools of black, luminescent black. *Sitting Pretty*. That's it. He has eyes like the painting I used to have hanging on the wall of my bedroom when I was a kid. A little girl with lovely black curls and a powder-blue dress holding a big straw hat. Black eyes that swallowed you up and lashes – long lovely lashes. Sitting pretty I could never be. Cut my blonde lashes when I was twelve hoping they'd grow in thicker and longer but they didn't. Have to blacken them with mascara or I look like my eyelids are bald.

I watch Mesut read through my script. I have the monologue for the competition memorized and hope this is the only coaching session I'll need. He runs a golden brown hand through his black hair. It looks soft. He has nice lips. Actually he'd be handsome if it wasn't for his clothes. Well, definitely that scarf has got to go and . . .

He looks up at me. "All right. We'll give it a run through. Let's see what you can do and then take it from there."

Suddenly I'm nervous again. Like I had never been on stage before. He sees my fright and does some warm-ups with me and then asks me to tell him in my own words about this girl I'm portraying and the man she loves that she's worried about.

In a few minutes I'm well into the character. He has me begin the scene. When I finish I feel good that I remembered all the lines and even got a bit of emotion going. Mesut is all business. He's on the stage beside me, blocking the scene, guiding my movements in response to particular lines. "Your timing is very good, but you need to build the emotion and cut down on all those unnecessary hand movements."

I try it again. It's better, I can feel it. He is pleased, but still critical.

"Genelle, you still are moving those hands too much. You distract from the mood and the emotion suffers. Here, use this bit of rope. Hold it in your hands. Let your emotion flow through your hands into the rope. Use it to build to a crescendo of feeling. Come on. We'll do it again. One more time." He puts his hand on my chin saying "Make me feel how much you love him, how you can't live without him. I know you can do it. Make me feel it."

We agree to meet for one more session. I know my performance has come alive under his direction today.

A week later, with a few drinks in me, it is easier to walk across the campus. He is pleased at how I have progressed with the scene. He is perched on a high stool by the window in the student theatre room, smiling with admiration as I finish my performance for him. He claps loudly. I do a

116

polished curtsy. He puts out his hand for me to come to the window. He says softly as he takes my hand "You're beautiful, you know".

He pulls me to him and kisses me. His lips are very soft and full. He has a strong aroma – salty, spicy, something I haven't smelled before. He kisses me again, more passionately. I struggle and try to pull back, but at the same time I find my lips responding to him. He is still sitting on the high stool. As he kisses my neck and lips, he holds me loosely between his legs. But the loose hold is deceptive because when I try to pull away, I find he has control of me, and restrains me.

"You don't really want to go," he says seductively. "Stay a while longer." More kisses. I feel something moving against my thigh. It isn't his leg. He hasn't moved on the stool. As he kisses my neck, I look down and see this throbbing, growing, aliveness moving down the inside of his loose-fitting jeans towards his knee. I am shocked and fascinated. He is seducing me right in this classroom in broad daylight and he hasn't even had a drink. Does he even take a drink? I don't even really know him. I'd like a drink. Fascinated and turned-on as I am, this is not how I intend to lose my virginity. At my insistence, Mesut lets me go. I gather my things hurriedly and leave, banging into a few chairs as I rush out of the room. Face is flushed and body is tingling. Run for the car. Run so I won't turn around and go back for another taste of those salty sweet lips.

The last rehearsal Mesut had with Genelle, he tore off part of his shirt and gave it to her. "Keep this with you. Have it in your pocket when you make your competition. Think of me when you touch it and that I believe in you. You will win. I know it."

Genelle returned to Pennsylvania for the pageant competition. She charmed the judges, remembered all the etiquette her parents had drummed into her. Wowed them with her performance. Her blonde hair and blue eyes made her look like the sweet-apple-pie-all-American girl, but she couldn't wait till she got out of there and back to DC where she could drink like she wanted to and curse when she felt like it.

She won the talent section and was first runner-up for Miss Montgomery County, 1963. Got her picture in the Mainline Times after all. Raised a few eyebrows for sure. Mesut was very proud of her. Genelle's parents asked only a few questions when she phoned him right after the competition. She told them that Mesut was her drama coach. She had learned well the lie of omission after their interference with Quan. She wouldn't let them stand in the way of anything or anyone again.

When Mesut and Genelle started spending time together they went to the films, foreign films mostly. Or they'd go to the park or the zoo, but they always ended up in his room. It happened very fast. Too fast to be safe.

Mesut's clothing still bothers me, but I'm ignoring it like I do with the state of his room. I seem to wear invisible blinders whenever I'm around him.

There aren't any paintings or prints on the walls of his place and there is only one window in the flat. It looks out on the alley. It's Saturday and I'm taking a break from my studies. I'm sitting on Mesut's bed. He's just gone out with a Turkish friend to go to the shops. I find myself staring at the yellow cracked window-shade. I have an idea. He has some charcoal pencils and crayons on the floor by a sketch pad amongst the clutter. I get the charcoal and begin to sketch on the shade. As I draw, I'm more and more energized, singing to myself and giggling. I rush to complete the drawing, coloring it in with the crayons. When I finish, there is a huge face – the face of a very young girl with large, haunting eyes and a whimsical smile on the shade. I'm really happy with my creation and decide to release the shade so that Mesut won't see the drawing until the next time he pulls the shade down. I giggle at the thought of the surprise.

We do little things like that for each other. Special little things that I keep tucked away in my mind. When my roommate at school says to me, "He's seems weird, Genelle. And the way he dresses! Why do you keep seeing him? It's a bit crazy, isn't it?" I pull out one of these memories and tell myself it isn't crazy, it's fun.

One time stands out vividly in my mind. The only chair in his room is very old. The chair is ugly and rickety. Its light-green paint is scraped off in places and one leg is cracked so no one ever sits on it. Even the magazines and clothes seem to avoid it. I tell Mesut how sad I feel for the chair and he is rather amused. It's just a few days after that when he phones me and tells me he has a surprise that should make me happy enough to cry. I'm right in the middle of studying. The night before we had a big blow-up, which is becoming a frequent occurrence now. We are both under pressure at our schools, and he knows I will be going home soon for the summer. That's the focus of our fights. "If you love me, you would never leave me," Mesut says. "You would stay with me now and forever and be my wife." Mesut doesn't understand that I need to go home to see my parents. He sees the real fear in my eyes about marriage though I try to hide it from him. I guess he is afraid I won't come back to him. Maybe he's right. But tonight, when he phones and has a surprise for me the anger is gone from his voice and his invitation is childlike and loving. I agree to go over.

When I get there, he has me wait in the hallway outside his door while he goes back inside to make sure everything is ready. Finally, he calls to me to tell me I can enter.

The lights are off. The rickety chair is placed in the middle of the room and hung on its back and round the seat and legs are Christmas-tree lights – the kind that sparkle on and off. In the middle of this is placed an adorable little teddy bear, all fuzzy and yellow and white. Mesut comes to my side with his panda eyes glowing softy, and smiles. *"Sssshh!"* he says with a finger to his lips. He takes my hand. "The king is thinking happiness."

For a little while the clothes, the smell, the final exams, and the emotional outbursts are suspended. We sit on the floor and watch the blinking colored stars, willing subjects of the king.

Mesut liked living on the edge, taking risks, welcoming challenges. He felt Genelle was playing hard to get, claiming to be a virgin still. Mesut didn't believe her. His friends assured him that a nineteen-year-old virgin didn't exist on an American college campus in the 1960s. Especially not one that liked to drink and party. He hated it when Genelle drank. He had to put a stop to it.

One night they had been out listening to some jazz at a club. He presented himself as a strict Moslem man when it came to drinking. As far as Genelle knew, Mesut didn't drink, ever. But she wouldn't hear of being in a nightclub and ordering a soda. She had several mixed drinks and was up out

120

of her chair dancing freely to the jazz, letting the music move her body. Mesut was enthralled when she was dancing for him in his room, but not in the club with other men looking at her. It was too much for him. Mesut took her arm roughly and left the club with her as she protested loudly. All the way back to his apartment she complained about his behaviour as she swerved in and out of traffic. He was silent. He was disgusted with her slurred speech and reckless driving.

"Just drop me off here," he said. "Don't bother to come in. I don't want you near me. You disgust me."

Genelle was shocked and hurt by this rejection. She didn't understand what he was so upset about. She didn't feel like she was really drunk, just feeling good. "Mesut. Don't be a party pooper. Don't be angry at me. I didn't do anything wrong. I was just having fun."

Mesut felt his power growing with his contempt. He looked at her and felt he'd been made a fool of for the past six weeks that they had been courting. "You tell me you're a virgin. You lie! You're a slut. I could see how you danced and looked at those other men. I could see your eyes. You . . . you'll make a fool of me no more."

These words went to the bone, the marrow of Genelle. They touched a desperate place in her. A familiar place. She reached over and tried to coax him, calm him. "Oh Mesut, don't say these things. They aren't true. I love you."

Mesut sneered at her and leaned closer. "You don't know what's love. I have no respect for you." She moved nearer to him to try and reach his heart, call him back from this darkness. Mesut looked at her face turned to his, at the lips he had kissed, the hair he adored, the eyes that he felt betrayed by and he spat on her. Spat right on her face. Then slammed the car door behind him and went up the steps to his apartment building.

Genelle wanted to die right then. She drove with the spittle on her face straight at the brick wall ahead. She felt so wrong. So bad. So ashamed. She didn't want to live. Somehow she turned the wheel just in time to miss slamming into the high stone walls that surrounded the zoo. She swerved and skidded across Adams Mill Road and jumped the curb before hitting a fire hydrant. Suddenly there was water everywhere.

✠ ❖ ✠ ❖

It's a terrible thing to be undone. It's a horrible sight to behold lemmings rushing towards the cliff to throw themselves into the sea. Whenever he mistreats me, Mesut comes back begging and pleading and in so much pain until I forgive him. Try to understand, try to love harder, better, clearer. Take on the responsibility myself, the guilt and the shame. "Not your fault, Mesut, mine. *Mea culpa, mea culpa, mea maxima culpa!*"

The last two weeks of finals, the stress of me leaving for the summer have combined to make the last twenty-four hours a nightmare. He has begged me to forgive him for his disrespect. He didn't mean it. How could he mean it? He loves me. He swears it. He begs me to come for a special meal he's preparing tonight. "Please. Please, let me make it up to you."

The dinner is my favorite – roasted chicken and steamed rice with sweet cherries on it. He won't let me wash up.

"I have borrowed Hikmet's record player. I want you to hear some beautiful Turkish songs now." I sit on the bed as he puts the album on.

When I had been going with Quan, he had always stopped his sexual advances when I felt we had gone far enough. Mesut has been much more difficult to put off. Tonight he won't be stopped. I try to stand up from the bed as he becomes more passionate with me. But he will not take "no" for an answer now. He presses me backwards on his bed, pushing against my lips hard. He takes my right arm out from behind me where I am trying to keep my body propped upright, and forces me down onto his mattress. I try to make him get off of me. I plead with him. Beg him to stop.

He rips the zipper on my slacks and pulls them down. I try to get up again and he pushes me down. I try to keep him from entering me. He's so strong – too strong for me. I bite my lip and then cry out in pain as he forces his way through my hymen. He doesn't stop. He won't stop. God, how he's hurting me. I'm crying and praying for it all to be over. He doesn't seem to hear my cries. His sweat drops heavily onto my blouse. Then his body begins to convulse. He writhes above me and finally collapses onto me. I'm still sobbing. When he sits up and sees the blood on himself and the bed, he is surprised. The blood keeps coming, staining his spread. Only then does he kiss me gently and see my tears.

"I thought you were lying to me, Genelle. I thought you were fooling with me. I'm sorry. Talk to me, Genelle. Say something, don't just stare at me like that."

I turn my head and look at my slacks. They are torn and laying on the floor. It hurts to walk. I move slowly, awkwardly, like a wounded deer, to the bathroom.

I watch the blood mix with water and swirl down the drain as I stand under the hot shower. I close my eyes and let the water pound on my forehead. I want to disappear. To dissolve. To be swept away down the drain into darkness. I don't want to get out of the shower. I don't want to see him. I feel so ashamed. I feel scared and alone. There's no going back now. "If you're not a virgin, no man will want to marry you – A good girl doesn't go all the way. She waits for marriage. Her husband must be the first – If you're not a virgin, you're a slut." Abusing myself with the words I have heard all my life,

123

I'm in a whirlpool, sinking fast. Spinning, being sucked down under to the bottom of the ocean. It's too dark to see. Just slimy feathery things brushing up against me before my lungs burst from the pressure of being down where I don't belong.

❖ ❖ ❖ ❖

Mesut walked the streets of Washington DC for two days and nights. He was beside himself. Genelle was leaving tomorrow morning and everything he had tried so far had failed to make her change her mind and stay with him, live with him. He was consumed by her. He didn't go to his classes. Didn't sit for his final exams. He had gotten someone else to work for him this weekend at Blackie's.

He was losing control of her. If she went back to her family in Pennsylvania for three months anything could happen. She could decide not to come back and he would be able to do nothing about it. He must figure out something, but what? She was still bleeding even though it was over two weeks ago that she had lost her virginity. He felt terrible about that. He should have known. He should have believed her. He shouldn't have hurt her like that. He would make it up to her if only she would marry him. He was panicking. He didn't know this friend of hers, Doris, who had come down this weekend from Pennsylvania to help her pack up her dorm room and travel back with her. Had Genelle done this on purpose to thwart him? Mesut was distrustful of Doris and resented her presence crowding him out. Crowding him out of the last night and morning they had to be together. He was sure it was part of Genelle's plan to get rid of him, to squeeze him out of her life.

Mesut had told Genelle last night that if she left Washington, she would never see him alive again. "If you leave me, you will destroy me! And I will destroy myself before I will let anyone else do that to me!" His self-control and logic had completely disintegrated. He was desperate enough to try anything.

✠ ✠ ✠ ✠

I move out of Mesut's shadow and gaze over the narrow ledge of the wall at the rushing water far below. I try to concentrate on some aspect of the waterfall's pool and to forget that he is towering above me, standing on the ledge swearing he will jump. Please God don't let him hurt himself. Please don't let him jump. He's just trying to scare me. He won't really jump. I hope. I can feel him staring at me and my eyes can't focus on the rushing water. My thoughts are swimming. I know he is exhausted physically, mentally, emotionally. I can claim little more myself. There was no sleeping for me in the hotel room last night with Doris. His incessant ringing of the room buzzer at six this morning has forced me downstairs and I have followed him into this park across from the hotel. Doris is sleeping upstairs in the hotel room, and my car is packed ready for the drive to Pennsylvania. I can't seem to think straight. The waters beneath me spin and twirl into fantastic shapes. I feel dizzy.

His voice startles me. "Look at me," he commands. "Look at me! What's the matter? Don't you like what you see? Don't you like what you've made me? Turn around and tell me who I am now. Tell me!"

I cover my ears and press my elbows against the cold stone of the ledge. I'm afraid to face him.

He jumps down from the ledge to my side and grips my arm tightly, shouting at me still. "Look at me, do you hear! I told you to look at me!"

I see his fist just before it hits the side of my head. Everything goes white. It throws me completely off balance and I fall to the ground. My face starts throbbing with pain and my tears come pouring out, liberating all the tensions of the past twenty-four hours. I feel relief as my body shakes with sobs.

Mesut kneels beside me on the grass. He starts to kiss my cheek where he has struck me and to kiss my hands. "I'm sorry, Genelle. Genelle, believe me. I don't want to hurt you. I love you. Tell me you love me. Tell me you won't leave me." He gives me his scarf to cry into and buries his face in my lap like a little boy turning to his mother for a reassuring touch to show that she cares and forgives him.

Automatically, I reach to caress his soft crop of hair, but my hand stops in horror. I know what he wants, but if I give him this it will be the answer he is looking for. I feel crazy for still loving him as hard as I try not to. I don't want to destroy myself for him. I stiffen my body. Take a deep breath. My body shakes with a final convulsion. "There's no going back. And there's nothing that can change it now, Mesut. We're not right for each other and we never will be." I feel unwavering.

He sits up slowly. His eyes search mine for a reversal of these words. My jaw is aching where he's struck me, but I meet his gaze steadily. The silence of the early Sunday morning hangs heavily in the air around us. He tries to speak, but can't find the words. Tears fill his eyes. He's trembling. Before I can say anything else, he leaps to his feet and begins running through the park. I watch him run right into the street. Cars swerve to keep from hitting him. He runs blindly across the next street and disappears from view.

I walk back across the park to the Meridian Hill hotel. My body weighs a ton. I drag it into the elevator. I enter my hotel room and shuffle wearily to the bed. Doris is breathing evenly in her sleep. Her dreams have not been disturbed. I light a

126

cigarette and touch my face. It hurts. My joints ache. The morning sun filtering through the dust-laden blinds is lost in the gray staleness of the room.

God, it's hot. Not even nine o'clock and it is stifling already. There's an air-conditioner in the window, but I would have to lift the blinds and that would probably wake Doris and all that dust would go all over and it probably won't work anyway. Nothing ever does in these crummy old hotels. I light a cigarette.

Lord, how I wish I was home. I try to remember something about Mom, but what comes careening into my consciousness is our kitchen table covered with white oil-cloth, cracked with use but immaculately clean. My father's face looms across it – his mouth is full but the words somehow fight past the barrier and tumble out forcefully . . . "How many feet in an acre? How many pounds in a short ton? 10,394 divided by 76, do it in your head! For Christsake, Winona, these kids are so dumb! What the hell are they teaching them in school, anyway?"

The phone rings. I don't move. My face is throbbing again. I wonder if it's swollen. I don't dare look into the mirror. The phone keeps ringing. Doris turns over and then sits up groggily. She looks funny, her eyes all puffy with dreams. The ringing stops.

"Boy, you look awful," she croaks with a voice hoarse from rest. "Didn't you sleep?"

I don't feel like answering her and take a drag off the cigarette instead. The phone starts ringing again. Seeing that I don't intend to answer it, she slowly rises, saunters over to the night table and picks up the receiver. She clears her throat and manages a "hello".

"It's for you," she says. I don't move. "Do you want to talk? It's Mesut, of course."

I take another puff on my cigarette and slouch lower onto the bed. What does he want now? "Tell him . . . tell him we have nothing more to talk about."

Doris repeats the message to him. I wait for her to hang up. She doesn't. "He says he has to talk to you. That he forgot to tell you something, and it's very important."

"I told you I don't want to talk to him. I'm not interested in anything he has to say. Just hang up!"

"I can't just hang up, Ellie. He sounds really upset."

Damn her. Why does she have to act like this, and why does she have to call me Ellie! I hate that name. I hate the way Doris says it. I look at her standing there with the telephone in her hand waiting, with her funny puffy eyes. Doris is so right, and prissy, and sweet – like her dog. I feel a wave of nausea sweep over me and I rush into the bathroom. I gag and choke and spit but feel no relief. Doris has dropped the receiver and is at my side. "Ellie, are you all right? What's wrong?"

I sway weakly above the toilet bowl. "I'm sick, that's all. It's this lousy heat."

Doris flushes the toilet and I flee from the sound. The receiver is dangling from the night-table. It looks like a microphone poised ominously in the gray air. He has probably hung up. I pick it up and listen. He hasn't. I can hear him breathing – waiting. The walls crowd in on me and my face hurts. I start to hang up, but then place the receiver on the table quietly. Getting another cigarette, I try to think. The receiver stares at me coldly. I go over and sit on the floor beside it. Doris closes the bathroom door.

A noise is coming from the receiver now. I lift it to my ear. He is coughing or gagging or something. When he stops he is breathing heavily. I become aware of my own breathing. He must know that I'm listening and waiting too. Doris is running the shower now.

"Genelle?" The voice comes soft and whispering through the coils of the cold receiver's cord. I inhale deeply, filling my mouth and throat and lungs with the thick cigarette-smoke and hold my breath as long as I can. I blow my answer into the black disc at my lips, "What do you want?"

It is his turn to pause, and I imagine his eyes closed in thought. I wait for them to open. "Well?" I'm impatient. I want to scream loud and long and shrill, but I know if I do he'll never say what he wants to. Besides that, Doris will probably come running out of the bathroom all dripping in a towel to see what is wrong.

"I called because I forgot to tell you something," he says cryptically.

"You said all there was to say. So did I."

He is coughing again.

"Are you okay?" Stupid question. I catch myself on my sentiment and immediately add, "Well, if you have something to say, say it! If not, I may as well hang up."

Regaining his breath he answers. "You're right. We did say just about everything. But . . . you see . . . oh, why don't you understand? You said you were agreed with me, but . . . " he pauses, sighing deeply.

"Mesut . . . "

"What?" His response comes fast and with hope.

I move my lips slowly. It is so hot. "Nothing. I mean . . . What do you want to say? What did you call to tell me? Something you had forgotten to say?"

"Yes, something I forgot to say . . . Goodbye, Genelle."

"What? You must have wanted to say something else. What is it?"

"Nothing more than that. I just wanted to close

129

everything for good. I want you to say it to me too . . . Say it, Genelle."

Everything is turning upside down. It's so damn stifling in this room. My lips move in a whisper, "I can't".

"What did you say?" his voice is anxious.

"I said 'Goodbye, Mesut'."

Silence. Then comes his answer. "Goodbye."

I hear the sharp, mechanical click and then silence. I sit with the receiver next to my ear, until the dial tone sounds. The phone is cold and dead in my hand, then it becomes heavy. I let it fall from my fingers and listen to the rhythmic knock it makes as it bumps up and down on the floor. I want another cigarette, but am too tired to get up for one. Doris is done with her shower now. The water has stopped.

"Is he all right?" Doris asks as she comes out drying her hair with a towel. "He sounded strange. I mean, well, he is strange, but he sounded like . . . I don't know . . . desperate, I guess. What did he want to talk about?"

"He wanted to say goodbye, Doris. At least that's what he said. And he wanted me to say it to him."

"But I thought you guys had settled all that last night. That you made it clear things were over and that's when he jumped out of your moving car, right? He jumped after you told him you'd never see him again."

Doris stopped drying herself for a moment. "You don't think he'd kill himself, do you Genelle? I mean maybe we should go over there just to make sure he doesn't do anything really crazy."

"Doris, you amaze me. You tell me you hate this guy's guts, that he's loony-tunes and he's destroying my life and I should stay away from him, and then you say let's go see if he's all right. What is it with you?"

130

"Genelle, I meant what I said. It's just I don't want to see anybody kill themselves, you know what I mean?"

"He is in a very dangerous frame of mind. It's strange, Doris. When I was talking with him on the phone, he was coughing a lot and he hadn't been coughing at all when I saw him a little earlier in the park."

"Oh my God, Ellie. Does he have a gas range? Maybe he's turned the gas on and is committing suicide right now. Try to call him, quick."

Dialing the number without thinking of the consequences, I feel a panic rising in my chest. The phone rings and rings without an answer. Now I'm scared too.

"Doris, you call the police and have them go to 81 Adams Mill Road, Apartment number 1C. I'll go and bring the car around and pick you up at the front door of the hotel."

When we arrive outside of Mesut's place, two police cars are already there. I make Doris stay in the car and I run. They are just forcing him out of his apartment. His dark eyes flash at me with crushing contempt as they push him past me down the hallway towards the street and the staring crowd that has gathered.

I lean weakly against the wall, my emotions on the brink of hysteria. The smell of the gas pouring from his room is filling the hallway and making me nauseous. One of the neighbors recognizes me and tries to comfort me, but I pull away. "Leave me alone. Can't you see what I've done to him? God forgive me."

When I get outside, I see the two policemen talking with him across the street. I run towards him, tears and stares blinding me. Brushing past the policemen, I grab hold of Mesut's arm.

"I'm so sorry, Mesut. I didn't want to do this to you. I just wanted to save you from hurting yourself. Forgive me, Mesut.

131

Please. I just wanted you alive, not this awful humiliation. I hate myself for all of this! Please. You must forgive me!"

One of the policemen tries to intervene. I hear Mesut's voice rising calmly above my sobs. "Let me talk to her for a moment. Please. We'll sit right over there on the steps so you can see that everything is OK. I need to explain to her."

The crowd starts to disperse. Mesut sits facing me and stares at his hand as he always does when he tries to collect and arrange his thoughts. He looks much older to me right now, and very tired. As he thinks, he rubs a bit of skin on the side of his finger with his thumb. Finally he lifts up his face, a soft half-smile on his lips. His eyebrows wrinkle together as he shakes his head. Reaching over, he tenderly touches my cheek. "I should have known. Life is so . . . crazy. You want to save me, you want me alive. But I am already dead. I died a long time ago. Before you ever knew me. Before I ever came here." Little droplets of water are collecting above his upper lip and across his forehead. "You were my greatest delusion. You were so free and full of life, so full of feeling, Genelle. So sensitive to everything around you. I believed you knew all about me without me having to say a word about it. How foolish I was. I'm not saying I'm sorry for what happened between us. I'm not sorry we met. I know it's all over. I know. I would have done so many things different if I had a better situation here." He looks at the policemen and the apartment building. The children have gone back to playing on the sidewalk.

He takes my hand in his. Mine look so white, so pale in his. "Leave. Go on and go back to your family, Genelle. I was wrong to do this. It's not your fault. I was lying to myself. Go on and go. I had turned the gas off before they came. Don't worry. I'll be all right. Just go now."

132

My heart is aching for him, for us. "Please forgive me, Mesut. Please."

"Genelle, there's nothing to forgive," he says as he stands up.

One of the policemen comes over to ask me if everything is OK. How can I answer that? My whole world feels inside-out. Mesut asks him to tell me what they found in his apartment when they got there.

"Well, the gas was off when we got in the door," the policeman explains. "The smell of gas was strong, but we opened up the window. Do you live there too, Miss?"

"No. She's a student. She just stopped to say goodbye to me for the summer," Mesut answers before I have the chance to. "And like I was telling you, I had put the oven on to get some chicken cooked and something must have happened to the gas while I was on the phone with a friend. I noticed the smell after a while and had just shut off the oven when you broke in. Go ahead, Genelle. Your friend is waiting for you. You've got a long trip ahead of you."

Guilty. Can't get it right, can I? Try to get over him. Go back to the Mainline and shut him out of my heart. Don't write to him. Don't respond to his phone calls. You can do it. It's too crazy. He'll get over you.

❖ ❖ ❖ ❖

Mesut's friends nurtured him back to sanity. He buried himself in work. He told himself that she hadn't been worthy of his love really. He worked seven days a week for months. Worked and slept, worked and slept. The chairman of his department at Howard University wanted to know what had happened. When would Mesut make up his final exams and do his final performance project for the semester? Mesut confided his heartache to him and Mr Turner took him under his wing.

Studies taken care of, work under control, Mesut appeared to be healed. Summer was nearing a close. He called the registrar at George Washington University to find out when their classes would resume and find out what dormitory Genelle was scheduled to be staying in. He was exercising again and feeling fit. He was sure that she would try to see him again. He imagined her coming with Barbara to Blackie's Restaurant, seeing him and falling in love with him all over again, only this time he would reject her.

But September came and Genelle never showed up at Blackie's. Mesut decided to phone her dorm. She hung up as soon as she heard his voice. It happened all over again. Mesut became obsessed with trying to see her again, dreaming about her, phoning incessantly. He even came to her dorm several times to try and see her but she barricaded herself in Barbara's room and wouldn't come out or let anyone in.

Mesut stopped going to his classes again. Stopped eating, and started wandering the streets. His friends tried to reason with him, tried to reach Genelle to no avail. It was well into November, almost Thanksgiving, when Mr Turner reached Genelle on the telephone. He had obtained her number from one of Mesut's Turkish friends.

Mr Turner tried to impress upon her the graveness of the situation. "My dear young woman, I'm afraid you don't understand how serious things are. Mesut seems close to losing his life. He's so despondent. He is unable to do anything. He's become homeless now because he's not able to work and can't pay rent. He's staying one night here one night there. He hasn't been to but a handful of classes all semester. You must do something to help him. He's refused to see a counsellor. Surely you can't hate him so much. If you just would agree to see him once, I'm sure things could be sorted out."

"I can't," Genelle answered. "I feel terrible to hear Mesut's condition, but I can't help. Maybe he would feel better for a little while if I agreed to see him, but I'm terrified of what it would do to me personally. I'm afraid for him, but I'm also afraid for myself. I'm sorry, Mr Turner, you have to help Mesut some other way. I can't be involved."

Mr Turner took Mesut into his own home. He made meals for him, took him to films, to theatre, became like a father. Gradually, Mesut wanted to be involved in living again He threw himself into his acting and directing classes with total commitment. By the following summer he was back on his feet, working as a lifeguard at a swimming pool by day and at Blackie's four nights a week. He had finished the spring semester with honors. And he met a girl. The daughter of a banker. She was a swimmer almost equal to his prowess in the water. Their bodies were well-suited, but he held onto his heart this time. He wouldn't be caught off guard or allow himself to be vulnerable again.

* * * *

I try everything. The green ones, the white ones, the black beauties, the dexies. Whatever my lab partner Benny holds out in his hand. Like candy to a baby they are to me. He looks like Dr Kildare. Handsome, blonde-haired, tall. Benny does Botany stoked to the gills. I haven't answered any of the calls from Mesut. I'm determined and desperate at the same time, but I work hard at not feeling the desperation. I drown it instead with beer or Bushmills whiskey or Benny's

Boilermakers. I don't know anything about Benny except that he lives in Maryland and commutes to the university. I don't care. Don't have his number, but he has mine. He's testing a new drug for the army out at the Walter Reed Army Hospital on the weekends. It's a gas. Well, not literally. It's a colorless, odorless liquid – a highly potent drug. Just need a drop of it on a piece of paper, eat the paper and blotto – poppo – magic-wando you're off the planet. Just what I need. They call it LSD.

He says he'll try and get me some. I feel so guilty about Mesut. I wish Mr Turner had never called me. I wish I didn't know how bad things are. I wish Quan wasn't seeing that Chinese girl Charlotte and would hold me and tell me how good I am. No, I don't. If he did I'd want to kill myself more than I do already.

I'm no good, I'm no good, I'm no good – baby, I'm no good.

Benny isn't in lab this week. Second week going. Wish I had his number. I'm not feeling very well myself. Lots of "Kissing Sickness" going around. Mononucleosis. It's sweeping the GW campus. Maybe Benny's got it or it has him. Maybe mono is what's making me nauseous and feverish too.

Home for the holidays. Happy New Year. "You do have mono, Genelle. A mild case. The steroids you're on probably have helped to keep it at bay," Dr Fitzgerald says. "Rest and eat healthy."

I return to Washington DC ten pounds skinnier and determined to put some meat on my bones and drugs in my blood. Benny is healthy again and we're in Zoology Lab together this term. Just can't seem to keep away from each other's side, though we're drinking and drugging buddies more than anything else. I eat fried chicken, fish and chips and drink Guinness stout day in and day out trying to fatten myself up for the kill. Brandy, Bushmills and Bacardi fill in the blanks.

Within a month I'm puking my brains out daily and peeing the color of strong tea. The pain in the back of my head is like someone pressing brass knuckles into my skull. So back to Philadelphia I go and into the hospital. Hepatitis. My skin matches the yellow of my bathrobe. They can't understand how I got it. "No shellfish? A dirty toilet seat, perhaps? Couldn't be alcoholic hepatitis for Godsake, she doesn't drink. Has a blood condition you know – can't." Wanna bet? Three years of heavy drinking on a liver already weakened by impure blood – well, well, I might get my death wish after all.

Not so fast. Put me in bed for three months at my parents' home. Feed me no fats. Thank God, the thought of butter or eggs or beer for that matter makes me want to throw up. The bad news is I'm going to live. I'm getting healthier. Doris, home for spring break from her college, takes me out of the house for the first time in over three months to see the film *America, America*. I laugh hysterically through it. Laugh so hard the tears roll down my face and my liver hurts. It's Elia Kazan's latest film. The leading man is Mesut's look-alike.

Don't drink again. "Don't drink at all" they had always told me – the doctors, my parents. I try to stay sober and enroll at summer school in Philadelphia. I date two young men. Both Jewish. Both acceptable, respectable, good-looking, intelligent. I sabotage both relationships. One before it gets off the ground. The other, well, the other gets to me sexually. He's seductive, Carl. He's a good kisser. He dates me for a couple of weeks and then meets me in New York City for the World's

137

Fair and afterwards, in a little uptown apartment he's borrowed from a friend, he gets me horizontal on the sofa. Gets me hot and heavy and excited and bingo – I start to cry hysterically. Can't stop crying. Don't want to. Carl lights a cigarette and tries to stay calm. He apologizes for his actions, apologizes for coming on too strong, too fast.

"It's not you, Carl," I tell him. "It's me. I'm no good. I can't do this. You should stay away from me. I just hurt people that care about me."

"What are you talking about, Genelle? Look, I've upset you and I'm sorry. Really."

I tell him the whole story of Mesut and how I drove him suicidal, how I hurt Quan, how I am poison to the ones I love. He tries to comfort me, tries to put things in a different perspective.

"Genelle, sounds like you've suffered enough already," Carl says. "I don't know about Quan, but this guy Mesut doesn't sound like he is playing with a full deck, you know what I mean? And he treated you terribly. I think you are lucky to be out of that situation. What do you want to be, the welcome mat for the United Nations? I mean, if you let people, they will walk all over you. You're not responsible for what happened to Mesut. He's responsible for that."

I can't hear him. I don't want to hear him. I don't want the arm he puts around me and I definitely don't want him to touch me. Can't handle it. I'm fried sunnyside-up.

In a month when I return to Washington DC, it takes me only two weeks of classes, two weeks of heavy drinking, two weeks of dancing with every black man I can single out at the campus mixers to get me to the point of kamikaze in combat mode. It is like I'm on a rollercoaster. A gigantic rollercoaster.

I'm in the lead car. It's just crested this humongous hill and is racing down at blinding speed. Only thing is the track ends at a stone wall. No one comes out alive. I figure if I'm going to die, I'm gonna control the crash. I'm gonna choose my poison. The poison I deserve.

I do the most destructive thing I know to do at that point. I go to Blackie's Steakhouse for three nights until Mesut's working. I touch his hand as he places the food on my table. Within three weeks I have dropped out of the university and am living with Mesut. I lay myself on the altar of his life.

We are wed. I am his wife. I am beaten as I should be. I am kicked down the street for being a "whore" because I had bare feet and had talked to a man with a newspaper while I was crying in the park. I had been sitting on the bench crying as I watched my husband of one month, who hadn't come home at all last night, saying goodbye to the young girl he has spent the previous night with. They are on the other side of Dupont Circle green. I have already approached them and Mesut has told me to wait for him across the park. I am kicked for three blocks from the park to our flat. Kicked in the back, in the legs so I stumble and hit the back of my head once. Kicked past on-lookers. All the time the words keep being hurled at me. "Dog!" *Kick.* "Pitiful excuse for a woman!" *Kick.* "Out roaming the streets. You should stay home and wait!" *Kick.* "Slut!" All the way to our apartment building. Pushes me inside our door and slams it shut and leaves me again.

Staring in the mirror, I look at the painfully thin body of a young woman with a twisted face. Wild uncombed hair, and blinding blue eyes that stare madly back at me. Daring me to try and pull the knife out of my third eye in the middle of my forehead. I see the handle of the knife but my arms are paralyzed and I lean on the top of the dresser and stare at my reflection. God help her this slow dying. God help me help her.

Gravesend

Last stop on the "A" train to Brooklyn. Avenue X and Ocean Parkway. High rises and row houses. Generation after generation holding on to their little piece of brick, their place on the block. Sicilian neighborhood, three decades now. Oh dear me, you can't laugh here or somebody will want to know what you've got up your sleeve or down your dress. Put on the blinders and pretend you see nothing, hear nothing, and above all speak nothing of what you didn't see or hear.

The walls have ears. Paper-thin. Buildings built at the end of the great depression to give men work and rekindle hope. The "greats" all blended together. The Great Depression, the Great War – the war to end all wars. The end. Grave's End. D-day. End of the war.

❖ ❖ ❖ ❖

I don't want to fight any more. I give up. You win. Do what you want to me whether I deserve it or not. I don't care if you never come home. I promise not to call the police any more. I know it's never true. My worst thoughts are always the best anyhow. Thinking that you have been killed in an accident or

141

mugged and left for dead because you haven't come home for days. I'm used to it now, Mesut. I'm looking at you sleeping there on the bed and for a moment, a brief moment, something like fire flashes through me and I think it would be so easy to kill you now. Now, while your eyes are closed and you're dreaming. But it's only lightning passing through me from somewhere else, charging me for a moment and then gone. Leaving me empty and powerless again.

The children. It's always the children I remember – cling to as my reason for living. Only two, but two is enough when they're both still in diapers. I've followed you. Acquiesced over and over. Relinquished the nest I've made for us as you trash yet another job because "They don't recognize genius". Let me count now. Is it eight? No, only seven. Just seven places we have lived since we were married four years ago. From New York to Washington DC to Virginia to Maryland, back to DC, then to Glenolden, Pennsylvania, and now to Philadelphia to this third-floor walk-up three-room flat on Osage avenue, West Philadelphia. I feel lost in this world of diapers, and bottles and flats that come and go like shifting sands. And you lay there so quietly, serenely, sleeping.

I can't even hate you. I think you are the king and I am a beggar outside the city walls of your world. I catch a glimpse of you when you come out of your gates and beg for a glance as your entourage passes. What am I thinking about? What am I talking about? I think I'm mad as you say. Insane. Babbling. Mumbo Jumbo King of the Jungle, and all the other kings of the jungle – *Mumbo Jumbo will hoodoo you. Mumbo Jumbo will hoodoo you.*

You stir. I know I should move, but I don't. I'm sitting on the floor next to your bed, watching you sleep. Everyone else is napping. Lela in her bed in my room, and little baby boy,

142

Ismet, in his cot in the kitchen. Please don't wake up angry. Please don't wake up.

"What are you doing, Genelle? How long have you been sitting there on the floor?" he says as he sits up and looks at the clock. "You should be preparing dinner. You know I have to leave in an hour to go to work. Look at you, you're pathetic!"

"Mesut, please don't leave. I need you. I'm so lonely. I feel like I'm losing my mind here day in and day out looking at these four walls with two small children. I need you. Talk to me. Just come home one night, come home tonight and talk to me. Please."

"Look at yourself, Genelle. Do you ever look in the mirror? You should. You should take a good look. Your hair is a mess. You're skin and bones. You look like death warmed over in that house-dress. Whimpering. That's all you ever do. Is it a wonder I don't want to come home? If you tried, just tried halfway to make yourself presentable!"

"Mesut, please don't raise your voice. You'll wake the children. I'll try harder. It's just . . . it's just I was so worried when you didn't come home again over the weekend, I just couldn't seem to keep anything together. And then I found those telephone numbers in your pocket as I was doing the wash, and . . . who is Linda? Who is Rochelle, Mesut?" I grasp at his shirt as he gets up to storm out. "Don't leave again, please. Don't leave me like this."

"You stupid jealous woman! I'm working, slaving to keep food on the table, to give something for those children in there and look at you. What kind of help and support do I get from my wife? A weeping, snivelling excuse for a woman. What man would ever want to come home to you? Let go of me!" The back of his hand I have come to know so well. It knocks me hard.

143

I hear my daughter calling from the bedroom. "Daddy, Daddy, don't be angry at Mommy. Mommy? Daddy?"

Mesut's eyes glare at me. He loves his children. Gives them anything. "You are driving me crazy, Genelle. You're destroying us all."

I go into the bedroom where Lela is crying and I try to calm her down. Try to hold back my own tears from wounding her again.

I hear Mesut throwing things in the front room where he had been sleeping. Ismet is crying in his cot in the kitchen now. Mesut is yelling loud enough to drown out Ismet's screams. Lela is shaking in my arms. I hear Mesut go rampaging into the kitchen. I'm afraid he might do something to Ismet or take him, just take him and disappear. I run into the kitchen with two-and-a-half-year-old Lela following me. Mesut is completely out of control. His eyes wild. He raises a large glass bowl that we were given for a wedding gift and smashes it into his head breaking the glass into pieces. Gashing his forehead open. Blood is gushing. Lela is screaming and holding on to my leg, as Mesut shouts loudly "You're killing me. You crazy woman. You're killing me. Look what you've done!" He grabs a tea towel to stop the spurting blood and runs out of the flat.

Finally, I phone my father. After the glass is cleaned up, the children quieted down. After not sleeping for three days, watching the clock, praying for Mesut to be OK, to come home, to try to get it right if he did come back one more time. And still no call or word from him at all. Yes, finally, I phone my father.

When Mesut rings at last, I have already phoned Dr Winters, the psychiatrist my father told me to see. Mesut agrees we can't go back to the way things have been.

Dr Winters speaks to us together briefly, then to Mesut

alone and then to me. He is very Mainline. He's in his late fifties. This doctor is definitely out of the reach of a waiter's salary. Good that Dad's paying for it, not us.

We sit before his large oak desk. The window behind Dr Winters overlooks his swimming pool and tennis court. I suddenly realize that I went to high school with his son. I recognize the graduation picture hanging on the wall. I'm full of shame. I can't even get a wife's role right. I cook and sew and make babies. I try to do as my husband tells me. I haven't had a drink since we were married. Our wedding pictures are a vivid recording of my last drunk. The little white pills are my mainstay, raised while pregnant to a much higher dose and reduced again a month or two after delivery. I cringe, sitting before this man in his three-piece suit, diplomas on the wall and successful children displayed in photos framed for posterity to show the world what normal is. Dr Winters shuffles his papers and clears his throat. He leans back in his leather swivel-chair and makes his pronouncement.

"I will speak frankly, Genelle and Mesut. After talking to each of you individually and weighing the pros and cons of your situation, also looking at your family histories, and your medical history, Genelle, I can make only one recommendation. It is my strong opinion that the two of you need to put at least one hundred miles between you for at least one year," he says and then leans forward in his chair to drive home his point. "Or one or both of you will be dead within six months."

Neither Mesut nor I speak. We sit and stare at Dr Winters as he takes his glasses off and rests them on the desk. The silence lingers. His intercom buzzer rings and he stands up, offers us his hand to shake and shows us out.

Mesut moves to New York City. We stay in West Philadelphia.

He has always blamed us for not being able to follow his heart in theatre and films. Years of blaming me and the children for hampering his creative talents being developed, and his degree in Fine Arts being used, are over. Now he has his chance.

I see counsellor at University of Pennsylvania department of psychology. In addition to the little white tablets that I've taken for years now, he gives me other tablets that make me feel like a zombie. Tablets to sleep and tablets to "even my moods". I hate how they make me feel. I hate lying down to go to sleep and feeling like the room has become a big well of blackness that is swallowing me up so fast I don't have a chance to breathe. The sleeping pills are the first ones I throw away. The mellaril tablets next. I can't stand the way they make my nose run and my skin feel. It's like I'm wrapped in glass wool, that prickly softness that makes me afraid to move but keeps me warm and filled with static. Once I find out my counsellor is just in training and that his teacher, supervisor or whatever is sitting on the other side of a one-way window that looks like a mirror that is rigged up in his office, I bolt and throw away the last of those tablets. I struggle for money and hate to get help from my father. I always feel like the dollars come wrapped in flypaper that sticks fast to my hands. A feeling that no amount of scrubbing seems to get rid of.

I get a part-time job as a secretary in an architect's office. Twenty hours a week. I hold the job. I can do what I'm told and receive a pay-check. Somehow I am useful. I can't talk to the people in the office. I just smile and do my work. Smile a plastered-on-smile that everyone knows is false but they leave me alone and don't ask questions. If they don't ask, they'll never know how defective I am. That I'm on my own with two children because I can't get it right.

Take the children to the park to play. I start to feel a bit more like I'm part of life, not just peering through a window at others who are living. I get bursts of feeling. I don't know what it is really, but I remember it – like the feeling I had after my first drunk. Like things are calling to me. Life is calling to me.

Coming back from the park one day I hug a tree. I feel its bark. My body tingles. I look into the tulip Lela holds up to me and feel a ripple of pleasure pass over my body as I see the brilliant red and then the yellow centre that pulls me into it and does something wonderful to my senses. Going to work, I am walking through an underground tunnel at eight o'clock in the morning and I run my hands along the cool smooth-like-glass surface of the tiles and feel my fingers tingling, alive with sensation.

Stay late in centre city one evening after work and go to a talk. "Overcoming Isolation." A tall man with curly frizzy gray hair wilder than mine rubs my shoulders and then I turn to rub his shoulders. We are partnered for the evening in exercises one after another geared to help people connect with themselves and others. Story is his name. He takes my number. James Taylor says it first and Story repeats it, *"You have a friend, Oh yeah. You have a friend."*

It's good to know I have a friend even if he leaves and goes to California – I still know I have a friend. First one in a long time. I get postcards from San Diego signed *Your friend, Story.*

Six months of separation from Mesut pass, dotted by visits from Santa Claus. That's what I call Mesut when he arrives every two months for a weekend to visit the children and me loaded with gifts for us all. Santa Claus with a Turkish accent and sandals and a headband. Mesut has joined the ranks of all the other unemployed actors in New York moonlighting as hippy cab-drivers. He is happy on his visits. Full of the excitement of New York City and pleased to have time with us. I fix myself up for twenty hours of work a week and Mesut's visits. He notices. He's affectionate. I don't ask any questions about where he's staying or who he's staying with. I'm happy to have him all to myself one night every two months. Crumbs from the king's table are a banquet to the starved.

✠ ❖ ✠ ❖

The sidewalks in Gravesend are lined with Chinese restaurants, Chinese laundries, Turkish carpet stores, Irish newsagents. Each of them has a tiny flag of Green Orange and White in the window. Proof that above all else, above whatever land the owners were born in, above whatever nationality their names over their shops tout, above the fact that they are on American soil, above all else this little flag shows they support the Italian Civil Liberties Association. They acknowledge that this is indeed "Little Sicily". And, if they do not want to sport the Italian flag in their shop's window, no problem. No problem in closing them down. A brick through the window. A horse's ear wrapped in butcher paper, a friendly note through the letterbox – a blank sheet of paper with a bullet hole in it. One by one the shop owners loved Sicily or they were gone. Brooklyn had a lot of neighborhoods. Another place to sell their goods could be found if they didn't like who the streets of Gravesend belonged to.

Mesut convinced Genelle to move to Gravesend with him to make a brand new start. "A great place near the beach at Coney Island" is how he advertised it to her. Told her she would love it. He would teach the kids to swim in the ocean like he had learned to when he was a boy in the Black Sea.

Things were so much better and they wouldn't let the same problems happen that happened before. He wouldn't be waiting tables. Driving cab was much better, and he had already had a bit part in an off-off-off Broadway play.

It was November of 1969 when they moved into the high-rise. Welcome to Gravesend. They lived on the third floor of a ten-storey building. Never met a neighbor. If they saw anyone in the elevator, there was never a word uttered.

Mesut fit right into the neighborhood with his dark eyes and hair, but Genelle with her blonde hair and fair skin stood out like a sore thumb. If she took the children for a walk and smiled at anybody on the street, all she got were suspicious stares. Mesut was gone fourteen hours a day. He told her those were taxi hours. It didn't take long before she was feeling isolated and lonely again.

Mesut had always held the money. In Gravesend it was no different. He took the family grocery-shopping, to the laundry, and every so often for a meal. Genelle didn't need to have any money of her own. After all, didn't he provided for all of her needs?

Mesut wasn't surrounded by Moslem friends any more. Instead, he lived in the wild world of Manhattan after dark where anything could be bought at a price. As a cabby, he got paid for a fare sometimes in hashish not cash, a bag of good dope, some cocaine or some sex. A cab driver in New York City sees everything and has a chance at whatever his pleasure is. One week he came home with a huge cheesecake from the famous Lindy's restaurant. Payment from a passenger. Another time with some vodka, a hefty bottle along with some Kahlua. The next day was his day off. He announced that his buddy from work, Seamus Haggarty, was coming over to help him put this gift to good use.

"What shall I make for dinner, Mesut?" Genelle asked anxiously.

"Swedish meatballs. They usually come out OK. And don't worry about dessert. We'll pick up Oreo cookies when we go to the shop. Seamus is crazy about Oreos."

I try to focus on the recipe on the page before me. Forget it. I bang the counter with the wooden spoon. Ismet is crying at my feet, pulling on my skirt, trying to get my attention. Lela is riding her tricycle around the small three-room flat. I've got to get this dinner right. This is the first time Mesut has invited anyone home for a meal in years. I pick up the letter from Aunt Margaret again and reread it. I can't believe my father is actually thinking of bringing another woman into the family home. A widow with three girls of her own, and my mother not dead for even a year and a half yet. How could he do that? What happened to the great undying love he had for my mother? What about all she put up with and suffered in the name of love. Is that it? Is that what it all boils down to? Put up with crap for twenty-five years, wait for the kids to grow up so you can share your golden years together only to die from too much crap – can't stomach any more, can't swallow your anger or your hurt any more. It eats a hole in your stomach and you're gone and in eighteen months you're forgotten like last years's clothes with a new woman filling your shoes. What am I doing here? What am I playing at? This isn't the little house on the prairie for sure and I don't want to end up like my mother or my grammaw.

Ismet has stopped crying and is sitting up on the floor at my feet clapping his hands and amusing himself. He crawls away into the other room to find his sister. I had picked out some cooking sherry when I was grocery-shopping with Mesut for tonight's dinner, thought it would pep up the cream sauce and give it a special flair for company. I take off the cap and take a deep breath. It's been a long time since I've had a drink. It smells real good. I don't pour it into a glass. I don't think about the consequences. I put the bottle in my mouth and drink it. Gulp half the bottle down. It's disgustingly salty to the taste. Oh, but that warm, soft glow starts spreading from my stomach up through my chest into my face. I'm OK. I'll be just fine. Blueberry-pie and apple-blossom wine time. Make that Swedish meatball dish swim in sherry. No one will ever know. After all the chef must always test the sauce. Get sauced . . . no, not yet. Keep the lid on it, Genelle, and maybe they won't finish all the vodka.

They both smell strange when they come into the apartment laughing. Something must be very funny. They fall onto the sofa in bursts of giddiness like two fourteen-year-olds just having pulled off a great joke on someone else. Are they laughing at me? Has Mesut been making fun of me? I hide in the kitchen and put the noodles on. I hear Mesut teasing Lela. I turn around in the small cubby of a kitchen to get out some lettuce and make a salad and come face to face with Seamus. His big form is filling the doorway. Tall and muscular, his great thick black hair falling almost to his shoulders and tumbling onto his forehead in a soft wave. But it's his eyes that stun me stupid. The biggest bluest eyes with light dancing in them to a mischievous beat.

"Tell me, luv, where you hiding the biscuits?"

"Oh, God. Biscuits. I didn't make any biscuits. Mesut didn't tell me to make biscuits. I've got some French bread and some butter – would that be OK for now?"

"Mesut told me he got two bags of Oreo biscuits – are they all gone?"

"Oreos? Oh, you want Oreo cookies? Sure, we have lots. But dinner will be ready in just about ten minutes, Seamus. That's your name, right? You sure you want them now?" I ask, not able to take my eyes off his.

"Sure, we'll have some now and some later. Got a case of the munchies, luv. Got to have some now. You smoke weed?"

"Weed?"

"Pot, you know, Mary-gee-wanna."

I know I'm red in the face. I'm stuttering now. His arms are tan and muscular and rippling the sleeves of his T-shirt.

"No," I say. "No, I've never tried the stuff. I don't smoke any more. Haven't smoked since I got married. Mesut doesn't approve of it."

He grabs the bag of Oreos and starts laughing again. heading back into the front room.

"Doesn't approve? You don't approve of smoking, Mesut. That's a gas. That's a fuckin' gas."

The table is set. The dinner is finished cooking. I call Lela to wash her hands and take the washcloth to wipe Ismet's fingers.

"Genelle, open the vodka," Mesut bellows from the sofa.

"The dinner is all ready. We need to sit down at the table."

"Genelle, I told you to open the vodka. Then you can sit down with the children and eat. Seamus and I want to have a drink first."

Opening the bottle I want to pour myself a drink so badly. My jaw is clamped tight and the muscles in my arms seem frozen. I sit at the table with the two children and eat the food with my back to the men who are sitting on the sofa drinking. Tears roll down my face and into my mouth. More salt. I'm where I belong. Just another child, not fit for adult company.

152

Not fit for anything but taking orders and crying. I'm always good for a cry. I can't even look at the children as I eat. Don't even know how it tastes. The noodles will be stuck together and cold. It all will taste terrible when they finally come to eat. I'll get beaten later probably for the horrible meal. I hate it. I hate it. I hate it. Mother, you lied. "The quickest way to a man's heart is through his stomach." There is no way to a man's heart. I can't stomach this. Trapped animal.

"Mommy, can I get down?" Lela asks.

"Did you finish your food?" Don't look up. If she sees my face she'll know I'm crying and say something.

"I don't want any more."

"Okay. Sure. Get down and go on and play."

Ismet is mashing his food into the tray of the high-chair. He gets more on his face and the floor than in his mouth. I don't care tonight. I'm like a robot now. Just clear their places and mine. Wipe his face, put him down on the floor and clean up the mess around his chair. The kitchen is a mess too. I stand gripping the sink and just wait. Wait for my thoughts to calm down. I see Aunt Doreen's letter laying on the counter. Water-drops have blurred some of the words.

Lela's coughing. "Daddy, that smoke makes me choke. Stop it, Daddy."

As I enter the front room of the flat, Mesut sits back up on the sofa a bit awkwardly. He has a hand-rolled cigarette of some sort in his hand which he passes to Seamus. I stare in amazement. Seamus inhales and holds his breath, stretching out his well-formed arm in my direction, handing the drug to me to smoke.

"She doesn't smoke, Seamus. I told you already," Mesut says reaching to get the smoke from Seamus' hand. Seamus teases him, moving his hand all around avoiding Mesut's grasp, chokes a bit and then exhales.

"There's always a first time, Mesut. Come on now. You wouldn't deprive your wife of a little fun, would you? What's your name again? Jemma?"

"Genelle."

"Right, Genelle. Come on – take a drag."

"Mommy, don't," Lela pipes up. "That smoke stinks."

I look at Mesut for permission. He's shrugging his shoulders and then gets up and goes to the table to eat something.

I look at Seamus' outstretched hand and his big come-and-get-me grin. I can't have the vodka right now. I know I'll have to bide my time on that. "I . . . I . . . "

"Come on now," Seamus says as he puts his beautiful arm around me. "Here's how it's done. Just put this end in your mouth and suck hard, then hold your breath a bit."

I don't like the taste. It's kind of sweet and dirty at the same time, like some dried thyme. I don't feel anything different. I wait and try it one more time. Nothing. Seamus is gone. He has taken it to the table and is finishing the smoke off with Mesut.

When I get the children to bed, Mesut and his friend are drinking the Kahlua. It smells too sweet. Like thick coffee with way too much sugar in it. One bag of Oreos is gone and they are into the second one. By the time I have the table cleared, they're gone. Out to some political rally, so they say. What do I care? Mesut gets one night off every ten days. He has promised to spend it at home with us. So much for promises. Whoopee.

I look for the vodka bottle. It has been forgotten at the side of the sofa. I embrace it. Sit in the rocking-chair and hold it in my arms like a long-lost lover come out of the grave to save me.

It was a warm night. Genelle had all the windows in the apartment open. It was just getting dark. She was hoping that there would be a bit of a breeze after the scorching sun went down. She heard the loudspeaker off in the distance and wondered what might be going on. People were gathering on the front stoop of their row houses in Gravesend, like children waiting for their father to come home from work. The noise got louder. Genelle, Lela and Ismet looked out the window from their perch on Lela's bed. Around the corner of their street came a flatbed truck, a small one that was dark in color and a bit rusted out and banged up. On the open bed of the truck was a huge statue of the Blessed Mother. Two men were holding the statue in place. Sitting on the sides of the truck were other men, all of them in dark suits and straw fedoras. The loudspeaker was announcing something in Italian. Over and over it was repeating its message. Genelle watched as women and men went into their homes and then came out holding up money. The men on the truck jumped off and ran to collect the money, took off their hats in appreciation, and stuffed the money into their pockets. Strange. Then, the speakers broadcasted Italian music. The people clapped. Old women wiped their eyes. The little girls twirled around. The truck disappeared around the corner to go down the next block.

Genelle watched from their third-floor window as if she was on an ocean liner passing through a strange port, looking at and listening to a people she didn't know or understand. The people on the stoops started moving as one mass, a throng filling the streets, laughing and joking and moving down the avenue towards the main street in the neighborhood.

Genelle took off the children's pajamas and dressed them in their clothes again. Put Ismet in the stroller and took Lela by the hand. But tonight she had never left the apartment without Mesut at night before. She was drawn to follow the crowd. Mesut wouldn't be home for another five hours. As she rounded the corner with her children she saw the streets from Avenue X to Avenue U hung with strings of white lights. There was music and laughter everywhere.

It was like Puerto Rico all over again. Nothing would have slowed her down. She was part of it now. Part of the crowd. Sparklers lighting up the night, twinkling lights, Italian ices, and zeppela – fried dough sprinkled with powdered sugar. It smelled so good. Children with cotton candy. It was a feast of some sort. Genelle wished she had money. The smells of the food cooking, the pizza baking in little portable ovens, and everyone so gay and happy. A young woman came over to her with a big piece of zeppela in her hand and a baby in her other arm.

"Hello. I live down the street from you. I see you when you walk the children every day."

Genelle was in shock. No one from this area had ever spoken to her before. Her name was Natalie and she bought Lela and Ismet some candy and Italian ices and shared her zeppela with Genelle.

"This is our patron saint's feast day. You must eat and be happy. No one should be sad or alone tonight!" Natalie said.

It was quite late when Genelle arrived back to the apartment. Ismet had fallen asleep in the stroller and Lela had to be carried home by Natalie's husband. Genelle hoped Mesut had not tried to reach her while she was gone.

She kept Natalie a secret from Mesut. She didn't mind when Mesut took Lela with him to go away for a weekend upstate New York with Seamus to visit a commune. Mesut had never taken Genelle away for a weekend. Had never even taken three days off work. But for Seamus he could do it. Genelle went down the block to Natalie's house and drank anisette without anybody looking over her shoulder, had all the wine she wanted with stuffed shells one night and chicken cacciatore the next. She spilled her guts to Natalie about the neglect and the double messages that confused her so much, and the beatings.

"Why are you taking that, Genelle? Hey, come on. This isn't the old country, ya know what I mean? This is America. You got rights. Don't let him abuse you and push you around like that. You don't see me letting Anthony treat me disrespectful, do ya?"

"I know what you're saying Natalie, but I have two kids and no money. Where am I going to go? And I can't say anything to my father. I mean I don't even want to talk to the man now that everything is upside down back there. I mean, my brother and sister are so mixed up and he's talking about getting married again and I just can't handle it. But, it really makes me think. Like, what am I sacrificing my life for? Just so Mesut can be with another woman when I die? That's a joke anyway. He sleeps with whoever he wants as it is. Just last month I was in the emergency room again – it's the second time this year with terrible pains in my belly, nauseous as hell – and I have to tell you when I came home I had the worst feeling that something had gone on between him and our baby-sitter."

"You don't need that, surely you don't, Genelle."

"But what can I do? Where can I go? And he is a good father, Natalie. I mean he loves the children so much and they're crazy about him. Besides, I don't think anyone else would ever love me. Mesut just barely puts up with me. I don't think I could live on my own."

Natalie handed Genelle another glass of burgundy and

157

patted her shoulder. "We'll figure something out. There's got to be a way out of this."

✠ ✦ ✢ ✦

They can't figure out what's wrong with me. I'm in the emergency room again. I'm in pain, throwing up and having chills but no fever. I feel paranoid and depressed. If only I could die. I haven't been able to keep any food in me for days. I'm very dehydrated.

They admit me into Maimonides Hospital in Brooklyn.

A doctor tells me that he thinks the steroids that I have been on for so long, my little white pills called prednisone, are killing me.

"Your mucous membranes are all stripped and you have almost zero level of potassium in your system. That's critical." The doctor speaks to me candidly. "I think it's the result of your long-term use of prednisone and we're going to take you off of them right away."

"But doctor, I was told that if I didn't take the prednisone, I would die. That's the only thing I thought was keeping me alive. How am I going to live without them?"

"Well, we just keep learning as we go. Over the past ten years medical science has learned that taking prednisone will not prevent a flare-up of your particular blood condition, and that taking prednisone over long periods of time could have severe side effects, like what you are experiencing right now."

They stop the prednisone. They put me on an intravenous solution of potassium and sugar-water for five days. I start having vivid hallucinations. The woman in the hospital bed next to mine is having visitors but I am alone. Every time I close my eyes there is a dazzling light so bright that it sends waves of pleasure through my body. The light is gorgeous to behold. I play with it by squinting to the rhythm of the music that is piped in over the hospital speakers. I see a woman in a sparkling midnight-blue gown covered with stars that spins out this dazzling blinding light as she dances. What power! If I open my eyes the light disappears. Close them and I'm travelling a stairway to heaven. And yes, it makes me wonder all right.

It's great while I think I'm in control. The terror starts when I want to go to sleep. It's late and I can't stop the show inside my head. I can't turn the images off. They've lost their beauty and brightness. Instead, grotesque gargoyles are inhabiting my mind. It's like a foreign army has taken up possession of my visual imagination and I am being held hostage. I start to panic. I wish I hadn't told the nurse. Now I'm afraid they'll come and get me and put me in the loony-bin.

The shapes get more menacing. Pick up the phone, Genelle, and ring Mesut. Don't try to eat the receiver. Keep it together. Don't throw the phone. Ring him and tell him what's happening to you.

"Fantastic, Genelle! You're getting a free trip," Mesut says. "I wish it was happening to me! Just lay back and enjoy it. Take it all in."

"Mesut, I can't. It has me really scared. I'm exhausted and I can't make it stop. They're horrible, terrifying creatures and they're out to get me. They're going to make me go insane. I can't control them."

"Calm down, Genelle. It's some kind of drug-reaction. People pay big bucks for what's happening to you right now. It'll pass eventually. But meanwhile, ride it out. Just watch the changes."

"What do you mean? What changes? They're hideous."

"Well, like where the picture is going to go next. Or look

159

for where the image is going to change. You're not seeing the same thing you were seeing this afternoon, right? The image has changed. Instead of freaking out and giving yourself a bad trip, relax and watch it. Be curious to see where it will change and what the next picture will be like. Lela's calling. Got to go."

I'm in the dark again with five ghoulish gargoyles in my head. I do what I'm told to do. I watch them and wait for them to change. I hate this feeling. Some of their faces start peeling off like masks. I try not to panic. I try to watch to see what face will be underneath. The doctor comes in and gives me a shot of something. I just keep trying to watch the creatures. Now they have become fantastically bright-colored. Their faces are twisted and gnarled with scars and puss-oozing boils. I'm still watching them when I fall asleep.

For the next few days, they give me valium by mouth and take me off the intravenous and start feeding me solid food. Thursday, they discharge me from the hospital. They send me home without medication of any kind and give me an appointment to see my doctor in two weeks.

Friday. Twenty-four hours after discharge. I sit looking at my children playing. Playing on the oriental rug, gift from Mesut's family. It has travelled halfway across the world and in and out of flats for the past four years. They are playing with wooden blocks. I'm sitting in the chair watching them. I am in my body but not connected to it. I am very frightened. I am sinking down somewhere deep. My body is getting thicker. My daughter comes to me to ask a question. I stare at her but don't answer. She pats my arm to wake up the sleeping mother whose eyes are open but no one's awake because someone is smoldering. Smoldering fire. Get away from me Lela or I will blow. Beautiful face looking up at me. Her father's face. It would be so easy to strike out now. Robot

160

space. Godzilla time. Monster woman destroys house and two children in meltdown. Read the headlines. I start yelling from somewhere deep inside. It's not me yelling it's something else that will break the furniture and these little bodies if it doesn't get out of the room. Children flee crying into the bedroom. I stomp on legs that have become tree-trunks. Stomp into the bathroom and slam the door. We're in trouble here. Look for Mesut's razor blades. Dizziness pulls me down onto the floor. Remembering carving the wooden cane I used to help me walk after the knee surgery. Sitting in Quan's car ages ago, high on Codeine cough syrup. Quan playing basketball and me waiting in the car, finding his jackknife and carving, tearing into the wood of the cane, ripping into the flesh of the wood. Lela is banging on the door. "Someone's here, Mommy. Someone's knocking on our door."

I don't want to see anyone. Ashamed of myself. Ashamed my daughter, my three-almost-four-year-old daughter must answer the door and point to the bathroom when Natalie asks "Where's Mom?"

"Help me," I say, as Natalie bends to lift me off the bathroom floor. "I don't know what's happening to me. It started this morning after Mesut left for work. I just sat staring at the wallpaper. I wanted to scrap it off with my fingernails. I hate my skin. My whole body feels wrong. I don't know what's happening. I want to hurt someone. I want to really hurt someone. I want to lie down and dissolve into darkness." She moves me into the bedroom carefully. "There's this big hole calling me to it and if I close my eyes I know I'll fall in."

"Genelle, you've got to call your doctor. Come on, tell me where the doctor's number is."

We phone the hospital. I try to reach my doctor. He's out of town they tell me. I have them page the other doctors that

161

had seen me in the hospital. Nobody responds to the page. I'm crying now. Natalie takes the phone from my hand.

"Listen operator, this woman was just discharged from the hospital yesterday and she must talk to a doctor immediately. She's having a very bad time and in a dreadful state of panic. If you don't get a doctor on this phone immediately, this hospital will have a lawsuit on their hands!"

A young resident gets on the line. He has never met me. When I describe the hell I am going through in my mind and body, he knows what's happening.

"They've taken you off the prednisone too fast. You've been on it for eleven years, you say. Five days to detox is just too fast for you. You're in acute withdrawal still. Tell me, do you have any prednisone in the house?"

"Well, yes. But, I don't think it can help the way I'm feeling right now. The doctors told me not to take them any more, that the drug was killing me."

"I understand," this stranger on the other end of the phone line says. "It must be very confusing as well as horribly scary for you. The problem is that the tablets were stopped too fast after eleven years. Just take a half a tablet now and three times each day until Monday. I am making an appointment for you with your doctors here at the clinic for first thing Monday morning."

My hands are shaking so badly that Natalie had to cut one of the prednisone in half. I'm frightened. What if it makes things worse? Natalie could only stay another hour, but in thirty minutes, I'm "flying". I'm on top of the world!

Mesut rings at suppertime to see how I am. I'm talking a mile a minute on the phone to him, so excited about what the doctor has said and how fantastically happy and energized I'm feeling. Mesut sounds worried. I can't understand why. He comes right home. A first. He won't let me take any more prednisone. He flushes them down the toilet. I hit him on the back and try to stop him from doing it, but he says I'm not taking any more of them ever again. He doesn't work for the next two days. I stay closed up in the bedroom, furious at him at first, then alternating between fits of crying and blank staring, hair-pulling craziness. He keeps the children away from me. Brings me in food. I don't want to eat or I'm ravenously hungry. The perspiration runs off me. I feel like all I'm doing is sleeping or bouncing off the walls. Mesut doesn't let me out of the bedroom except when I have to go to the toilet and then he stays in the bathroom with me. I'm under house arrest. That's OK. I don't trust myself at all.

Monday. Mesut drives me to the hospital and leaves me at the door of the clinic.

There they are. Four doctors sitting across from me in an antiseptically white hospital room in their white coats and white shirts and dark ties. I'm still shaking. Still feeling crazy from the rollercoaster ride of mood swings that the weekend has been.

The room is cold like the steel of an operating table. Here they sit in their clean coats telling me – telling this twenty-eight-year-old skin-and-bones woman – that they are sorry. Clinical, cold, sorry.

"What you're going through is withdrawal from addiction to the medication we just took you off in the hospital last week. The medication which you had been told was necessary for you to take in order to live. It would have killed you if we left you on it. Like I said, we're very sorry."

I swallow with great difficulty. I'm dizzy with the whiteness of the room and the fluorescent lights. "How long will I feel like this? How long will these crazy feelings that I've been having last?"

They look at each other anxiously as if drawing straws to

see who would have to tell me the truth. They say nothing. Finally, my internist speaks up.

"It will probably be nine months to one year before you have any real mental or emotional stability," he says calmly, almost nonchalant.

A young intern in the room adds hastily, "Eat plenty of bananas and oranges, and, oh yes, tomatoes. That'll help replace the potassium that's been stripped out of your bones by the prednisone." His eyes meet mine. He looks down.

Like white ducks in a row, they stand up together.

I watch them file out of the room. Stunned, enraged, powerless, silent, I sit and stare at the cold, gleaming stainless-steel tray with the cotton wool and antiseptic lotion on it. Better safe than sorry. Clean up the blood and move the next one in. Don't worry, I'm leaving now. Sorry.

❖ ❖ ❖ ❖

It is grave's end. Time's up. End of the line, no more prime time. Genelle couldn't go home again. Not to the Mainline anyway. Didn't visit her mother's grave on her anniversary. Couldn't face what was going on in her father's house. Struggled with bouts of depression and severe mood-swings. Mesut got more heavily into hallucinogens. Sometimes he'd come home high as a kite and Genelle would try to stay out of his way and keep the children occupied. He was frightening when he was stoned and he was frightening when he was straight. Money problems got worse. The telephone was cut off. No money to pay the bills.

Then, the sky opened and the good fairy showed up. Magic wand time. An acting job for Mesut. Mr Turner sent a letter that arrived three weeks late after having been forwarded from two former addresses. He had gotten a Ford Foundation grant and was leaving Washington DC for New York City to start a repertory theatre in Harlem. He wanted Mesut to be part of it.

The offer brought structure into their lives again and Mesut cleaned up and settled down. Weeks later Genelle worked up the courage to ask Mesut if she could attend a therapy group she had seen advertised. She was prepared with arguments if he said no.

She had figured out how she would pay for it. Her father was bound to send her some money for her birthday. She'd use that. But before she had a chance to ask Mesut, he sat her down with a very serious look on his face.

"I have something important to talk with you about, Genelle. You know we've been working on developing the theatre troupe, and I told you that we've begun to work on our first production. Well. All the roles have been filled except for one. Mr Turner has auditioned every female in the troupe for it, but he just isn't happy with any of them in that role. The part is difficult and frankly, he's very stressed about finding someone for it. I suggested he audition you."

"You what? Mesut, what are you saying?"

"I told him to give you a shot at it. I told him you were great and I was sure you could do the part."

"Mesut. I haven't acted in years and years. I'm still on a rollercoaster half the time and just trying to keep my head on straight. It's only five months since I got off the prednisone. I don't think I have it in me."

"Genelle, don't embarrass me. Don't let me down here. I'll work on a piece with you – a monologue. I know just the right one. You audition with that piece and I know you'll be in. It'll be like old times. I know you can do it."

"But what about the children? We can't afford a baby-sitter?"

165

"Listen, it's only three days a week and one of those days you can bring them to the theatre, I've already checked. And we'll get Kathy from upstairs for the rest of the time. Won't your father send you some money for your birthday? We can use that if we need to. Besides, you'll get paid for this. He's got a grant."

"Paid? You didn't tell me you were earning money there."

"I didn't? Oh, it must have slipped my mind. Anyway, you can't let me down. I've already promised Mr Turner that you'll audition for the troupe."

In like Flynn, Genelle was Julia in *Bury the Dead*. How fitting. Genelle's part was no stretch for her – a hysterical woman who commits suicide when she receives the word that her soldier husband has been killed in the war. He and the rest of his regiment refuse to be buried as a protest against the war and the society that has created it. He won't come home and he won't be buried and she wants to die. Sounds familiar not strange. What was new to Genelle was the experience of receiving compliments. To be praised for her talent and commitment to the project.

Mesut was too proud of himself and his possession to see the end coming. He flirted with the other females in the cast right in front of Genelle. He whipped her once in a improv scene with his belt, hurting her hand. But that was what the scene called for, he felt. What else would a lion-tamer do with a tigress that was regaining a sense of power?

Other cast members stayed out of their business. Genelle's confidence grew in spite of the intimidating tactics that Mesut could muster at the drop of a hat. She'd go over and over the bits of praise in her mind. She travelled the "A" train into Harlem twice a week to get to the theatre as Mesut would come to rehearsal directly from work. She had some coins in her pocket for the first time in five years. She was out of the house on her own. No children. No husband. Even if it was just from Avenue X to 145th and St. Nicholas and then a three-block walk. It was liberation to her and she cherished every moment of it. She heard the applause swell as she took her bow after the performances. She was starting to feel like a human being again – like an adult, not an erring child to be kept in line.

Mesut didn't allow her to go to the cast party. But she didn't mind. She sat home with the children and remembered the stage lights and the hugs from the other actors after it was over. But most of all she remembered the applause. One of the actors rang her from the cast party. He told her he missed her being there, thought her performance was great and wished she was at the party.

"Maybe we can meet for a drink some time, Genelle. One of the nights Mesut has to get back to work, you know. A quiet spot – just you and I."

She was flattered and scared. "No. No, I don't think that would be a good idea, but it's something special to me that you asked."

"Hey, the offer's always there. Think about it," he said. "Mesut doesn't seem to be thinking about you on your own, and you're a good-looking woman. So next time I see you I'll give you my number and we can stay in touch."

It was only two weeks later, at rehearsal, that Mesut blew up at Mr Turner. It might have been all right if it had been in private. But it was before the whole repertory company. Mesut refused to take direction from him. Then, to make matters worse, told him in no uncertain terms that his skills as a director were lacking and he ought to let someone with more talent, more modern ideas, work on the direction of the new production.

"An original script like *The Moneymaker* needs someone with style, not an old-fashioned gray-hair who isn't up with the times," Mesut roared with theatrical gusto.

Genelle sat trembling watching first-hand what must have happened over and over in jobs her husband had lost. Mesut ended up cursing at the man who had been like a father to him. Cursing, throwing a chair, then storming out. In the pregnant silence that followed, Genelle felt like all eyes were on her. She didn't know what to do. She knew if she ran after Mesut, he would physically attack her. She decided to try and defend him.

"Mr Turner, I know he didn't mean what he said. He's been under a big strain with driving cab and being in the troupe and then I haven't been well in the last year. Try not to be so hard on him, please."

Mr Turner turned his humiliation and frustration on her. "Be so hard on him? After the way he's behaved he can never come back to this theatre and work for me. And if you think that's being too hard, well you can damn well follow him out the door!"

"No. I didn't mean you were being too hard. I was just trying . . . "

"Now *you're* going to talk back to me! Go ahead and get out of here. Now! I won't tolerate any insubordination in my theatre. There are actors all over New York City dying for some paying work. I'll replace the two of you in a heartbeat.

Genelle sat on the "A" train and watched the color of the faces change. Black, black, black, black, white, black, black, black, white, white, black, black, white, white, black, white, black, white, black, white, white, black, white, white, white, black, white, white, white, white, white . . .

Stars they come and go, they come fast they come slow. They show up in a blaze and then they're gone, but they've always got a story. At least there was some glory. At least it had begun. The end of the grave was the answer. To act or not to act wasn't the question. Or was it?

Christmas

Where's the manger? Never was one. Never had one. Only trees. Big, bigger, biggest. Crowned with a fibre-glass star. Santa Claus and reindeer on the roof. 'Twas the night before, never the day after. Never even had a chimney until Santa Claus was dead and buried already. Boxes wrapped in colored paper. Ribbons. Bicycle. There must have been Christmas. Don't remember it at all as a child. Where was I?

Photos save the day and fill in the blanks. But there was only one of Christmas. Tree, boxer puppy, me in a bathrobe by the tree, must have been about seven or eight years old. The blanket around me told me I was carried out of bed for the picture. Must have been sick again. Merry Christmas it's supposed to be, and yet I wonder if it ever was. Why can't I remember?

I do remember Tino in the back alley killing Santa Claus with his laugh. I cover my ears and tell him to stop! I tell him he is lying, not my daddy and mom.

"Where do you think your little bicycle came from, Genelle? Santy? Don't be such a baby. There is no Santy Claus. That's all made up for silly little babies like you, if you believe in him."

169

"Tino, you're going to be in trouble now. You shouldn't lie like that. You'll get coal for sure in your socks. Mommy says God hears everything."

"Cry baby! Silly Genelle! You believe the lies they tell you. You don't even have a fireplace and you think Santa Claus comes to your house. You're so funny," he points his finger at me and laughs.

"I'm not silly, you are. And you're not going to get anything next Christmas you wait and see."

"Yes, I am, because my father or my mother or my sister or brother are going to go to the store and buy me something. Go on. Ask your mother to tell you the truth. Stop being a baby and grow up. Santa Claus is dead."

"He's not!"

"He is!"

"Is not!"

"Is too!"

I throw my skate key at Tino and he laughs and walks away. I go running into the house to find my mom, rollerskates in my hands.

"What's wrong, Ellie?" she asks.

"Tino says that Santy Claus is dead. He said it's all lies. That there never was a Santy and I'm silly to believe it. That's not true, is it Mommy?"

"That wasn't nice of Tino to do."

"He was lying, wasn't he?"

"Well, sweetheart, he wasn't exactly lying. I'm sorry you had to find out like that. Your dad and I were going to talk to you about it next Christmas if you hadn't figured it out for yourself by that time."

"Then, Tino's right? Santy is dead?"

"Ellie, there really isn't any Santa Claus. There never was so he didn't die. He never ever was a real person. It's just a story that parents tell their children so they can be happy and excited about a surprise and gifts from a special magical person."

"It is a lie? You lied to me? Tino was right, you lied! I don't want Christmas this year if Santy isn't real."

I cry on my bed with my skates that Santa didn't give me under my arm. *Better be good. Better not cry. Better be good I'm tellin' you why* . . . it's a lie, it's a lie, it's a lie.

Learned to play the piano when I was sick in bed from five-years old to six and a half. All the kids were playing kickball and swinging on the swings, sliding down the slides and I was inside learning to play the piano. Too sick to go outside. I'd come downstairs for my lessons sometimes in my bathrobe. Allowed out of bed just long enough for the lesson, and to practice fifteen minutes a day.

By the time I was a ten-year-old, I was proficient enough at the piano to play classical music. I took lessons from an accomplished music director in Philadelphia. Mom left me alone with him in a funny-smelling room. The window was never opened. The air in the room looked yellowy, like teeth that aren't white any more, stained from the good life or the dead life. It felt dark in there and old. Mr Thomas was stern. If I played well for him and he made a good report to my mother when she came back to pick me up, I'd get to have a hot fudge sundae with chopped walnuts on it and a cherry sitting on creamy, creamy whipped cream at Whitman's Sweet Shoppe.

It was dark in the Sweet Shoppe too. The only light seemed to be from the windows. The counter was chrome and cold. We sat on little stools that were connected to the floor. Everything in there was black and chrome. Icy cold, like the ice cream served in the chrome dish, but the hot fudge was still warm. It was oh so gooey, and sweet and yummy. I could forget about everything eating it. The butterflies I had in my stomach before my lesson. The funny feeling I had when Mr Thomas leaned close to me and turned the pages of the sheets of music.

I hated when he put on the metronome. *Tic-toc-tic-toc* like some giant clock about to strike me over the head if I didn't keep time with it. Mr Thomas knew I hated it. I hated the way the music sounded when it moved to the ticking and tocking. Hated the way the metronome had a life of its own just waiting to be freed by the thumb of his right hand. It would sit there quietly threatening me if I stepped out of the boundaries laid out on the sheets of music I had practised for weeks. I wanted to play it like I dreamed it. Like I played it when no one was home. Like I danced it. It was mine then. It was mine and I was free to feel it with every inch of my body and sing it with my heart. Instead, for a scoop of yellow rich vanilla and warm thick chocolate with whipped cream I betrayed my heart and marched to the lines of the sheets before me. If I strayed, the metronome sprang loose to command me in its goose-step gestapo unflinching unvarying ever-vigilant cadence and I would get a bad report and go home with nothing. We'd walk by the Sweet Shoppe not into it.

Ten-year-old me played the Christmas carols my mother selected when my great-grandfather, Paishe, came to visit us in Overbrook Park. It was the one and only time I ever saw him. I was dressed in green with a red ribbon as a headband in my blonde curls. I was practicing the carols before he came. *"O come all ye faithful . . . "*

Dad shouted to Mom as he was going out the door, "Pour the Schnapps I bought as soon as he comes in the door and hand him the glass. Oh yes, and keep the bottle on the table so he can see it all the time like I told you. He'll leave if we don't have Peppermint Schnapps out."

They were very nervous. My baby sister rocked in her playpen and I concentrated harder on the music. For what? The old hunched-over man didn't speak to me at all. He said only a few words, in a language I couldn't understand, to my father. Great-grandfather looked at me once but his eyes had a cloudy look, filmy, like he couldn't see me at all. Dad led him around by the arm. He smelled like candy canes and peppermint patties. The Schnapps bottle was empty when he left. He didn't bring us a present. His face was like the skeleton on Halloween – paper-thin skin stretched taut over the cheekbones and skull. *"Jingle bells, jingle bells, jingle all the way."*

❖ ❖ ❖ ❖

Stockings hung by the chimney, now that we had one, out on the Mainline. I'm all ready to play the carols for the family to sing tonight, Christmas Eve. Afterwards, we'll go next door for the open house. I'm wearing some heels tonight. I've been practising walking in them. I'm a tall and skinny thirteen-year-old walking around the house with an encyclopedia on my head to improve my posture. Mom always tells me I walk like I'm behind a plough. With these heels on I feel like I'm walking on stilts in sand dunes.

Dad sits on the piano-stool with the light shining down on him and tries to move his big fingers over the piano keys. He's using only his right hand. Mom has put the old note-chart up over the keys and written the name of the note above each key and over every note on the sheet of music he struggles with – Bing Crosby's "I'm Dreaming of a White Christmas". It's embarrassing to watch. I want him to stop. It sounds so bad and he looks so silly.

"Dad, come on. It's almost time for the carols and we're all ready to go to the party next door. You should just give up with that. Honestly, it's pitiful."

He keeps playing, making more mistakes now and getting frustrated. I don't read the barometer on the wall above his head. I'm too busy being the authority, the pianist looking down my nose at the giant that has always put me down. My moment of triumph.

"Face it dad, You don't have what it takes for that. Your fingers just don't work right to play music. Slide over and let me show you how it's done."

Fist pounds down with a crash on the ivory. Cover slams shut over the keys. I turn to exit fast and twist my ankle in the heels. He catches my arm, grabs my shoulders, shakes me and pushes me towards my room. "You can stay in there for the night, Miss Know-it-all. And forget about having any dinner too. See how you play that tune."

✠ ❖ ✠ ✠

From the age of thirteen all Genelle remembered about Christmas was her father blowing up and her crying on Christmas Eve. It was like clockwork. You could bet money on it. Without fail Genelle would be lying on her bed wishing she was dead while the rest of them were singing "Joy to the World".

Her family always opened their gifts on Christmas Day before breakfast. Genelle would put on the brave front, pretending the night before hadn't happened and that she was overjoyed with the gifts she received. But inside she wanted to run away to some other family where the gifts really meant something. She didn't want cologne or a new jumper as much as she just wanted to feel a bit of peace in her heart. A bit of love. Genelle wasn't sure exactly what happened year after year between her father and herself. He was like a volcano that exploded every December 24th and she was always right there pushing him to it or innocently standing in the line of the molten lava's flow.

She expected it to be different when she was married, but it wasn't. The first two Christmas holidays Mesut and Genelle celebrated with her family. And each time, true to form, she had a row with her father and was in bits by the time Christmas Eve rolled around.

The first Christmas that Mesut and Genelle spent on their own in Washington DC, Lela was just nine months old. Genelle wanted a tree.

"It isn't Christmas without a tree, Mesut. We have to get one."

"Genelle. Look, I have to work all Christmas at Blackie's and Lela's too small to even know what day it is. What's the big deal? We don't have any money. You know we're just scraping by. It just doesn't make sense."

"But, it's so depressing. I look out the window and see the lights in other people's windows on their trees and feel miserable. I feel lonely, I guess."

"We've been over this already. I told you that you could go back up to Philadelphia and spend the holidays with your family."

"No. You know what always happens with me and Dad. Besides, we're a family now. I want to stay here."

Two days before Christmas Genelle was still moaning about no tree. They took the baby in the stroller and went to a big park to look for a branch large enough that they could use it as a tree. It was cold. Genelle felt exhausted and dejected. She sat down on a bench with Lela who was asleep in her stroller. Mesut arrived back fifteen minutes later with a huge branch off a beech tree. The leaves of course were off of it, but it was almost as tall as himself. He dragged it home behind them. That night Genelle cut thin strips of newspaper and hung them from the branches. Mesut brought home a candle from Blackie's Steakhouse, and she put it in the window.

Christmas Eve it started to snow. Genelle started to cry. Lela was asleep in her cot. Mesut was at Blackie's. Genelle sat by the candle in the window with all the lights in the flat turned off, and looked at the strange tree. She knew there'd be no Christmas dinner, and no gifts under this make-believe tree. It was quiet. She imagined that everyone else was inside their homes with family and friends. She felt like she was the only one that was alone. She began to dive into the self-pity that had marked the passing of each Christmas for the past ten years.

Lela stirred in her sleep. Genelle went over to her. How peaceful she looked. Her thin black curls, her soft cheeks and little bow of a mouth. She was so precious. She stirred again. Genelle stroked her back gently and sang softly *"Silent night, holy night. All is calm. All is bright . . . "* How is it a child could make everything seem right?

✣ ❖ ✠ ❖

Lela's second Christmas. We have moved from Washington to Glenolden, Pennsylvania. Mesut has found a job as a waiter in Philadelphia and is also taking a film course. He is home very little. Lela has become my whole world. I love being with her as she discovers things for the first time. It's such a joy. It's just when Mesut gets in very, very late that I worry. Sometimes I don't sleep at all until he's home.

Mesut has promised us a real tree this year but it's almost Christmas and we haven't gotten one yet. He's late tonight.

Very late. I'm worried something's wrong. I phone the restaurant. No answer. It's closed already. It's three in the morning. I'm afraid he's been in an accident with the car. So late. There's a lot of drunks on the road. Anything could have happened.

I call the police when it gets light outside. It's the first time in a very long time that he hasn't come home at all. They tell me there's nothing they can do unless he's missing for several days.

"But something terrible must have happened. He didn't phone. He didn't come home. What should I do?" I ask the officer on the phone.

"Well, lady. Look, it's Christmas time. He probably went to a party after work and fell asleep there. You know, had a bit too much to drink. It can happen to anybody. Just sit tight. I'm sure he'll show up soon. And if you haven't heard anything in three or four days, give us a buzz back."

I try to stay occupied. I make Christmas cookies with Lela looking on. I roll out the dough and put her hand on it, pressing it down a little. I do the same with mine. I cut the dough hands out and bake them along with the cookies shaped like Christmas trees and snowmen.

It's gotten dark again. Still no word. It's a day and a half since I've last seen or heard from Mesut. I call the restaurant. They say he has worked day-shift today and is off this evening. I put Lela to bed early so she doesn't see my crying. I watch the clock. I work on finishing the dress I'm sewing for Lela for Christmas. It'll look so lovely on her. Mom has given me a good-size remnant of red velveteen and I'm almost done fashioning it into a lovely full dress for Lela. I'll make a little white bib collar for it. My tears are staining the fabric. Take a deep breath and blow your nose. There's some explanation I'm sure. He'll be home any minute.

It's almost midnight. I'm clearing up the sewing stuff. The dress is finished and laying on the bed. I hear the key turning in the latch. I sit down on the bed. I pick up the little dress and examine the hem. I don't know what to do. I don't know if I should go out to the front room or just wait for him here. I don't know what to say to him. I don't want to get hit. I don't know what kind of mood he's in. At least he's home – just be grateful for that, Genelle, and don't say anything. My body has started to tremble. He's at the doorway of our room. His eyes are burning.

"Well!" he says challengingly.

"Oh Mesut, you're home. I'm so glad, I've been so worried," I say, instinctively clutching the newly made little dress to my heart.

"You, worried? You've got nothing to be worried about! I'm the one with all the worries," he says belligerently and moves towards me.

"Where were you?" I ask timidly.

"Shut up," he says slamming me back on the bed.

"Mesut, what's wrong? Why are you mad at me?"

He's not listening. He's looking at me like he hates me. He's unzipping his slacks. I start to get up and he pushes me back down on the bed. He throws up my skirt and yanks down my tights and panties and forces himself into me.

"Mesut. You're hurting me. Wait. Wait for a moment. I don't have any birth control. Just wait, honey, please. Wait for a second. Ough! Stop, please. You're hurting me!"

He slaps me and yells at me, tearing into me with his penis like it's a weapon fashioned for injury not love. I don't know what I've done. I don't know why he hates me so. I can't make him stop. I can't stop the flow of my tears. I hold the little velveteen dress in my fist, crushing its fresh white collar.

Don't speak of this. Not to anyone. Don't cry again this Christmas. Don't say a word.

Christmas Eve the tree appears. He sets it in the corner when he comes home from work, with a box of shiny silver-foil icicles to hang on the tree's green branches. Lela smiles in her soft red dress. The collar just doesn't lay quite right. *"Oh Christmas tree, Oh Christmas tree, your branches green delight me . . . "*

❖ ❖ ❖ ❖

Children ask questions. They always want to know.

Lela was bright and inquisitive. "Where does the rain come from?" "How did the baby get stuck in your tummy, Mommy?" "How do birds fly?" "Why are you crying?" "How come you have yellow hair and Daddy and I have black?"

Christmas cards brought more questions. "Who's that baby?" "What's the circle around the Mommy's head and the baby's head?"

"When's Daddy coming home?"

"Why are we moving?"

"When will Ismet talk like me?"

"Why do you and Daddy fight, Mommy?"

"Why is Mommy lying on the floor, Daddy? Is she dead yet?"

"Mommy, why do you look so sad?"

Because. Because. Because . . .

Christmas in Gravesend was no different than anywhere else. 1969. Christmas eight months off prednisone is like seeing my reflection for the first time in a round mirror. I don't like what I saw. I'm ready for my life to be different. I don't know how to do it. What action to take. I wish I was still in the repertory company. That had felt so good. Just getting out of the house had done wonders. But that is over. Mesut is forbidding me to even talk to Natalie now. He refuses to let me look for work. He is trying to push me back into the box I've been in before. His temper tantrums are worse now that he is more deeply involved with street drugs. But he doesn't rage at the children, only at me.

Thirteen days later on January 6th, a fight is brewing. I can sense it in Mesut's eyes. It is shaping up to be a good knock-down drag-out. I feel the anxiety mounting in my stomach. Lela starts riding her tricycle around the flat as I'm trying to hoover. I ask her to stop and wait until I finish the room.

Simple request. All hell breaks loose.

"Nag, nag, nag. That's all you're good for, Genelle. Look at you? You can't even organize a house and you want to go out and work someplace? You should clean while the children are asleep and not disturb their playing."

"Oh, and I suppose you think they'll sleep through the hoovering?"

"Bitch! You have an answer for everything! You think you're so smart. Well you're not! You're disgusting. Good for nothing. Not fit to be a mother or a wife! And you think you're going to get away with talking to me like that?" He's off the sofa and moving towards me. I know he is going to start hitting me.

"Mesut, please. Not now. Not in front of the kids. I feel like I'm going to flip out. I can feel my head starting to go. I don't want to lose it in front of the kids. Don't hit me. Don't hit me now. Please, just get them out of here. Just give me some time to pull my head together."

He stops and looks dead straight into my eyes. I'm hiding, hoping, dodging the bullet behind the insane mask my face is wearing.

He listens to me. Why I don't know and don't care. He gets the children out of the room, puts on their jackets and ushers them out the door of the apartment.

I look out the window. When I see them come onto the

sidewalk in front of the building, I grab my winter jacket and shoulder-bag. Pull on my boots. Get out of the apartment.

I run down the inside fire-exit stairs hoping I won't run into the building manager. I dash past his office and out the back door of the building. Even though I'm walking fast, I can still feel my body shaking. I don't look back. I cut through the alleys and sidestreets to the subway station at Gravesend.

I see an old woman standing in the line waiting to get a ticket. I start rummaging madly through my bag for the money I know I don't have. The woman watches me. I go over to her panic-stricken.

"Please, can you help me? I don't have any money and I have to get out of here quickly. I've got to get to a safe place. My husband is going to beat me again if I go back home right now. Please, lady, just enough for the train, I beg you!"

She is frightened. She doesn't want to take out her wallet. Maybe she's afraid I'll rob her.

"I'll get you a token at the window," she says. "That's all I can do."

I want to kiss her hands and feet. I ride the "A" train all the way through Manhattan. I take the subway as far as I can go on that one token. Jerome Avenue. The Bronx.

I know I'm crazy for sure now. It's January. It's cold. Very cold. I'm twenty-eight years old, a wife and a mother, and I'm running away from home. I don't want to get beat up again. I don't want to scream like a crazy woman with eyes wild and mouth twisted. I don't want to live like that any more. I don't know where I'm going, but I have to get out and away.

I cross the Jerome Avenue bridge. I walk along a major highway with lots of traffic. I put out my thumb and hope my hand doesn't freeze before I get a lift. I make it to the Sawkill

Expressway going north. My toes are frozen. I'll go wherever the next car that stops is going or I'll freeze to death.

A car-load of people in their late teens stop to pick me up.

"Where you headed?" the young driver asks.

"Wherever you're going," I say.

"Hey, cool. Join the crowd. We're headed for New Paltz and then skiing up in the mountains."

New Paltz. That's where Seamus is living – some commune called the Red House. I start to feel a bit delirious. The kids in the car are smoking hash and they pass me some. "No thanks. That stuff doesn't do anything for me," I say.

Someone offers me a bottle in a brown-paper bag. "Take a swig of this. It oughta help you thaw out."

Two hours later I get dropped off at the Homestead Bar in New Paltz. "It's the biggest hangout in town. You're bound to find a place to crash for tonight in there," the fellow driving says to me as I get out of the car.

The golden light from a winter sunset is hitting the front door and windows of the bar. I know the cold will really set in once the sun goes down. I feel like I have been travelling for days, but it has really taken me years to get to this place in time.

The bar is dimly lit. Lots of smoke mixing with the light of the sun's last glow makes the air thick and golden. Several men are sitting at the bar. I walk up by the one that's sitting with his back resting against the bar directly in front of my line of vision. He is slumped forward with his beard resting on his chest. He's wearing an old felt hat and his face is completely hidden. I wonder what the barman will say when I ask for a drink of water. I have no money for the kind of drink I want. As I climb up on the stool, my shoulder-bag knocks against the slumped man at my side.

"Sorry," I say.

He raises his head like he is pulling himself out of a deep fog and looks in my eyes. I'm startled. I know those eyes.

182

"Holy Shit. Seamus? Is that you? Do you remember me? We met a over a year ago out in Gravesend, in Brooklyn. Genelle's my name."

"Course I remember, luv," he says slowly, very relaxed. "Where's Mesut?"

My face flushes. "It's a long story. I'm just here by myself for a while, I guess. I was hitching and the people that picked me up were coming to New Paltz so – here I am."

His eyes take me in with a long look. I feel awkward and self-conscious.

"You're on the run, aren't you?" he says. "Must've been pretty bad for you to do a runner like that."

"It was."

He studies my face and takes off his hat, tousling his hair roughly, then puts his hat back on. "You've had a long day I bet. Listen luv, have a beer on me and I'll take you out to the Red house. Don't worry. You'll be OK there, and you can stay in my cabin as long as you need to, no questions asked."

I'm relieved. I can't believe the coincidence of walking right up next to him at the bar. It feels great to hold a bottle of beer in my hand again.

When we leave the bar, he explains "I'm supposed to go to the movies with this girl Sue tonight, but I'll take you out to the place and get you settled first." Seamus picks up some hamburgers, fries and a six-pack of beer on our way to his little cabin right behind the Red House commune.

There is nowhere to sit inside the one-room hut, except on the bed or on an old hassock that is covered with his clothes. The cabin is very lived-in with newspapers strewn about, logs and kindling for the little woodstove that heats the cabin and a few cardboard boxes with books in them. The bed takes up most of the cabin. It is a double-bed mattress on the floor and has lots of old quilts and blankets tossed about on it. There's a lovely smell in here – like coffee, wood-fire and beer. But there is also a sweetness in the smell. Maybe he has lots of sugar in his coffee when he drinks it. Sweet and light.

He sits down on his clothes on the hassock and I on the bed as we eat the hamburgers and fries and drink the beer. He throws some logs on the woodstove. It's cozy and warm in here. I take off my boots and wet coat and stretch out my feet towards the stove to dry my socks a bit. I cry some as I tell Seamus bits and pieces of the struggle life with Mesut has been. He listens intently. He doesn't say anything, but nods occasionally.

He moves over onto the bed and lifts my hair up off my forehead. "I'm sorry," he says. "I'm sorry you've had such a rough time, luv. You stay here as long as you need to."

He lays back on the bed, his head relaxing on his arms, looking up at the rafters as he smokes a cigarette. The food has filled me up and I feel tired. The beers have relaxed me. It's dark in the cabin except for the glow coming through the open door of the woodstove. I lay on my side and watch the smoke curl up from Seamus to the rafters above. My eyes are heavy. In a few minutes they close completely. I don't know how long I lay like this. I know I am just dosing off to sleep when he begins to gently stroke me. His beard and mustache are soft against my skin as his lips brush my cheek. I love his smell.

"Just lay there and relax," he says softly. "You look so comfortable."

He takes off my heavy socks. He strokes my legs and gently massages my feet. I haven't been touched so tenderly since I was in Quan's arms and that seems like another lifetime now. I know I am married, but it doesn't matter to me right now. It doesn't matter that he is Mesut's friend either. I'm hungry for loving, for gentleness. He holds me for a while, just stroking my back.

When Seamus gets up to go to the film with his friend, he covers me with some of the quilts and adds a bit more wood to the fire, closing the door of the stove. He calls his dog in from outside. "She'll keep you company while I'm gone. Will you be all right?"

"Yeah. I feel more all right than I have in a very long time," I say smiling gratefully.

"The bathroom is in the main house, just inside the backdoor to the left. Oh, and if you need to use the phone, go ahead, luv. It's right in the big room where the bathroom door is. I don't think anyone's around this evening so you won't be disturbing anybody."

He picks up his coat and gives a last look around the cabin. "The stove is loaded up, so it should be fine. We're going to the second show, so I'll be back late. Sweet dreams."

I really don't expect Seamus to come back. I figure he will stay in town with his date. I snuggle in under the layers of covers and doze a bit. I rouse after a little while and realize I better go into the bathroom before it gets really late. There is a light on in the main house that I can see through the cabin window. I put on my slacks and grab one of Seamus's heavy sweaters that is laying on the floor and go out into the cold January night. The moon is up and big flakes of fresh snow are falling.

I hear voices in the big room while I am still in the bathroom. I feel a little uptight. I stand inside the bathroom not wanting to come out and talk to anybody. I think about my children and decide that I really should call and let them know I'm all right. I come out of the bathroom just as two men are leaving through the kitchen door. I call out to them self-consciously, "Seamus said I could use the phone. You don't mind, do you?" They don't even bother to turn around and look at me, one just motions with his hand that it's OK.

When Mesut answers the phone, I'm curt. "I don't want to talk now, Mesut. I'm just phoning to let you know I'm OK."

"Where the hell are you? Do you know what time it is? I had to get the kids' dinner. You know I was supposed to work tonight! Where are you?"

"I'm upstate. I'm at the Red House."

"Oh, great!" he says, sarcastically. There's a long pause. "When are you coming home?"

"I don't know."

There's another long silence. "Look, you're a mother, or did you forget! You have kids here that have been wanting to know 'When's Mommy coming home?' What the hell am I supposed to tell them?"

I see Lela and Ismet's eyes behind my closed eyelids. I know that fearful questioning look in their eyes so well. I feel a bit of a lump in my throat.

Mesut's angry voice interrupts the vision challengingly. "Well, just what do I say to them?"

"Tell them what I always say when you've been gone for days and haven't even phoned me and I don't even know where you are or if you're alive and they ask me 'When's Daddy coming home?' Tell them 'Don't worry. It'll be soon, real soon.' Goodbye, Mesut."

When I go outside there is already a thin layer of snow spreading a soft blanket of white under the moonlight. The cabin is warm. I nestle under the quilts and listen to the sleeping dog's contented breathing. I feel safe and protected in this cozy little place.

I don't hear Seamus come in. I wake to him kissing my neck and pulling me closer to him. "Wait a minute. Don't get going, Seamus. Remember I told you I don't have any birth control and I don't want to get pregnant. "

"I stopped at the drug-store on the way into town and got some condoms. Don't worry, I won't get you pregnant. I heard what you said. I just want to make you happy. I want to make love to you, give you the kind of sweet loving you deserve and see you smile."

Well, Seamus Haggerty, you certainly know how to make a woman smile, and sigh, and laugh and feel really loved! Lying in your arms after making love I feel like a little kid who finally gets what she wants for Christmas.

"Mesut's crazy," he says quietly. "He's crazy to be running around with other women on you, and beating you. And he's a fool, luv, if he lets you go. You're one really special woman, Genelle."

That night as I sleep next to Seamus, I have a dream. It's very real. I dream that it's early in the morning and everyone is still asleep. I go outside and walk back into the meadow away from the Red House and the cabin where Seamus lies sleeping. The meadow is filled with snow. In my dream, I sit down cross-legged in the snow, enjoying the silence and the trees swathed in whiteness as the dawn's first light appears. I feel warm inside and at peace. After a few minutes, I see out of the corner of my eye a young doe approaching. I sit very still and feel love pouring out of me like a fountain. The doe comes up to my side and lays down next to me, putting her head in my lap. She rests peacefully with me. Her big brown eyes look up at me so lovingly, so trustingly.

I wake up with this dream vividly in my mind. I know I will leave New Paltz and go back to Gravesend, but I feel no fear. I'm at peace. I'm going to be OK. If Mesut wants to take Lela as he has threatened to do, or if he beats me, or just disappears and leaves me and the children, I know I'll be all right. What I have inside me he can't get at any more. I won't let him get at it. It's mine, all mine. A gift.

Epiphany.

Begin a new life. Start a new tradition. Develop new rituals. Make a family out of just the three of us – Lela, Ismet and myself well before single-parent families are acceptable. Pop the corn. String the cranberries. Bake gingerbread men and buy candy canes. Christmas is coming. We're living on the dole in New Paltz after Mesut has left us. He's gone to live on a hippy commune in Denmark.

New friends, new ways, new hope.

"It's coming on Christmas, they're cutting down trees, putting up reindeer, singing songs of joy and peace . . ." Decorate the little Scotch pine in the corner of our sitting-room with everything edible – cookies, candy canes, garlands of strung popcorn and berries. It smells so sweet in our front room now. I have candles everywhere. We love to sit in the room with the fireplace lit and the candles glowing, looking at the tree. The kids cuddle up close and sing "Jingle Bells" and "Santa Claus is Coming to Town". Only it's Mesut that shows up wired to the gills and wants to sit into the picture of happy family – snap the photo – after being away for six months, writing once, sending no money. I'm not buying what he's selling when he knocks at the door in the night-time, two days before Christmas.

Surprise, surprise. Christmas is over before the gifts ever get opened. Mesut is bellowing like a madman. Children screaming, clinging to me as I finally find my voice and yell at him to get out and leave us alone.

He picks up the Christmas tree and hurls it across the room, knocking over candles and the table displaying Christmas cards received. Hot wax all over the walls. Red and green wax sealed into plaster and floor where it's splattered.

He storms out leaving our sitting-room like the wreckage of a ship that's been torn apart on the rocks after a high gale.

I sit on the floor and hold the children. I rock back and forth with them in my arms. The sound of the hearth fire is all that can be heard.

That's it, I decide. I'm finished with Christmas. I'll never have another Christmas tree. I'm not buying any more presents, sending any more cards. Not trying to do it right any more. Merry Christmas, Deck the Halls, *fa-la-la-ha!* It belongs to other people not me. It's not for us, kids. It's a farce. It's all lies, lies, lies. Welcome to the real world. Anytime things look to be going well, the rug will get pulled out and you'll be looking into the gaping hole of hell. So, just stay tanked up on booze and don't try to pretend you're normal any more, Genelle. You're not. We're not.

I give up trying to be good. The perfect present for me right now would be an ounce of Columbian Gold. I'd work my way through it and make it work for me. I'll learn how to get high off the stuff or die trying.

❖ ❖ ❖ ❖

December 24th. Five years of living in New Paltz had finalized the divorce, but had not softened Genelle's heart with forgiveness for Mesut. Genelle's home was empty. No tinsel or tree. No colored lights in the window. No children. Lela and Ismet had left in the afternoon to spend Christmas in New York City with their father and his new girlfriend.

For the first time in her life, Genelle was alone on Christmas Eve. She cleaned the house. Scrubbed the floor. Laundry was done and put away. She tried to watch some television, but the shows were all guaranteed heartbreakers, Christmas sob-stories. She had enough of her own.

She finished the bottle of brandy on the kitchen shelf. It had begun snowing in the late afternoon after she had put the children on the bus. The quiet closed in on her. She looked at the clock. Almost 11pm. She was wide awake and edgy. She decided to go into town. It didn't phase her that she didn't have snow-tires.

She bundled up in case she skidded off the road and got stuck. "May as well be stuck on the side of the road as be stuck inside this empty house on Christmas Eve," she told herself. "Besides, if I take it slow and easy on the roads, I'll be able to get in and have a drink or two at the bar."

She hadn't ever been out on Christmas Eve. Always had to mind the kids and get them settled in early since they'd be up first thing to attack the wrapped boxes and play with their new toys.

Not this year. There wasn't a soul on the roads as she drove the six miles into New Paltz village. The mountains were silhouetted against the sky and a new moon showed itself. Colored lights glowed under their blanket of new-fallen snow on the bushes and trees outside of houses along the road into town. Genelle felt lonely and sad. The road was icy and she hunched over the wheel trying to anticipate the upcoming curves and little hills that she normally sped over.

In the village everything was closed. The Homestead Bar, St Blaise Pub, North Light, even P & G's – the hard-core pub – was locked up tight. It looked like a ghost town lit up like a Christmas tree with nobody there to see it.

Genelle passed some cars. They were turning down Route 32. She decided to go up by the college and head back down to her house on the back roads. It would take longer and kill some more time.

Lots of cars came into view. Like a stream of lemmings wearing red and white lights, cars were converging on the church below. St Mary's. Genelle had never been inside a Roman Catholic church. She parked the car and watched. The dark night winter landscape had become alive with movement. Cars and people streaming toward this lighted church.

"It must be Midnight Mass," Genelle thought. She had always wondered what that was like. When she had overheard her friends talk about going when they were all in her teens it sounded like something magical. Like at midnight something mysterious happened that only a select few got to witness.

She wondered if she would be allowed in. "Got nothing to lose," she told herself. She joined the men, women and children ploughing through the snow-covered sidewalks towards the blue light of the stain-glass windows.

It was crowded inside. All the seats were filled even in the balcony. People stood around the sides of the church and at the back in rows two or three people deep. Genelle squeezed in next to an elderly man and a young woman at the back of the church and leaned against the wall. The familiar smell of brandy and beer filled the air as carols were sung.

It was a few minutes before Genelle spotted the manger. It was at the front of the church, on the right-hand side. A beautiful crib fashioned of wood and fir branches. Inside were candles lighting the life-size forms of mother and father. She stood on her toes and strained to see the infant child. She was shocked. The bed of straw was empty. "Oh, my God, someone's stolen the baby," she thought.

Then the procession entered the church. Shepherd's crook in hand, the robed priest with a baby doll in his arms walked through the church for all to see . Genelle stood on her toes to watch as the baby was laid on the bed of straw. Tears of joy surprised her eyes. A young man sang *"Oh holy night, the stars are brightly shining . . . "* with the voice of an angel. Some of the crowd pressed forward after the service and she followed them. Followed them up to look at Mother and Child, Father and shepherds. Little lamb resting at the foot of the baby's straw bed. Children and their parents alike paused. They stared with wonder at the scene.

"What is it they're so taken with?" Genelle wondered. "These are just statues, like the statues of Santa Claus and the reindeer placed in Penny's Department store window. Why is something stirring in my heart? It's got to be just another lie," she thought. She looked again at the doll laid in the bed of straw, lying there with open arms. She remembered her favorite doll Sniffles. How she loved that doll. She remembered how Tino had grabbed it from her, teasing her, taunting her by spinning around with it, and how he had smashed Sniffles' head against the garage door by accident as he spun. She had sobbed and yelled at Tino, cradling the doll with its smashed head in her arms. "It's just a doll," Tino had said, when his apology hadn't stilled her tears. She knew Sniffles was more than a doll to her. Sniffles had been her companion through months and years of sickness, of being confined to bed, her playmate when she couldn't go outside with the other kids. Genelle looked at the baby, this doll in the straw reaching out to embrace her. "You've got beautiful blue eyes like my Sniffles," she said softly and left.

All the way home, Genelle felt a calmness growing within her. She thought again of the dream she had years earlier. She remembered the doe's eyes as it rested its head in her lap.

The silence that greeted her when she entered her home wasn't ominous any more. It was comforting, and peaceful. She took a pillow off of the sofa and placed it in the middle of the living-room floor. She lit a candle and placed it in a saucer, setting it down before the pillow. Genelle sat on the pillow in the stillness and gently sang *The first Noel the angels did say was to certain poor shepherds in fields where they lay . . .* "

Granpaw

Lean. Lanky. Level-headed. Joseph Butler looked like a long drink of water on a hot Kansas day. At only age fourteen, he was already almost six foot tall and still looked to be growing like a weed. Had the Butler eyes all right – bluest of the blue, like the mid-western sky on the fourth of July. He was primed. He was ready. He could ride a horse faster than his older brother, Caleb, or his cousin Elroy. They were all going. All the Butler men were going to be in the saddle that day – the day of the big Oklahoma land rush.

Cherokee, Choctaw, Chickasaw, Osage and Creek Indians would be pushed out again. The five civilised tribes of the eastern states had been promised this land by President Jackson for "as long as the grass is green or the water runs". Well, the Cimarron River hadn't dried up yet, but there was something other than water that was about to run, and its running would drive the Indians off this piece of dusty earth.

Indian Territory was about to become Oklahoma Territory. Any able-bodied man, woman or child could stake a claim. All they had to do was be there and ride until they found a plot that didn't have a stake flag on it and they could claim it for their own. No money needed – just sweat, and courage to throw caution to the wind, and a hefty piece of land could be had.

April 20, 1889. History in the making. Joseph was so excited he could hardly keep quiet around the campfire and listen to his father's last-minute instructions. His uncle and cousin Elroy had joined his dad, Caleb and himself. They had left his mother and baby brother as well as three sisters in the buckboard in west Kansas. Five Butlers on horseback, pistols in their hip holsters, and two shotguns between them as well. Their saddlebags carried only water, some brown bread and bits of dried smoked meat for the journey.

"Listen up, Joseph. Tomorrow, when we get to the Oklahoma line, folks'll be thicker than flies on molasses," Jason Butler said. "You won't even be able to hear yourself think, so pay attention, son. Here's what we're gonna do."

The Butler men agreed. When "the run" began, they'd ride till the sun was nearly down, sticking together and keeping going until it got close to dark. They wouldn't even look at land close to the line. "Folk'll be fightin' over the stuff close to the border. You boys are liable to get hurt. They'll be knockin' people over left and right. Just keep a-ridin', hear me? And don't look back. It'll be hard enough to stick together."

His father was right. The Oklahoma line looked like the State Fair only dirtier and bigger. No one was dressed up in their Sunday best at this event. Joseph had never seen so many people in one place at one time. There were buckboards with families in them. Chickens and livestock, people selling grub and household wares. There were snake-oil vendors, guaranteeing to cure whatever ills a person had. It was a real side-show. It looked to Joseph like some people had been camping there for weeks waiting for the big day.

Hustlers, rustlers, farmers, vendors, money-lenders and

speculators of a wide variety competed with squawking children and chickens, makeshift clotheslines and restless horses to make deals and seal promises. The excitement in the air was fierce and everyone – man, woman and child – was dreaming their dream. The great dream of *"land lots of land under starry skies above"*. If the poorest of the poor were prepared to steal a horse or make an honest walk of it, they could stake a claim and have their own little piece of Oklahoma sod. The land was there for the taking.

April 22. The sun had just come up.

Horses, men and their womenfolk were chomping at the bit. Hooves, toes, wagons on the line waiting for the gun-shot that would turn them loose. The concrete markers had all been put in place the month before. Neatly measured-out plots forty by forty, a hundred and sixty acres in a plot with a concrete post at each corner. Land was sectioned off for towns as well as farms. There was something for everybody. Those whose dream was to have a dry-goods store, or blacksmith shop, or saloon and such wouldn't be left out. Guthrie, Norman, Stillwater, Oklahoma City, Tyler were just roped off barren space this morning, but by nightfall they would be tent-cities of folk vying to be the barber, the butcher, the tailor, the doctor, the barkeeper. Well, whiskey would already be flowing from barrels brought in buckboards to assure the provider's place in the menfolks' favor.

Fifty thousand people lined up along the plains waiting for the bugles to blow and the shots to be fired. Picture it. Horses, covered wagons, buckboards with everything a family owned strapped to them. Men on foot and horseback, why there were even some on bicycles and one man on an ox. They had come from all over. Even overseas. The Irish, the Scotch, the Bohemians lined up in heat the likes of which they had never felt before. Steaming heat. And dust, lots of dust. Spring rains might as well have been just a memory and the red clay soil was hard-packed and dry. Cracking under the ninety-degree heat.

High noon was the time when life as Joseph Butler had known it back home in Missouri would be changed forever. He couldn't wait. He stroked his mare. She was fast. He pushed his hat down snug on his black hair to try and cut the glare of the sun. The Butler men were ready. Everyone's ears were cocked. A great hush fell over the waiting thousands, like a giant beast holding its breath as its prey came into sight.

The bugles blared, revolvers were fired into the air. A great *"Whooooopee!"* filled the air and the crowd lurched forward, cheering, yelping, crying, straining to be the first, to get the best, to beat the rest, to get their piece of heaven.

Joseph set the pace for the rest of the Butlers. He was out in front of them. He had the green and yellow flag that his mother had sewn for them to use to stake their homestead tied to his back and it was flying. That boy could ride. They kept the colors in sight and followed him over the plains. They passed people coming to blows, and men already with shovels in the ground turning over the baked land. They saw the roped-off areas with makeshift signs naming the towns that would someday flourish there. They kept going.

They rode for five hours, stopping but once to cool the horses in a bit of shade in a grove they found. They hadn't seen many trees. They didn't have time to even get comfortable though. Two men rode up on horseback, pointed their Winchester rifles at them, and told them to leave. "This here land's already claimed. You'll get on outa here now, if ya know what's good fer ya!"

The Butlers didn't have to be told twice. They rode on until the sun had become a red-hot ball of fire over their right shoulders. It was getting real low in the sky. Joseph slowed

196

down and waited for the others. "OK," his father said. "The next marker we see, we claim."

There were a few riders left, but they were far enough behind them that they looked like dots on the horizon. There shouldn't be a battle. They fanned out to ride on and kept their eyes sharp for a bit a concrete sunk into the ground. It was Caleb that let out a whoop. He'd spotted one. Joseph rode to him. Jumped from the saddle and pushed the stake down deep into the red clay. The brothers jumped for joy and hugged each other. Their dad stayed in the saddle after he had rode up to join them. "OK lads, well done," he said. "Take the rifle, Caleb, and the two of you stand our claim. We'll go and check out the rest of the spread. Your uncle and cousin need to stake their claim." The three rode off.

Around the campfire that night they recounted the day's adventures. Joseph's father beamed about their spread and the one his brother had claimed the next lot over so the Butlers had just gained three hundred and twenty acres between them. Raw-tired and dusty, Joseph still couldn't stop grinning. He took his mare for a walk under the stars and felt proud. He felt happy, real happy. Glad to be alive.

✜ ❖ ✚ ❖

I sit next to the cottonwood tree. The petals of the buttercups tickle my legs. Granpaw's fixin' me a swing. I watch him. He rubs rough paper over the piece of board that I'll sit on. He looks up at me and grins. I know my granpaw loves me lots. He never gets cross at me like Grammaw does sometimes. He's got the ropes tied up on the big branch and gives them a tug. The big branch shakes a little, not much. There, he's got the board on. He slaps the board and grins at me. I know he wants me to give it a try. Granpaw doesn't talk much. I know what he wants most of the time by how he looks.

His big hands hold the seat and move me back and forth slowly. It's my first time on a swing. I like it. The swing's just right. He pushes me a little and I giggle. He laughs. Mommy's gone again so long.

Grammaw's voice. "Joseph Butler, that's a fine day's work! Now if you're done playin' games, you can fetch me some things from town."

Granpaw gives me another good push and heads off to get her list. I hold on to the rope and lean way back and look up at the sky through the leaves. I try to make the swing go, but I can't. Still, I like just sitting on it and walking my feet on the ground while my bum is on the swing. Chippy, my doggie, comes over to my side and I sit on the swing and pat his puffy fur. I give him a big hug. Grammaw's calling me. Maybe it's time to eat.

The kitchen smells yummy. "Ellie, I want you take these cookies over to Mrs Love while they're still warm. All you have to do is walk across the front yard. You remember her house, don't you? The one with the blue painted around the screen-door. Go on over with them and when you come back I'll give you a big glass of Bessie's milk and some of the chocolate-chip cookies I've saved for us. Now run along and don't drop any of them."

They smell so good. I carry the plate up close to my face. I walk really slowly, biting my bottom lip. I want to have just one. I want to sit on the swing and have just one. But I know I must do what Grammaw tells me. Besides, I see Mrs Love standing with her screen-door open now, watching me coming to her.

"Well, well Ellie. What've you got there? Careful now. Let me help you," she says, coming to my side. Mrs Love walks all bent over and she smells funny, like dark places that don't get much sun. She pats my head and asks me to come inside. I point at my swing instead.

"Granpaw fixed it for me. I'm gonna swing more."

Grammaw gives me fresh milk and three cookies. I take them to the swing and sit on it eating. The chocolate is warm and gooey. I love the sweetness. So does Chippy. I give him one, and split my last one in half. "Half for you and half for me." I sit on the swing till Granpaw comes home.

✤ ❖ ✤ ❖

Joseph Butler's formal learning was over when the family left Missouri and started homesteading their newly claimed land. It was a good piece of land with a few little rises and some tamarack trees, cottonwoods and even a few locust trees. There was even a stream running through it. They named it Coyote Creek.

There were seven children in the family now. Five girls and two boys. Joseph was the quiet one. Seemed he could have fun just working, or whittling, or whistling a tune for his little sister to dance a jig to. He loved music. Whenever his father would let them go, he would head off with Caleb and the older girls and go to a "hoe-down". He loved listening to the fiddle playing almost as much as he loved to dance. And the thing about Joseph was that he had no favourites. He'd dance with every girl there – pretty, homely, ugly, fair, old and young. He just loved to dance and hated to see anyone with a long face on when it was time to have fun. When the girls would see that Joseph Butler was at a dance they would all be happy because they knew they'd have a good spin around the floor. And at the Sunday church socials, there would always be a few box-lunches made up for him by young female hopefuls trying to capture his heart.

It took Annie Russell's stubbornness to challenge his ingenuity and get him to courting. He had heard folks talking about her. She was the new schoolmarm who was up in Drummond Flats. A Missouri gal, folks said. He hadn't seen her at any of the dances yet.

He was riding his mare and taking its three-year-old in to get it shod one morning when he came across a two-wheel buggy that was askew in a ditch. The heavy flash rain the night before had made some mean ruts in the Oklahoma clay and the buggy's wheel was good and stuck in one along the side of the road. Something must have spooked the horse and made it veer off the middle of the road. The buggy had landed in the ditch. A young woman dressed all in black was trying to make the horse pull it out. She was quite agitated that her efforts were to no avail and only worrying the animal further. Joseph saw the problem immediately as he rode up and offered to help.

"Looks like she's tore the trace strainin' to get you out. Let me see what I can do," he said.

Annie was infuriated that she had to have help. She was used to managing things on her own. She watched as he tied his horses to a tree and took a bit off the end of his rope with his knife and threaded it through the trace of her rein, plaiting the broken pieces and calming her horse with his low voice and steadying pats on its neck.

He looked up at her and studied the proud woman with gray eyes and dark brown hair tightly knotted into a bun at the base of her neck. She turned away from meeting his gaze.

"You must be the new schoolmarm I've heard about. Joseph Butler's my name. Glad to be of service. Slide over and I'll coax her outa this ditch and drive you on down to the school. She should come out easy enough now that I fixed the trace."

Annie glared back at him. "That won't be necessary. I can handle it on my own now, I'm sure. I'm quite late as it is, Mr Butler, and I shan't delay further by chatting. The children are waiting."

"Well, I'll follow on behind you just in case you have any trouble and that weavin' doesn't hold. Wouldn't want those kids to be left too long on their own. Right?"

"Suit yourself," she said curtly and flicked the reins on the horse's croup and the animal pulled the buggy out squarely and headed on down the road.

She was quite contrary, Joseph thought, but he followed on the mare much to Annie's consternation and tipped his hat as he left her at the door of the little one-room schoolhouse made of sod. Her face was beet-red as she saw the children whispering to each other and looking at the man who was trotting away with the spare horse alongside him.

Several days later, Joseph received a short note in the mail.

"Mr Butler, thank you for assisting me. A. Russell."

It was her aloofness more than anything else that Joseph found curiously interesting. He liked challenges. He was almost thirty by now and knew how to keep a good farm going and had broken a few mustangs in his time. He reckoned Annie was a challenge he shouldn't pass up. Besides, it was about time to think of settling down and starting a farm of his own. His father had given Caleb a good amount of acreage when he had gotten married two years earlier. Joseph had no reason to believe he wouldn't do the same for him.

Joseph brought Annie flowers. He came calling one evening just after supper with a freshly picked bunch of Kansas Cornflowers in his hand. He was fresh-shaven and he had on his Sunday-best shirt and trousers. Of course he had on his felt hat. Joseph Butler never went anywhere without his hat. He wore it cocked to one side with the brim bent down in front. When Annie came to the door, he took off his hat and made a grand bow. He'd practiced that a few times on the dirt road coming over. Then he stood up tall and handed the bright big-faced flowers to Annie, staring straight into her eyes with a mischievous sparkle in his own. "Stopped by to see if you had anything else that needs fixin'," he said and grinned.

She looked at his thick black crop of hair and the scrubbed clean face and wondered what to do next. Joseph Butler was the first man to come courting her. She didn't like his impudent smile or the twinkle in his eyes. It was like he knew all about her. But she was already twenty-one and people were beginning to wag their tongues about her being an old maid. She took the flowers, didn't invite him in, but came out to go for a walk in the lengthening May night.

He was gentle. He was quiet. He let her do all the talking. He liked the rustling sound of her starched slips against the black taffeta skirt she wore. She used words he'd never heard of before. When he got home he'd look them up to find out what she was on about.

Months passed but she never let him get quite close to her. He had tasted her mouth all right, though she had held her lips quite tightly together. That was enough for him for now. She'd make him a good wife, he reckoned. She was educated and could handle kids so she'd be a good mother. And once he had her as his wife, he'd wear away her contrary ways. All she needed was some careful handling and some good loving he was sure.

He got his parcel of land. He got the ring. He got her. But she was more than he bargained for. She wasn't a scared wild thing that he could tame, she wasn't a hard field that he could plough and work and fertilise and make yield. She was armored, icy, demanding and rejecting. She didn't dance. He stopped.

Somewhere after the sixth year of marriage his patience wore out and he gave up. They had Clinton, Doreen, and Dirk by then. It had only been a handful of times Annie had let him enter her in those six years. The last time had been so hurtful to him he couldn't think of trying again. She had gotten quite heavy. Seemed like all she did was cook, sew, and eat. He was lucky to have the three children, he reckoned. He figured he shouldn't press her any more. He didn't want to argue, and he couldn't bear the rejection. Whatever she demanded he gave in to. She didn't help on the farm any more. She had always done it under protest anyway. She weighed almost twice his own weight by now he was sure. The more she ate, the less he consumed. Neither had a clue she was pregnant already.

It was a shock for both of them to find out that she was almost eight months pregnant with their fourth child and due in a month. She was carrying so much fat even she hadn't noticed there was anything strange. And since she had begun putting on the weight her periods had become quite irregular so she never paid them much mind.

In March of 1923 their last child, Winona, was born. The baby filled up the void that was broadening between them. She slept in the bed in between her parents. She was sweet and quiet and both of them poured their frustrated love into her. She took after her mother in sewing, cooking, baking, and added the finer arts of drawing, music and poetry. She won her daddy's heart by raising chickens, milking the cows and going fishing with the boys.

Joseph hated to see her grow up. Was miserable when she left for Tyler to go to college. Devastated when she took off for her big-time office job in Washington DC. Heartbroken when she came home with that big lump of a city Jew that couldn't tell his ass from his elbow when it came to rounding up cattle or planting a field.

Joseph hardly spoke to any of them. Just worked sunup to sundown and sat in the chair outside, soaking his feet, eating the bit of a dinner that had been kept warm on the woodstove for him. That's why when he heard little baby Ellie cry for the first time after Winona brought her home from the hospital, he woke up. He listened to the bit of new life in the small little farmhouse with joy down in his bones, bones that he thought were dead already.

All my memories of Granpaw are pictures in my head and feelings in my tummy.

Granpaw's arm around me always makes me feel safe. Granpaw's back is warm from the hot sun and makes my tummy feel happy resting against it. I lay on his back as he bends over and works the potato beds. I feel sleepy and happy. His shirt smells like sunshine. I rest my cheek against it. I'm coming on three years old.

Even younger – I'm fretting about something. I don't want to sit up at the table and eat my dinner. My mommy is patting the chair's seat. "Ellie, be a good girl and stop your whining now. Climb on up here next to me and have some food." Her body feels hard and funny to touch – like a wall.

"That child is always frettin' about something," Grammaw says as she sets a bowl of potatoes down.

I'm standing at the corner of the big wooden table. It's higher than my head. I look at the white bowl Grammaw has just set down. I see the steam rising from the white mounds. I rub my eyes. I'm not hungry. I feel fussy. My grammaw's big body brushes by me and I see into the porch doorway. I see my granpaw down low to the ground out on the porch. He's smiling at me. He puts a finger to his lips. I know what that means. *Shhh*. It's gonna be a whisper. Don't tell anybody. Just you and me know. He waves me to come over to the doorway. I go on tiptoes. *Shhh*.

"Ellie, where you going? Come over here," my mommy says.

"Oh, yer father's up to his ole tricks. I can see him from here, Winona," Grammaw says. "You may give up on that young'un. He'll have her ruined."

My eyes are on Granpaw. I go out on the back porch. He's sitting on the floor next to a wooden crate I didn't know was there. He puts his arm around me and pulls a glass bottle up out of the crate.

"Sodie pop," he says grinning. "Grape sodie pop if you eat yer supper, Ellie. Go on now."

The bottle is cool against my tummy as I carry it over to the table. Mommy takes it from my hand and gets me a glass. It is bubbly and sweet and makes me giggle when I take a sip.

Mommy's been gone a long time. Grammaw came back last night. I come to the kitchen from the day-bed where Granpaw and I sleep to see what's wrong. Grammaw's cross and shouting at Granpaw. Sunlight's streaming into the kitchen. Grammaw breaks branches and throws them into the cookstove. Fire shoots out close to my face. Angry words keep coming from her, as she slams the pots and pans around. I look at the fire that's warming my left side. I'm just as high as the flames shooting out. I look at my granpaw standing by the screen-door. He looks so sad. Like he's gonna cry maybe. He looks at me in my nightie. He rubs his bald head with his big hand and reaches for his hat that hangs on the nail by the kitchen door.

He turns and holds out his hand to me. "C'mon, Ellie. Let's

go see ole Bessie and see does she have any milk for us."
Grammaw's still saying cross words to him.

Ole Bessie is big, black and white and silent. She turns her
head toward us as she hears us coming. Granpaw picks me up
in his arms. He doesn't try to milk her. He doesn't even have
me pull up a handful of grass and feed her like he tells me to
do sometimes. He just holds me up in his arms standing right
next to Bessie and he leans against the fence post and looks
out across the fields. He holds me a long time. I lay my head
on his shoulder and close my eyes. I hear Bessie moving away,
the dry grass crunching under her as she goes.

✠ ❖ ✠ ❖

The house was empty. Joseph Butler sat in his big old armchair
alone. His wife, Annie, was in Tyler working away every week,
coming home at the weekend like she had done for years now.
Clinton was long gone. He had a family and a business in
Oklahoma City now. Dirk was working his own spread, but
always helped Joseph out at harvest time. Doreen stayed in
touch. She moved around so much with that husband of hers
that they never knew where she'd be next. But she was good
about ringing regular like.

He missed his little Ellie. Missed those blonde curls and big
blue eyes. He smiled thinking about her. Remembered holding
her on his lap driving the tractor, ploughing a field under. Best
company he ever had. He smiled thinking of the time they
played basketball in the kitchen. Annie would have had a fit if
she had found out. He had turned over the three-legged stool
and tied some old rags together weaving them in and out of
the spokes. Then he got Chippy's chewed-up rubber ball, gave
it to Ellie, and watched and laughed and clapped as she tried
to throw the ball into the "basket".

God, how he loved that child! How could Winona be making her perform like some kind of wind-up doll? He had been so angry when his daughter had brought four-and-a-half-year-old Ellie back to Oklahoma for a visit and had her down to the school dressed up like Shirley Temple doing tap dances to "The Good Ship Lollypop".

"That child's too young to be taking dancin' lessons. She's not a plaything, Winona. It's not right making her do all that stretchin' and splittin' and carryin' on. Her little body's not strong enough for that. She needs to be playin' not strivin'. She'll have the rest of her life for that," he had said angrily. And he refused to go see little Ellie perform. He had stayed home and had walked out and cut some timber up instead.

Now, he sat in the big ole arm-chair, remembering. He was tired. His prostate surgery last year had taken a lot out of him. For some reason tonight, he didn't even want to get out of the chair and fix something to eat. Didn't even want to turn on the radio. Just wanted to sit and rest. Just go to sleep right there in the chair like he had done a lot lately. A drink of water'd be nice he thought, but didn't move. The picture of him in his overalls with his arm around Ellie and her little arm around Chippy floated through his mind. He laid his head back against the chair and fell asleep. He didn't wake up.

❖ ❖ ❖ ❖

I've been sick in bed almost a year now. I got sick after Granpaw died. I wanted to go with him. I'm almost six years old. It's night-time and I've just had a bath. I'm still sick. Behind my bedroom door is a vent where the heat comes up from the cellar. I'm cold and huddle by the heater as I get my jamas on. I don't want to leave the warm air that's coming through the vent so I say my prayers next to it tonight.

Mommy's taught me to say *"Now I lay me down to sleep . . . "* then to ask God to bless my family.

I think of Granpaw tonight. I miss him. If I can talk to God, why can't I talk to Granpaw too? Mommy says he's with God now. Kneeling by the heater I say "Granpaw, I wish you were here with me. I miss you lots. Are you still angry with me?"

The room starts to get much lighter. My mouth opens wide, but I'm not afraid. I'm excited. "Granpaw, can you hear me?"

The whole ceiling is shining bright like the sun now. I see my granpaw's face real big, as big as the light, and I then hear Grandpa's voice. He says "Ellie. I love you. Very, very much. I want you to be happy and get well."

"But I want to be with you, Granpaw. Take me with you."

"No, Ellie. You can't come to where I am. Not now."

"Granpaw, I don't know what to do. I'm sick."

"Be a good girl, that's all, Ellie. Just be good. And remember I love you."

I feel very special and safe when I get into bed. The light is gone. I'm not dreaming. I'm looking for his face again.

Mom comes in to say goodnight. I don't tell her a thing.

"Did you say your prayers, Ellie?" she says.

I nod my head and close my eyes. I feel her lips kiss my cheek. Behind my closed eyes I see Granpaw with his finger to his lips. *Shhh.* I won't tell anyone, Granpaw. It's a secret. I promise.

❖ ❖ ❖ ❖

Thirteen years later, when Genelle is eighteen, she goes back to Oklahoma. Her family had gone out ahead of her. She was still in Washington DC taking her final exams at the University, completing her Freshman year.

Flying on her own for the first time, she felt quite the grown woman. High heels, lilac-colored jersey dress that clung to her body and drew the stares from men in the airport. She felt good all over. Quan's loving, gentle stroking and appreciation of her form had done wonders. From DC to Chicago on a jet was easy enough. From Chicago to Oklahoma City on Braniff Airline's two-propeller plane shook her up. Sounded too much like *"Brand If"* for her. Couldn't wait for that leg of the journey to be over and her foot to touch solid ground again.

Uncle Dirk and his wife collected her at the airport. Unsettling. He looked so much like Genelle's grandfather when she saw him, that she stood stock-still staring. Bald, bony and tall, but baseball cap instead of felt hat cocked to the side saved the day from dissolving away for her. The uncle explained the rest of the family had gone over to a picnic in Laughton with the cousins and they would take her there to join them.

Genelle looked out at the Oklahoma flatlands and tried to find something that said "home" to her. Her grandmother was at the picnic passing around her famous fabulous fried chicken. No one could fry chicken like Grammaw, everyone in the family agreed. No one could put it away like Grammaw either, but nobody ever mentioned her weight. Like a big hot-air balloon parked in the front garden that nobody talked about but you couldn't miss noticing.

Sleeping on the floor in the front room with her cousins was not what Genelle had in mind for a week's holiday after the pressure of finals. She had slept troubled and now the rooster was carrying on as if no one knew that the sun was throwing light into the east window. It was shining right into Genelle's eyes.

Her grandmother came into the room. Genelle turned over,

pretending to be asleep. "Ellie, c'mon and get up. Help me to feed the chickens. I'll have my hands full with tryin' to catch two and make a batch of chicken for the pot-luck over to the church tomorrow night."

"Aw, Grammaw, I hardly slept. And besides, I don't know how to feed chickens," Genelle said.

"Time you learned. I can't do all this myself. And your brother, sister and cousins are too small. C'mon now. I don't want to have to get cross first thing in the mornin'. Get a move on."

Genelle was depressed for days. Some holiday. Something wasn't right inside. It was Saturday and they were all going out to the West place, the old farm. She refused to go. Said she was tired though it was just gone past mid-day.

The house was quiet with everyone gone. She lay across the bed in her grandmother's room. Granpaw's picture on the wall caught her eye. She sat up and stared. Stared long. As if by looking she could understand, reach inside, reconnect, find her way back. Nothing there. She fell back on the bed, on the white-on-white bedspread that smelled of bleach and Oklahoma sun and she stared up at the ceiling. In her mind, she saw the windmill above the blowing corn. It was gone now. Her grandmother had town electricity. Didn't need a windmill any more. Genelle saw the pump. The hand-pump, handle painted green and the gray metal pail under its spout. Saw her hand, small hand on her grandfather's large hands pushing, pushing, pumping, pumping – helping him to make the water gush and splash and fill the bucket with cool water. He always spilled a little from the pail on the dusty ground for Genelle to make mud-pies with.

None of it was here any more.

She lay on the bed and moved her hands slowly up and

down over the raised tufted white balls of the spread's design, like she was a little girl laying in the snow making a snow angel. Her arms stopped. Rested in the silence. No more images. Her mind was blank. The tears came, then the sobs. She turned on her stomach and cried like a little girl.

❖ ❖ ❖ ❖

The first thing I notice about a man is his eyes and his hands. Quan's eyes – a mysterious land, his hands dry and soft, too old for him. Mesut's eyes dark with passion that could melt or terrorise, his hands brown, smooth-skinned, so soft, so deceiving. Will's eyes a kaleidoscope of color, green-blue with yellow flecks, hands large and music-making. Daniel's. Daniel's eyes were the softest doe-brown love-me eyes, forget-what-I-do-let-me-love-you eyes and gentle hands caressing my body to erase the truth of what's happening. Always looking at the eyes and hands. Always trying to find my way back to rescue those eyes that loved me first that I abandoned. Those hands that held me safely that I left.

New Paltz

New start. New place. New people. New freedom. New lifestyle. Welcome to Upstate New York. Welcome to New Paltz. Quiet town. Old stone houses built in the 1700s by French Huguenot families. The Dubois, DeFrees, VanHoeucks, and LaFevres still lived in the town two hundred years later.

It had been Indian land of the Iroquois nations. Thanksgiving had meaning here when the settlers listened to the Indians who counselled them to build their stone houses on the ridge on the other side of the Wallkill river – farm the lowlands but live above them. There were many among the Huguenots who didn't want to trust the ruddy-skinned natives they encountered. Sang the *"only good Indian is a dead Indian"* refrain. But their tunes were changed when the spring rains fell and the flatland were flooded for weeks on end under a foot of water. When the river water receded the corn and wheat could be planted for a rich harvest.

The Dubois and DeFrees learned the art of peaceful coexistence. They had fled the continent for religious freedom. But the Indians weren't tied to the valley. The spirit guided them and they migrated north and west. But the Huguenots' stone houses were built to last. They stayed.

Now, centuries later, a new group of free spirits arrived to camp on the lands in and around the Shawonghunks mountains of New Paltz, New York. And the LaFevres and Van Hoeucks looked on at the invasion. Their sleepy little town saw barns being claimed for hippy communes, old camps becoming artist colonies, and their main street looking like a carnival or circus side-show.

It was a perfect town for a hippy invasion. A college town. Just a small teacher's college founded by the Huguenot families a century earlier, but it became the scene of demonstrations. The takeover of the faculty tower. The proclamation of student demands. The small local police force had been asleep for years and now had to wake up. Then "Woodstock" happened a stone's throw away and it was all over. New Paltz was on the map.

When Genelle and her two children moved from Gravesend in Brooklyn to New Paltz, they arrived on a Saturday in May, 1970. That same day the New York City *Daily News* devoted the full front page of the paper to the headline: NEW PALTZ, THE DRUG CAPITAL OF UPSTATE NEW YORK! The article sealed the town's fate and Genelle's too. If there were druggies out there that didn't know before, they knew then – New Paltz was the place to be for the summer of 1970.

Fly the flags "full-tilt boogie" or "let it all hang out".

Long hairs mixed with short hairs, love-beads and leathers, Jesus freaks and Hare Krishnas, drug-pushers and college drop-outs galore, drugs to be scored in every alleyway, nook and cranny. Pub after pub took over old vacant buildings, candy shops, or hardware stores. Who needed a butcher when you could pour Bud by the pitcher to pull in money? In the two-block-long village centre there was now nine, count them, nine pubs. Mind-altering, mood-changing, back-bending was the order of the day.

During the daylight hours the streets weren't too crazy. But at night they disappeared – the streets that is. They were chocker-blocked with people of every size, color and shape. From sidewalk to the middle of the road was wall-to-wall people – hash-smoking, beer-drinking, acid-tripping teenyboppers to hardcore users looking for the dealers that were weaving their way through the crowd. It was a happening scene.

Genelle ended up house-sitting for a college professor who made a planned escape from the village for the summer and left her with a lovely two-bedroom house to mind just two and a half blocks from the wildness of Main Street.

On the dole, on a roll – a drum-roll, really, of freedom. In New Paltz, Genelle was free from the bonds of marriage. Mesut had grown his hair long, tied a bandanna around his head and made off for the tall blondes of Denmark and their hippy-run island of "Christiania". Parting words: "Don't wait up, I may not come back this time."

Freedom – from the shame of being a single mom. She met other women in New Paltz who were estranged from their husbands and the straight world they had been connected to. They herded their children from one house to the next on the weekends so three out of four women were free of children and could experience the joys of sex, drugs and rowdy rock-and-roll.

Freedom – to burn the bra and Genelle's self-consciousness about no cleavage and let the nipples say hello to the world. Let the hair friz into the fullest, wildest, curliest, tangled, untameable bush it wanted to.

And, freedom to dance. Oh yeah, dance! She had forgotten how much she loved to dance. Dancing, drinking, drugging, drumming, strumming, smoking her brains out in the pubs, in the mountains, in the house, in the trees. Hop, skip, clap can

214

happen to someone as naive as Genelle and it did. She drank to shrink the shame and waited for the day her prince would come and wash it all away with some really good "sunshine" or "windowpane" acid.

One, Swanee Drive. The third move in Genelle's four months being in New Paltz.

"Wow. This place is really homey. I think we've landed," she thought to herself. Genelle's children loved this new apartment. There was a fireplace, a big country kitchen, and two bedrooms. Genelle had it all figured out. She couldn't afford it on the dole, but if she rented out one of the bedrooms and slept in the front room on the sofa-bed, they'd make it fine.

There were a few other children around in the other flats in the house. Each flat had its own entrance with a bit of garden. Genelle loved their garden. It had a big weeping-willow tree. Their flat even had an enclosed porch. It felt like a dream come true. It was their first real home since Mesut left them for parts unknown.

Genelle was psyched. A young man, Dennis, who she met on the street, wanted to rent the room in her flat. He had dreamy eyes, but he didn't seem to like kids. She knew he always had good dope. He promised her that he wouldn't deal out of her house. She believed him. Who wouldn't believe those eyes? Genelle thought he wouldn't do anything to hurt her. She was sure.

A steady stream of people coming to the door looking for Dennis led her to clean his room when he was out one night. Lucky Genelle. A brown-paper bag stuck under the bed by the back wall. She now had a twelve-ounce – neatly wrapped in cellophane ounce by ounce – bonanza of pot. She put it in the top shelf of the kids' closet, out of reach, and waited for the fireworks to start when Dennis came back from town and went to his room looking for the stuff. He was out on his ear. Shame about those eyes.

Housemates came and went. Some Genelle slept with, some she didn't. She got a job waiting tables at Good Food Restaurant. Like "Alice's" you could get anything you wanted there. She spent her breaktime down in the cellar getting high with the dishwasher and assistant cook. It was a haven for health-food nuts and hippies with the munchies. Everyone there worked for a dollar an hour, even the cook. The tips were split between everybody. And no one ever went hungry at Good Food. Genelle worked there four times a week and got all the leftover soup, veggies and rice her family could eat.

Six months of freedom under her belt, and she sure didn't want Mesut's madness back in her life when he showed up. Christmas or not he could learn to use the phone and just not arrive on the doorstep unannounced and destroy everything. That's how she felt. He'd been selling acid all over Europe and now he wanted to make a pit-stop to see his kids. Well, he could make a time and have them for a weekend or a day or an afternoon, but he couldn't arrive back in and want to play Happy Family or try to control her any more. Genelle was not getting back into the cage or the box or the bin – for him anyway.

She had found her knight in shining armor. Well, maybe the armor wasn't so shiny but she was good at wearing blinders and missing the growing rust-spots on his metal exterior. Will Harding was the man of the day, to Genelle anyway. She ignored that his hands shook in the morning with alcoholic tremors as he tried to drink his coffee. She didn't listen to her friend Colleen who knew the scoop on everyone who had ever walked the streets of New Paltz. She had told

Genelle about Will's history in the town as a heroin addict and drug-dealer. He had disappeared for over a year and lots of people had thought he had been busted and sent away. But he told Genelle he had signed himself into a hospital in a little town in Maine to kick the habit himself. He didn't shoot drugs any more, he swore, only smoked dope and loved booze. But then so did Genelle.

She loved his body. It was as beautiful, as perfectly formed as Michelangelo's David. She saw no flaw in it. Will was an artist himself, a painter who of course didn't paint any more. Just got sidetracked like a lot of talented people in the '60s. Making music was his thing at present and getting high. But now that he was trying to clean up his act and appear legit, he'd decided to get down and dirty and fix people's pipes. Sinks, tubs, toilets. He was a handy man with a wrench. His white charger was a robin-egg-blue Volkswagon bug.

Sitting by the fire, wrapped in a cosy haze of burgundy and Afghany gold, Genelle lapped up the words of "Wild Horses" Will caressed her mind as he played his guitar. His eyes by any light were a painting in themselves – changing color with whatever he wore, but always the finest brush strokes of golden flecks were there. Will was sexy and strong and definitely into Genelle, which she desperately needed.

❖ ❖ ❖ ❖

After cleaning up the steam table and salad area, putting away the leftovers from the evening, I decide to have a cup of Bancha tea with the other waitress before I go home. It's been a busy night at Good Food. We're all happy. Good tips for a change. Will's home minding the kids and I feel like unwinding a bit before I join him.

"Hey listen, Leanne, tomorrow's Thursday. How about we ditch the guys for one night and go to Joe's for a Ladies' Night on our tips?" I ask.

She laughs. "Sounds like a plan. I'll talk to Carl about it in the morning and let you know."

Good Food is mellow, real mellow. I love working here. Where else could you get high, make friends, eat great food and make a bit of money? It's a real laid-back atmosphere. I couldn't waitress in a regular-type place. I don't have the skill. I'd be fired the first week.

I think of Will at home. He'll have made a fire, have the TV on and a nice buzz going. Making love with him is a dream. It feels great to be desired so strongly. He makes me feel so sexy. I glance at the clock. Eleven. He'll be watching the late news and finishing up his six-pack. That's it. Time to go home and get some loving. I say goodnight and head out.

My old gray Chevy, "St Francis" I call it – a gift from my dad, is parked right outside of the restaurant. New Paltz is free and easy. Nobody bothers to lock their cars or houses. Nobody really has much anyway.

The sidestreet is empty. No cars or people. I get in, start the motor, and pull out from the curb down the slight hill toward the traffic-light a block away. Suddenly, hands are around my throat trying to strangle me. I gag and choke. I'm terrified.

I slam on the brakes and throw the car into park, which knocks my attacker off balance and forces a brief release of his hands on my throat. I jump out of the car and he is right after me. Mesut! He must have let himself into my car and been hiding for God only knows how long on the floor of the backseat. His eyes are ablaze. I don't know what I'm doing. I'm just running – running around the car with him chasing me. I'm strictly on automatic. Survival instinct.

I jump back in the car, locking the doors as his hand clasps the outside handle trying to get in. I sit there shaking as he pounds on the glass.

I start screaming. Open my mouth and eyes in fierce, frightening roaring screams. Screaming at him insanely to scare him away. I'm sure his next blow will shatter the window.

I start the car up again. No more screaming. I'm like a zombie as I start to drive towards the traffic-light. Mesut runs in front of me immediately, blocking me every way I turn the car. He's crazed and not about to stop. Something inside of me goes completely cold and lifeless though my limbs continue to shake.

I drive the car down the hill slowly, determinedly, right towards Mesut. He stands his ground and I keep coming. As the bumper and Mesut collide, he leaps up onto the hood of the car and grabs the wiper-blades, twisting them in his grip, glaring murderously at me and howling. I don't stop. I don't even stop when I come to the red light. I turn the car and he rolls off the hood onto the street. In the rear-view mirror I see he is up off the road and running towards me. I turn on the speed. I don't look back. I drive the two and a half miles home.

When I get inside, I'm still shaking. I can barely talk to Will who sits on the corner of the sofa-bed, his arm around me. His warm alcohol-steeped breath covers me as I just stare into space, feeling numb. The phone starts to ring. "Don't answer it, Will. It's Mesut. I know it. Please. Just let it ring. He just tried to kill me in town. Hold me, Will, please."

✠ ✤ ✢ ✦

Fleeing in the middle of the night, hiding out in another state, threats of suicide, and drug overdose were too much for Will to handle on a regular basis. His armor rusted out and fell off.

Genelle was left alone while Will took up with a woman that owned a pub and had a nose for blow. It was a pub that Genelle had hung out in quite a bit and so she still frequented it. She couldn't blame him for leaving her. Who could handle that kind of madness?

Miraculously Mesut found another woman to distract him. The woman was quite young and a hot item. Genelle was grateful for her reprieve. But it wasn't for long. One afternoon as the children were napping and Genelle had laid down for a rest herself in the spare bedroom that was temporarily unrented, Mesut showed up. She hadn't heard him come into the house. When she happened to turn over and open her eyes, she saw Mesut standing next to her bed, taking off his shirt.

"What are you doing here?" she said startled. "Get out. Get out right now."

Mesut sneered. "I just came by for some sex with my wife."

"I'm not your wife any more, and you're not getting into this bed. Now get out of here before I start yelling and wake the kids up."

"You don't care about the kids. You don't care about me. You're a whore!" he said pulling his belt out of the loops of his jeans.

Genelle panicked and tried to get up and out of the bed, but he started lashing her left and right with the belt. She screamed for help, for him to stop, for mercy. The children awoke and came crying into the hallway. They grabbed hold of their father's legs begging him to stop hitting their mother.

He turned on them. He didn't strike them, but looked at them with nostrils flaring. "You're not my children! You're not my children if she's your mother," he said and stormed out.

Genelle held the shaking children. The welts on her back and arms were burning. She took Lela and Ismet to Colleen's house. Then she went to the movies on campus to try to calm down. She sought solace in the darkness. *Bonnie and Clyde.* More blood and gore. She was still shaking when she left the film and went into the pub. She ordered a double brandy and a beer chaser. She didn't dare look to her left or right or in the mirror before her. There was a welt on her cheek, she knew, from where the belt had glanced off her right shoulder. Her body ached from the beating.

Will watched her from the end of the bar. He was talking to some friends but he saw how her hands were shaking holding the brandy. He still loved her. He just couldn't handle the insanity. He was worried about her now. He knew something desperate had happened. When he found out that Mesut had beaten her again, he said quietly to her, "The bastard won't get away with it this time".

People on the street that night had to pull Will off of Mesut. He had found him walking into a pub with a woman on his arm. That didn't slow Will up. He tore into Mesut, intent on beating him to a pulp. As people stopped the fight, Will yelled at him a final threat, "Get out of town, Mesut. If you're not out of New Paltz by the morning, I'll kill you. I mean it. You won't touch her again. You can't do that and get away with it!"

Genelle heard about the fight. She didn't expect it would have any effect on Mesut, especially since he knew that Will wasn't with her any more. But it did. He left New Paltz and didn't live there again. He moved in with the woman he had been seeing who lived about six miles outside of town and he steered clear of Genelle for a long time.

She went through a series of men, a string of one-night stands, friends that became lovers when they hit her front room with too much booze in their belly. Sometimes they left smoke for her. Sometimes a load of firewood. But when one of them, a friend, put some money on the coffee table "for the kids", her stomach turned and she wanted to run.

But there was nowhere to run. She missed Will like crazy. Every so often he would surface for a little while and then he would split. Couldn't handle the kids, or Genelle's moods, or his own fear of commitment and he'd be off again.

✠ ✠ ✠ ✦

The landlord's wife has come to the door. I know I look frazzled. I'm still emotionally fried from the overdose Mesut took two days ago. Why does he have to show up on my doorstep when he's getting ready to die? Twelve hash brownies could kill a horse, but not Mesut. He's survived, and I have delivered him from the hospital to his lover's door, but I'm bushed. Hope the landlady doesn't want to raise the rent. We've been at Swanee Drive eighteen months now. It's really home. I try to smooth the wrinkles out of my clothes as I go to the door. They're the same ones I had on yesterday. I had fallen asleep in them last night on the sofa.

I open the door. There she is – all crisp and fresh and proper – standing in front of me. Her mouth is tight and her lips thin as she speaks to me with obvious disdain. Not a strand is out of place in her short gray permanent wave. I run a hand over my unruly tangle of a wild mane in embarrassment. Somewhere in the back of my mind is the memory of how to look presentable.

Her words are short and clipped. "We're tired of you here. We've had too many complaints. Men in and out at all times of the night. Loud music. Drugs. Take your kids and get out. Go back up in the mountains where you belong!"

I feel attacked, punched me in the solar plexus and the breath knocked out of me. I can't breathe right. My brain is gasping for words as if they are the air that has been knocked out of me. She looks like a grandmother whose brood is threatened and she has taken a broom in her hand and will sweep the place clean of any and all "undesirables".

As she turns to go, my words finally come blurting out. "Wait. Wait a minute. I can't move out, I . . . I have nowhere to go! I have two children and no money right now. You can't just put me out."

"That's your problem isn't it, not mine," she snaps efficiently. "You have to be out of here in a week or we'll throw everything you own out on the front lawn. We've already rented the place to someone else and they're moving in next week. If you don't want criminal charges on you, too, you'll be out!"

The porch door slams behind her as she leaves. I stand there barefoot watching her walk across the yard, the yard I love. The kids are down playing on the tire-swing that Will had rigged up for them last autumn. I just want to disappear and die and not hurt any more!

I need a drink. I need a man. I need help. I call Colleen and pour out this latest disaster to her and wait for her healing direction. What I get is not what I want. What I get leaves me feeling judged, deserted and lost . . . *Sometimes I feel like a motherless child, sometimes I feel like a motherless child. Sometimes I feel like a motherless child, a long way from home – a long, long, long way from home* . . . Yeah, what I get is Colleen's voice on the other end of the phone saying "One of these days, Genelle, you're going to be willing to give up your suffering".

I sit on the fold-up, second-hand sofa-bed and cry. Hugging one of the throw pillows, I start to rock as I sob. I want my mother. I want my mom. I want to go home. Oh, this is an old, deep pain. I weep until the tears don't come any more. Lela has run in from outside to tell me something and sees me crying. She silently goes back out. My fists are clenched as I get off the sofa. I shout out in a voice hoarse from crying, "Damn it, I want to live. I'm sick of this dying. I want to live, not just survive. I want to live!"

The room is empty – not a soul in earshot. I walk over to the mirror in the corner of the room and look at myself. My eyes are a very light blue – the color of a dull sky – the blue they always get when I'm distraught. My hair is a wild, shoulder-length bush of waves and tangles. I look at myself straight on and lay it out clearly "No more trying to be the nice one. You're really a bitch underneath. You're really furious with the whole friggin' world. Well then, be yourself! Be the bitch! And let them all deal with it. Come on out and live once and for all! Do it!"

When the kids finally venture into the house for supper, I don't pretend to be other than I am. I'm angry and preoccupied. Dishes are not being placed gently, and pots and pans are being slammed down.

"The landlady says we have to move out. We have a week to leave. I'm upset and don't want to talk about it. Got that? I'm trying to figure out what we will do." I can't look at their faces as I state these cold facts. I don't sit down at the table with them but stand by the sink staring out the window going back and forth between tears and anger.

The kids eat in silence. They're upset. They love this place too. They have friends here in the building. The school is close enough to walk to and the playground. After supper, they go out to share the news with their friends. I watch the long faces from the kitchen window as they walk off down by the well to talk.

I'm glad I'm not going out. For the first time in a long time I want to be home with my children, rather than running away. Something's shifted. Can't quite grasp it.

That night we three sit on the sofa-bed watching the TV. We don't talk. We sit close. My arms are around them. We'll be all right. We'll deal with what comes next, even if it means being homeless. We'll get through it.

I put the kids to sleep in their bunk beds tonight, and I sit on the floor and take time to sing to them. They both love this, though most of the time I'm too high or too busy with people that are over at the house to tuck them in this way. Lela's request is first. She peers over the edge of the top bunk that she still prefers even though she has fallen out of it a couple of times. Maybe she feels safer up there, further away from the goings-on in the house. She is all eyes as she peers down at me. She looks like all the photos of the waifs of the world. She challenges me a lot with big searching dark eyes and awakes guilt and fear in my heart. I'd often avoid their gaze or lash out verbally in self-defense. But tonight, her eyes are scared and needy. I sing her favorite song . . .

I went to the animal fair. The birds and the bees were there. The big baboon, by the light of the moon, was combing his auburn hair. The monkey he got drunk, and fell on the elephant's trunk. The elephant sneezed, fell on his knees, and what became of the monk- , the monk- ? And what became of the monkey?

Ismet lies still in the bottom bunk. I wonder how much he understands of all that is going on around him. He's only four years old. For now, he seems OK lying peacefully under his sheet. He's waiting quietly for me to sing his favorite lullaby. The African one about the sleeping lions – *Awimboweh.*

Homeless.

For over three months, Genelle, her two children, and the

dog lived out of the car. She stored their furniture in someone's old barn. Colleen gave her a big piece of foam rubber that she could cram into the trunk of the car and it became their travelling bed.

"It's summer. It won't be really like we're homeless," Genelle told herself. "We'll just be camping out for a while."

She had a plan that seemed good and solid to her. She'd keep the car stocked with bread, peanutbutter and jelly, and a jar of apple-juice. There was a summer arts and crafts programme for the kids at the middle school. She'd drop the kids off in the morning with their sandwiches and, if she wasn't working at Good Food that day, she would look for a place to live the rest of the day. She just needed to pick the children up by 4:30pm.

That was the plan. But Genelle was hitting bottom with her addiction, so forget the plan. When she wasn't waitressing during the day, she'd start out with the best of intentions. She'd get the newspaper and then go up into the mountains to read it and think about what their next move should be. She'd go to Smitty's Hotel and hang out at the Falls or go up to the "secret place" by Lake Minnewaska. Either way, it was the same. She'd end up getting high with the rest of the hippies up there and lie out on the rocks, soaking up the rays and watching the clouds make pictures in the sky.

So much for finding a place to live.

On the weekends, she'd take her children there too. Lots of dogs, kids, food, drink, and drugs. Jones Beach for the flower children. Lela and Ismet didn't seem phased by the nudity of others. They seemed to love running around on the rocks free of their own clothes.

They "crashed" a lot of different places that summer. A night here, two weeks there, five days in another person's house. Places that were just being built or abandoned – it didn't matter as long as a roof could be over their head, they'd bed down for the night.

When Genelle's other grandfather died, it took Colleen's husband a day to locate her and give her the news. They had been living in an abandoned cabin for a week, with no running water. Colleen took the children for the weekend. Genelle went south for the funeral. She took a flask and a load of valium with her to get through it. The first night in her father's house was like landing in heaven – especially having a warm shower. She stayed under the hot running water for ages. They were almost ready to send in the navy after her.

There were many close calls that summer, the summer of 1975. Genelle was so strapped for money and so uprooted and stoned that she found herself in very dangerous situations. Cocaine dealers wanted to put her "on the street", strip joints offered big bucks to women that could do neat tricks while dancing nude. Then an offer of a house on Main Street – the Tobacco Road of Rosendale.

The street looked like the film set for a wild-west ghost town. Genelle knew deep down in her bones that if she moved onto that street it wouldn't be guns she'd be shooting up, but something else. She'd hold on just a little bit longer.

James Street. Finally. Just what the doctor ordered. They rented the whole downstairs of a house there. Lots of space. Respectable part of town. Nice neighbors. Children. A breath of normalcy in the nick of time. An anchor in a sea of uncertainty and change.

Will he, won't he? Will's in. Will's out. He landed for awhile, helped them renovate the house, then disappeared again. Each time Genelle's heart ached till he came back.

Hospital trips had begun again. Pains in the abdomen. Blood in the stools. The doctor took Genelle off red meat, caffeine, all raw fruits and vegetables, and alcohol. Big lumps started appearing all over her body. Good Food buddies told her it was the toxins being discharged now that her body was cleaning itself up.

Genelle felt like one huge raw nerve-ending. Every time Will popped a can of beer she wanted to kill him. His drinking had never bothered her before, but all of a sudden she was counting every can he drank and making a big deal of it. She lay next to him in bed unable to sleep and listened to his regular, peaceful breathing. He was sleeping like a baby while the smell of alcohol oozed out his pores. She set about trying to make him stop drinking. He set about leaving again.

She stayed off red meat for seven years, and off of alcohol long enough to tidy up her life a bit. Got her divorce finalised. Got back to college. Got her BA in English. Got into therapy. Found Ram Dass, and *Be Here Now* became her Bible.

For three years James Street was home. Roots went down at last and fruits were ripening. She still looked like a candidate for Hippy-Mama of the Year, but mega change was happening under the surface. Binge-drinking would happen when Will would leave again or Mesut would show up and rattle her some more. But she had stopped smoking hash and cigarettes for a year now. Major shift.

✤　✤　✤　✤

Bioenergetics breaks through the armor I didn't even know I was wearing. Works on the invisible iron band girding my loins giving me narrow hips, imaginary leather straps binding my breasts keeping them from developing fully or me from breathing. My therapist says my face is also armored. It's a mask of running sores that I have been wearing since Mesut and I separated, guaranteed to push any healthy man away.

Will tells me he doesn't even notice my facial sores. He's got some serious blinders on. Psychodrama sorts out my rage, my grief, my longings and gives me a chance to ventilate, aerate the wounds. Let them breathe, let the pain out. Let the pus run. Hope all this therapeutic pain is worth it.

Cheryl, my psychotherapist, is sitting across the room in her chair. I'm lying on the twin bed in her office and staring at the ceiling. I've been working for the past few weeks on blocks to my sexuality. It's news to me. It's the one area of my life that always has seemed to be in good working order. She's told me I'm holding a lot of anger, possibly rage in my womb, that's why my hips are so narrow. My pelvis has never opened up fully, or so she says. I think I'm very open sexually. Could stand to close up a bit. Relearning how to keep my legs together and not have my womb so open seems to me what I need to gain, but Cheryl thinks something else is going on. All I know is that since she's started working with me on this issue, it's screwed up my screwing. I mean, I used to have orgasms even just kissing, multiple orgasms through intercourse, now I'm lucky if I have even one. It's a struggle, even with Will.

"All right," Cheryl says, "make fists of your hands and start raising up one of them and bringing it down to pound on the bed at your side while you lift the other one then and do the same. Come on now – right arm, left arm, right arm, left arm. Get a rhythm going."

This is easy enough, though I don't see the point in it. At least it doesn't strain me physically like some of the other exercises have.

"Good. You're doing good, Genelle. Now start moving your legs too. Alternate them left, right, left, right. Lift your whole leg up, don't bend at the knee. Come down on the mattress with your heel like it was a fist too, keeping your legs straight. Come on. Try it now."

This is a bit hard to synchronize. My arms and legs moving up and down, trying to get them into some kind of rhythm. I can't believe I'm paying money for this. Well, I'm not. Medicaid is. But still . . .

"OK, Genelle. Now, while you're moving your legs and your arms, start moving your head from side to side, like you're shaking your head 'no'. That's it. Now, pound that mattress with your heels and fists. Keep it going. Harder. The box-spring and mattress will hold you. Go on!"

Something has clicked inside me and I'm flailing the bed with my arms and legs like my body has a mind of its own. My head is moving back and forth wildly. I don't think I can stop it even if I wanted to. There's something my body's got a hold of and it's not going to give it up. Five minutes. Ten minutes. How long can it go on?

I'm exhausted when my body finally slows down and stops moving. I hear Cheryl say "Breathe. Keep your breathing open".

I lie still. Breathing. Sinking deep into the mattress like it's a cloud bed. Something is moving inside me. I focus my attention. I'm sensing something moving in my vagina. It's startling. I pay attention. It feels pleasurable. I feel confused.

"What's happening right now?" Cheryl asks from across the room.

How does she know something is going on from over there?

"There's this sensation happening," I say. "It feels real, but it can't be."

"What are you feeling?"

"Well, I feel something moving inside my vagina. Something small and thin, like a pencil."

"How does it feel?"

230

"Pleasurable. It feels tingly and pleasurable."

"The size of a pencil?" she asks.

"Yes, like a pencil or a finger. Oh, my God. I think it's a finger."

"Whose finger, Genelle?"

"I don't know. I don't know. I don't know."

"Stay with it, Genelle. Just stay with it."

An image does appear. I cover my face to try and block out what I see. Cover my face. Clench my jaw. Move my head back and forth rapidly. Try to blank it out – get it out of here. Get it out of here!

Cheryl rushes to my side. "What is it, Genelle? What did you see?"

"It can't be true. It can't. It can't!" I twist and turn on the bed in horror. Cheryl strokes the hair back off my forehead. She brings me a drink of water and has me sit up to sip it. When the image comes back in my head again, I try to shake it away.

"Genelle, I can't let you leave here in this state. You've got to let me help you work through this, whatever it is."

My jaws are clenched so tight it is difficult to get any words out. God knows I can't walk out of here like this. But how can I speak the unspeakable?

Cheryl tries to help me. "Just shake your head if you can't speak. Just try to answer my questions. Did you see an image of someone?"

I nod "yes", shivering as I sit there.

"Was it a man?"

Still nodding, I stuff my hand in my mouth, horrified.

"Could you see his face?"

I shake my head "no" vigorously and try to push Cheryl away from me.

"Genelle, I'm trying to help you. Don't push me away."

I want to tell her, but I'm afraid to even think about what I saw let alone speak it. It's too awful. "Not my granpaw – please God, not Granpaw."

"What's that you're mumbling? Did you say grandfather? Was it your grandfather you saw, Genelle?"

"I don't know. I don't know!"

"Something made you think it was your grandfather, Genelle. What did you see?"

"The hat. I just saw the silhouette of a man's shoulders, and head with the sunlight shining in my eyes behind him, making his face too dark to see. But the hat. My granpaw always wore a hat like that. Oh, my God – no. Please no." I shake my head trying to force the image out of my mind.

"Genelle, perhaps your grandfather . . . "

"No!" I yell. "My granpaw loved me! He would never hurt me, never do anything wrong like that. No!"

"I know you're upset right now, Genelle. The idea is horrifying to you, and seems impossible. But the sensation was very real and then the image came. If it was possibly true that it happened, how would you handle it?"

"I'd flippin' want to kill him! He's already dead. How can such a thought even come into my head. I hate myself for that image even entering my mind. It's not true. Don't you see. It can't be."

Cheryl has me stand up and face the bed. My legs feel like jelly under me. She gives me the glass of water to drink.

"Now, Genelle. I want you to make fists with your hands and I want you to try and discharge some of the emotions that you're struggling with now. Put your fists over your head and come down hard with them on the bed. That's it, only bend your legs and not your back. Hit the bed hard and say 'no' as you hit it."

I start pounding on the mattress and saying "no". Then the image of the man's silhouette comes back into my head and my arms become like steel. I start pounding the mattress and roaring my head off. Yelling at God, at my granpaw, at the idea – the horror of the idea that anyone could have violated a little helpless one like me – only three. My chest and upper body are just exploding with rage. The boxspring has moved into the centre of the room from the force of my blows and Cheryl has to pull the mattress back up onto it often as my pounding continues. My arms feel like there is enough strength and power in them to dismantle this whole room, probably this whole building.

Pieces tumbled into place. Like why Genelle had ended up hopelessly in love with men that abused her, who couldn't seem to love her like she needed to be loved. Or men that she tried to fix, to rescue. Why she wore blinders, heavy blinders when it came to love. And also why she hated herself so. But she rejected the new pieces of the puzzle. She refused to accept on a conscious level the image of her granpaw as someone who could have violated her. Without his love and affection, she believed, she wouldn't have survived. How could she live if he had violated her? But on a sub-consious level the image was eating her away. She was filled with shame at the possibility – the horrible possibilities her thoughts had presented her with.

So she punished herself some more. She got pregnant.

She wasn't sure who was the father of the child. Was it Will, who didn't want any children, or a friend she had spent a few weeks with as a lover? So, after much soul-searching, including going to spend a day with her then guru, Baba Ram Dass, seeing a psychic reader, and talking to her psychotherapist, she reached her decision. As a final blow to her sexuality, she had an abortion.

233

Within half a year of the abortion, Genelle and her family were put out of the house on James Street. Her landlord wanted to move back into the place. Will had broken up with her yet again. And in two weeks she was to start her first official job in ten years. She had been offered a teaching assistantship in the English department of New Paltz college with a scholarship to do a graduate course. She reckoned she was the only college professor in New York state that was drawing the dole. Her world was whirling around. She felt ready for none of it.

Daniel

Sensuous. Sensitive. Soul-wrenching. Seductive. Soma-seeker who ended up a small-time thief in a big-time prison. Addiction threw away the key long ago. "Free Bird." He could play it on his guitar but couldn't make the flight. Melted-down macho man moved through the desert on a pony with no name. On the street they just called it "horse".

Daniel Falcone. Born the only son of an Italian father and an Irish mother. They had five daughters, but Daniel came at last, the flag-bearer to carry the Falcone name forward. He was the apple of his mother's eye and spoiled rotten by her and his sisters. Even as a child, women commented to his mother on Daniel's eyes. They were soft brown, the color of a fawn, with a soulful dreamy look. "He's got real bedroom eyes, that boy," they'd say. "He'll be a lady-killer when he grows up!" His mother would just smile.

Princeton, New Jersey. Prestigious town. Daniel's father was a college professor there. His mother, a lush. Daniel was wild and loved taking risks. He was intelligent, but never took the time to apply himself in school, much to his father's annoyance. Daniel just skimmed through on his good looks and brains – no time taken to study or do any homework at all. Couldn't be bothered. He might miss out on some fun.

His mother preened him and put ideas in his head before he was ripe enough to understand what was going on. She used him to get at her husband and played them off one another. It was Daniel she would show her affection to or her new dress, to ask his opinion on how it fit her. It was him she would call into her bedroom and ask to zip her up while her husband stood and watched. It was Daniel's mother who boasted about his ability to handle wine at twelve. After all, she'd been pouring him glasses of it since he was nine. He should have been well able for a bottle.

Surrounded by six women, Daniel saw lots of the female anatomy and loved what he saw. He read a lot, too. Not the stuff the teachers assigned. He read *Lady Chatterly's Lover* and short steamy stories by Guy de Maupassant. He had discovered the joys of masturbation at twelve and soaked up every word he heard older boys saying when they talked about sex. Somewhere along the line, he read a description of narcotics, of the feelings they produced. The warm, womb-like feeling that flooded the body and flushed away any pain, creating pure pleasure – like an orgasm in every cell. He daydreamed about getting that feeling. That ultimate rush.

On his thirteenth birthday he drank a bottle of burgundy and got laid. A girl three years older than him took him by the hand and led the way up to a storage space in the top of her garage where an old mattress lay waiting for them. He loved every minute of it. As often as he could sneak out to be with her, he did.

Eventually his father found out and grounded him. Daniel climbed out of the window then. His mother applauded. His father fought with him. Sometimes father and son came to blows. Sometimes it was a battle of words.

"I'm the man of this house, Daniel Falcone, and don't you forget it," his father said. "You're too damn big for your britches. Wet behind the ears and think you know everything about everything. Any jackass can stick his cock into something wet and warm. It's not your cock that's going to get you anywhere in life, but your brains. Try and get that through your thick skull!"

"Yeah. I see where your brains have gotten you, Dad. Why don't you try making Mom happy for a change instead of worrying about impressing your students. You never even give her the time of day!"

"You keep your mother out of it. This is between you and me. And as long as you're under my roof, you'll listen to me or get out!"

"Can't wait," Daniel muttered.

"What was that you said?"

"Nothing!"

Daniel had his first taste of heroin at fourteen. Skin-popping or smoking opium became his thing then. He loved the floating feeling that shut out whatever craziness was going on around him. In a college town in 1964 pushers were plentiful. Whatever drug was wanted, whenever – it was available as long as the money was.

A year later, at fifteen, Daniel fell in love. Marla was pregnant within two months of going out with him. Her parents and his father wanted to kill Daniel. His mother wanted Marla to go away and put the child up for adoption. Daniel's response? It was the response of any good macho man. Put the woman up on your horse, shoot your gun in the air, and ride off into the sunset to prove them all wrong. But of course, he couldn't do that without first having a fist-fight with his father, throwing things into a suitcase and leaving his house with sisters crying and mother pleading.

He didn't need any of them. He was a father now – that made him a man now in the world's eyes, as well as his own, he figured.

Marla and Daniel lied about their age and were married. He stole some jewelry and found a fence to sell it for him and they took off for the steel mills of Pittsburgh, Pennsylvania. It wasn't long before he was the father of two children and working forty-five hours a week stoking the furnaces that melted the ore in the big steel works.

He drank some on the weekends. He smoked a little pot with his wife for fun, and skin-popped heroin with a friend a couple of times a month.

He worked hard. Played hard. But most of all he prided himself on bringing home that pay-check and being the man. He was seventeen going on thirty-four, and he loved it. He loved coming home from work, opening the door of his own apartment, and smelling the dinner cooking. He loved being all dirty and sweaty from the steelworks – dirty like his father never knew how to get – and it not stopping Marla from kissing him and hugging him. He loved the kids being all happy when they saw him. They'd look up at him and grin. It was dark and lonely down in that pit, or up on the trestle bridges stoking the fires. But the loneliness was all gone the minute he stepped into their flat. His walk was steady, his arms strong. He was set. He was a man and he'd let no one push him around or tell him what to do again.

Then, he was put on the graveyard shift. 11:00 at night to 7:00 in the morning. The children were just waking up when he was coming home to go to bed. He had a bowl of cereal while his small sons were fed their breakfast, and then he'd go off to sleep. They had their afternoons and evenings together, but Daniel hated leaving them at night. He hated leaving Marla, not sleeping through the night by her side, not holding her close in the darkness. But *a man's got to do what a man's got to do*, even if he still is but a boy.

The steel works looked like Hades at night. Black smoke from the huge furnaces billowed up hiding the stars. Floodlights cast gigantic shadows from the molten giants down on the men that labored in the pit, loading the iron ore. The white hot iron flowed out of the bottom of the massive ten-storey-high blast furnaces while the steaming slag streamed down cast-iron gutters to the huge waiting cauldrons below. Men slaving in silence – shovelling, pushing, pulling, or watching the molten liquids, the bubbling surfaces, the flaming cauldrons like they had some power. Like warriors poised on the rim of a volcano, watching it bubble and boil as if there was something they could do if the lava started to rise. As if they had some power to stop the flow once it started. Faces lit by fierce, awesome fires or stark floodlights. It all had an eerie, ominous feeling at night.

It was dark and dirty and all the equipment was heavy cast iron. Tons of raw ore were loaded into large cast-iron wagons and conveyed up steel trestles. Pulled up by winches to arrive at the steel platform bridges that spanned from one furnace to the next. Furnaces that were 100 feet high and 120 feet round at their base. Furnaces that housed the hottest fires man could create in order to produce that strongest thing man had yet to discover – steel. And the men who worked there in the belly of the monster stood in awe of it and yet were called to mind it, stoke it, manage it. Keep it under control.

Daniel trembled at times before the great fire, but felt his muscles and mind strengthened by the power of it at the same time. He was working up on one of the platform bridges now. There were three men up there usually. Two to manage the mechanism that reversed downward to make the lid of the great furnace lower itself. Daniel's job was to release the front

239

of the ore wagon, once the lid was lowered. By releasing the front panel, the tons of raw iron would tumble into the mouth of the furnace. He would use his shovel to clear out any ore the lingered in the huge wagon and feed it into the furnace's mouth.

January 14, 1968. 3:00 in the morning. One of Daniel's mates on the bridge was out sick. The other fellow he worked the platform with had gone for a fifteen-minute break after they had finished emptying a load. He told Daniel, if any wagon arrived before he was back, to hold on. There was usually twenty minutes in between loads. Daniel leaned on the steel railing and had a smoke. It was cold. An icy night. But the heat from the furnace when the lid was lowered kept the bridge railings and platform warm enough so that no ice could form.

He watched the men below. They looked like roaches illumined by candlelight. He heard the familiar roar of the great blast of hot air from the pipes at the base of the furnace and saw the light cast out upon the sand-covered ground as the base of the furnace was opened and the molten liquid poured out into the well-formed rivulets in the sand to cool into pig-iron. His thoughts drifted to Marla. To her sweet even breathing as she lay sleeping. He thought of the softness of her thighs. Of pressing against her. Then he heard the iron wagon approaching. He straightened up and got ready to do his work again. He got his shovel and waited for his mate. No sign of him. Daniel knew that the loads were timed and that the empty wagon needed to roll back on down the steel trestle and be pulled into the loading pit, out of the way of the next wagonload to be hauled up. He couldn't delay much longer or there would be trouble. There could be a collision.

He was sure he could handle his mate's job. He'd watched them do it often enough. He knew where the switches were and he was agile enough to squeeze by the opening of the furnace when the lid was down if he clung onto the railing tightly. No problem. In fact the challenge of it excited him. Time was essential. Not a minute to lose now.

He heard the great rush of flames as the lid responded to the switches shift and lowered itself into the ferocious heat. Daniel couldn't resist looking down into the intense belly of flames as he maneouvered around the lip of the furnace. He sighed in relief as he reached the waiting wagon filled with tons of ore. The boiling bubbling surface of the fire was sending rushes of heat up into Daniel's face. He pulled out one of the heavy iron pins that held the huge wagon's front panel in place. The other pin seemed to be jammed. He couldn't budge it. He climbed up on top of the wagon, and lay across the ore. He grasped the loop of the big pin and tugged with all his might. "Damn you," he said. "Damn you, you friggen pin, come on and get the hell out of there!" He was up on his knees now on top of the raw iron, cursing at the pin that was saving his life. He hadn't thought it through. If he dislodged the pin he would tumble into the furnace with the ore. Oblivious to the danger he was facing, he sat down on the wagonload, exasperated. It was then that he realized the huge wagon was moving backwards. The winch must have slipped. He grabbed at the railing to swing off of the wagon, but too late. The wagon was off of the platform bridge, hurtling down the steel trestle. A thirty-ton uncontrolled mass tearing down the track at break-neck speed. Daniel gripped the edges of the monstrous wagon with every ounce of strength in his body. He knew he was finished. He knew he would be dead in a minute or two. This had to be hell after all.

He heard the yells of the men down below as they saw the runaway ore wagon heading at full speed for the ground below and the ore pit. Daniel screamed out in terror as the wagon hit and flung him into the air. Pain shot through him, then total blackness.

They started him on the morphine on the way to the hospital. The pain was excruciating. Only a shot of morphine every four hours enabled him to bear it. For a short while he could float away into a fantasy world, drifting in and out of consciousness, until the pain again would start to curl the edges of his dreams.

When he finally got to come home to Marla, he still had to be flat on his back. He couldn't believe he was actually alive. He was sent home with an open prescription for painkillers. He started waking up sweating and yelling from nightmares so the doctor gave him a script for sleeping pills too.

He hated having to lay helpless in the bed while Marla took care of everything. The cooking, the shopping, the cleaning, the children. He couldn't lift them up or have them climb into the bed with him though he longed to hold them. They were too little to understand that they couldn't jump on the bed or roll against him playfully as they once did. It killed him that he couldn't make love to Marla. He longed to give her loving. He cried inside when she would lay her head on his shoulder at night. He would not touch her body at all or even fantasize about being able to give her pleasure because he didn't feel like a man any more. He was an invalid. A pathetic child who could not even go to the toilet by himself.

In a couple of months, he was in a wheelchair and managing his way around the apartment. Work was out of the question and bills were piling up. Marla talked to him about getting a part-time secretarial position. She had the skills. There were lots of jobs in the paper for office help and he would be able to look after the children a few hours a day, even in the chair. His upper-body strength was back, and he had the use of his legs though he couldn't really stand for long and definitely couldn't lift anything. Daniel fought against her going to work but in the end gave in because he knew there was no other way. His pride wouldn't let him ask his father for money.

He felt like he had been in the bowels of hell battling with the Devil himself and that the Devil had won. Daniel Falcone had died that January night. The person in the wheelchair was somebody else, someone who really didn't even want to be alive either, reduced to wiping running noses of little children and sitting in a wheelchair watching *Sesame Street* or *Captain Kangaroo*, his wife working. He started eating the painkillers and sleeping pills two and three at a time, experimented mixing them with beer. It made the days pass quicker and his morbidity dull into a blue haze.

One day, while he was baby-sitting, his friend stopped by with some heroin. Skin-popping did nothing for him any more. He'd been on painkillers too long. But his friend showed Daniel how to tie himself off and shoot up.

Wow. Mainlining. Moonlight. *Misty roses – too good to be true but too beautiful to leave alone*. He got out of the wheelchair and up on the "horse" and started to ride again. *It felt good to get out of the rain. La, la, la-la-la-la, la-la-la, la, la.* Yeah. Hey, Jude – welcome to la-la-land. Milk and honey, don't be worried about the money. There'd always be a way to score and get more once you were in the game.

❖ ❖ ❖ ❖

Going back to school was easy, this is hard. When I was a student at New Paltz college I blended right in with all the other students. Nobody would have guessed I was ten years older than them with children of my own in school. I looked like one of them. Felt like one of them. Got high and partied with them. But this is really difficult. Standing up in front of a classroom teaching when I'm just finding my own way in life feels very strange. There ought to be a law.

September 3, 1976. The first day of class. I write on the board the name of my course. *Freshman Composition – Drama.* I'm wearing my professor disguise. Tailored trousers, an Oxford shirt and a conservative cardigan. I've practically shaved my head. My hair is shorter than ever before except perhaps for the first year of my life. My wild mane is in one of the garbage bags that the barber put out for collection yesterday. When I run my hand over my hair I think I'm touching someone else's head, a man's. It's quite startling for me. This whole scene is startling.

Students look up at me expectantly. My hands are shaking. I hope my voice doesn't crack as I speak to them. "Chill out, Genelle," I tell myself. "You've been on stage lots of times. This is nothing new for you really. Step into the role and run with it."

I begin. Give them an overview of the course. Then ask them to write a composition on "The Drama of Life". I sit down in my chair behind the big oak desk at the front of the class and look at them in amazement. They're actually writing. Twenty-two students sit before me writing diligently. They think I'm a college professor. Uncanny. Then, it occurs to me that perhaps this is happening elsewhere in the world. That there are men dressed up like priests and people reacting to them as if they really are something different than themselves. What if there are doctors who really aren't sure of what they are doing but they show up and put on their white coats and people come in to see them as if they know how to cure them? What if the president really doesn't feel sure of himself at all, but everybody is relating to him like he knows what to do? What if everybody in the world is only playing a role that they've been handed and they are just going through the motions and others are responding with reciprocal emotions? Everything just cardboard-cut-outs of reality. Scary thoughts. My students are still writing – that's even scarier. I want to run out the door but that's not in the script so I wait for the clock to run out.

Amazingly, two years of graduate studies and the contract for teaching freshman composition pass very quickly. It's been great. I've loved teaching, really loved it once I got used to being myself before the class. I've even accepted that I have something of value to teach. But it's all over. The contract is up and non-renewable. Teaching assistantships are only retained for two years.

Not sure what I'll do. The therapy and meditation stuff has done wonders to build my confidence. I've even been getting training in how to run therapy groups and do counselling myself. That's a blow-mind altogether. But hey – anything is possible.

That's the truth. I'm facing going off the dole now. Both kids are well along in school and I've got a graduate-level college education. Guess it's time to be a grown up and *"Get a job, shah-nah-nah shah-nah-nah-nah-nah"*. But first I intend to enjoy my summer.

Beers, barbecues, boyfriends and baseball. Ismet, Lela and I all are playing ball this summer. It's crazy trying to juggle each of our rosters, have a bit to eat, and cover the bases. Hash is in the air. I keep passing that joint saying "no thanks" but it's smelling better and better to me. I'm four years off the stuff. Just drinking beer has been good enough for me. But I can almost taste the hash again when it's being smoked so close to me.

Bingo. The buzzer goes off and the telephone rings before I join the ranks and inhale.

"Hello. Is this Genelle Basharan?" the male voice asks.

"Yes," I say cautiously. It's still my knee-jerk reaction to expect the worst when a stranger phones.

"Well, my name is Ed Wegsheider. I understand that you have been in a training group with Sandra, one of the drug-abuse counsellors from my clinic. She's spoken very highly of you and your skills."

"That's nice to know."

"Sandra's given her notice to me today that she will be leaving permanently in a month. She doesn't want to return after she gives birth to her baby. She mentioned your name as a possible replacement. I wonder if you'd like to come in for an interview?"

"Gee, you've kind of taken me by surprise. I'm not sure what Sandra has said to you. But I haven't had any training as a drug-abuse counsellor."

"That's OK. Why don't you come in to the office and talk to me. I'm interested in finding out more about your other qualifications. We can always educate you about drugs."

※　※　※　※

Daniel Falcone was out of the wheelchair, up on his feet, out the door and into other people's houses through their windows. Marla was working full-time. He still watched the children for her, but now also cooked the meals, did the laundry and hoovered. He hated being a house-husband. He was riddled with guilt. He should be the one getting up and going out to work supporting the family, not her. Instead he slipped out of the house, while the children were napping, and into strangers' homes to steal whatever he could to support his heroin habit.

Marla was distressed but stood by him during his first time in jail. Petty larceny. The charges were eventually dropped. Insufficient evidence. Even the second time. Burglary. She was faithful, and brought the children in to visit. But the third arrest, possession of a controlled substance, was the line she refused to go beyond. She took the children and disappeared.

Daniel Falcone learned how to play the jail game but he hated being behind bars. Hated the jailers, the cons, the blacks, the Puerto Ricans. Most of all he hated himself. He was hooked badly. It broke his heart to lose Marla. But to not know where his boys were or if he would ever see them again tore him apart. He had sworn to himself that he would be a better man, a better father than his own dad. He had the brains and the heart and the talent. But regardless of the strength or the goodness of his intentions, white powder had a hold on him and wouldn't let go. It made him violate his dreams and all he valued.

He wrecked cars. The jaws of death had to pull him out of one wreck. Lost his spleen in that one. His sisters wrung their hands and prayed, baked him cookies and came to visit the hospitals, rehabs, and prisons that housed him. His mother and father pointed the finger of blame at each other and divorced. But neither of them could visit him without feeling guilt or crying when they left whatever insitution he was in.

In 1974, when he was in the Woodbine Correctional Rehab Centre two things happened. He sold his guitar for a balloon of hash smuggled into the facility, and he was introduced to the wonders of methadone. Synthetic opiate. Legal liquid gold for the veins of a junkie.

Designed to satisfy the drug-addict's urge for heroin. It did. Shoot enough heroin on the street and a dope fiend could get on any legal methadone clinic in the country. And even if methadone did have some bad side effects, what was more important – the health of a drug-addict or the safety of society?

Daniel knew the theory. He was a smart man. Had read all the articles on it written by its promoters which denied the medical research that indicated possible severe liver damage or deterioration of bone marrow due to prolonged usage. He loved to read all the case studies that talked about the ex-junkies who now held responsible jobs and had happy families to come home to, and all they had to do differently than their neighbors was to call into the methadone clinic on their way to work and take their daily dose.

Methadone was big business for the government and addicts flocked to the clinics. Not because they wanted to get clean, but because methadone was a great high. And if you were on the dole, it was given out at no cost. The dose they gave at the clinic would just maintain a consistent level of opiate in the body so they wouldn't go into withdrawal and get sick. But take a regular dose and then boost it with booze or valium or barbiturates and *ooh-ooh* baby we got a *goooood* buzz going.

If anyone needed a TV, stereo unit, or anything – just pass the request along the waiting line of addicts queuing up to get their dose of meth and some Santa would supply it next day. Dr Dan, as his dope-fiend pals named him, always had a good supply of pills for purchase outside the methadone clinic. He got real good at forging prescriptions. He'd go into the emergency room with a complaint about his old back injury, and while they had him waiting in the casualty unit he'd locate the doctor's prescription pads and tear off a couple of sheets. A simple game of fill in the blanks and forge a doctor's signature. Their writing was always illegible anyway.

There were plenty of short stays in jails. Three months. Five months. Nine months. Lots of petty crimes. It was the felonies that evoked fear in Falcone's heart. "Three felonies," his jail-time buddies told him, "And they send you to the big-time prison and throw away the key."

Daniel was living in Ulster County, upstate New York, when he was convicted of his second felony. November 18, 1978. Couldn't beat the rap. He was caught red-handed running out of a drugstore at midnight with two grocery bags filled with pills – barbiturates, tranquillizers, painkillers.

He met Genelle when she and another drug-abuse counsellor, Ralph, came into the jail to start a group for the inmates. If either of them had been seasoned counsellors it might have been different. Maybe not. Genelle had just finished reading a book, *Inside Out,* written by some Ram Dass followers who worked with prisoners. She was inspired and wanted to save the world. What she really needed to do was save her own ass. She was headed for the falls without even an oar in the water.

They started interviewing potential group members at the jail on February 11th. Daniel Falcone was the third person on their list. He had a bandanna tied around his head. He was wearing faded maroon corduroy slacks, a dark flannel plaid shirt with the sleeves rolled up, and leather bedroom slippers. No socks. He looked at Genelle only a few times during the interview, but his big beautiful reddish-brown eyes captured her attention in those few moments and roped her in.

"Interesting man," she commented to Ralph after Daniel had left.

"Yes. He seems more intelligent than some of the others. This ought to be a difficult group, but good."

Daniel did the rap group, the Hatha Yoga group, and afterwards even joined the small meditation group Genelle offered to the inmates. The beauty of his spirit struck her deeply. He was glowing when she'd bring them down from the guided imagery. The whole room seemed filled with light after the group meditation. It was always a bit jarring when the guards would bang on the steel door of the library indicating it was time to end the group. Daniel's eyes talked to her as he left the library to go back to his cell. "Don't forget me," they seemed to whisper.

Ralph and Genelle began to counsel inmates on an individual basis in the small rooms downstairs that were normally used for lawyer visits. It was summertime now. Genelle was Daniel's individual counsellor. She looked forward to seeing him each week. They worked on his troublesome relationship with his father mostly, and some struggles he was having with his girlfriend, Sonia.

Genelle knew she was attracted to him. Her feelings were starting to spill over into her dreams. Yet she told herself she could handle it OK. He was going to be transferred in a few weeks to high-security prison for the last three months of his sentence. But it was during a session when he was upset about a letter he'd received from his girlfriend that Genelle knew she was in over her head.

"Here, read this. You read it and tell me what you think is going on!" He tossed the letter to Genelle angrily. She looked at the signature *Love, Sonia* and swallowed hard.

"Look Daniel, I don't think your girlfriend would want you showing her letter to other people. Why don't you just tell me what you're feeling."

"I'm feeling like I wish I could get the hell out of here and strangle her! Please read it. Tell me if I'm going crazy or if she's screwing me over."

Genelle sat staring at the letter. She tried to focus but couldn't. She was shocked at her own thoughts. She wanted to side with Daniel, put Sonia down, suggest he break up with her. She looked at Daniel's face. It was strained. His whole body was tense and leaning forward intently.

"Daniel, look – I have to tell you something. I can see you're really upset about this, and I want to help you with it but I can't. The fact is, I can't be your counsellor any more."

"Genelle, what are you talking about? You've been a great help to me. Don't let this little thing throw you if you can't figure it out. It's just that I know Sonia and her devious ways. So I know something's up. It's okay if you don't really understand this one. I do. I feel better just letting off steam to you about it."

"Listen to me, Daniel. I can't be your counsellor any more because I've lost my objectivity with you."

"Hey, everybody has their bad days. I should know. I get plenty of them in here. You're being awful hard on yourself, like you're always telling me I have a habit of doing. Ease up a bit."

"I guess I'm really going to have to spell it out for you, Daniel. I can't be your counsellor any more because I have feelings for you. Feelings as a woman for you as a man. I'm sitting here reading this letter feeling jealous of Sonia and wanting to manipulate you about her. I've got to stop counselling you and let somebody else work with you who can be objective and help you."

"Genelle, you're blowing me away. I've been attracted to you from the first time I saw you, but I never dreamed you could dig me. Listen, you don't have to stop seeing me. You could still come in like we were having a session, only we'd just hang out together."

"No. I couldn't do that. You're about to get out in three or four months. You'll need to work up a plan for re-entry and all. You need to have a counsellor who can really help you."

"Hey, you're the one that can really help me. I won't see

anybody else. That's final. I mean it, Genelle. Either I work with you or I don't work with anyone. What do you say?"

"I can't do that," Genelle said seriously, avoiding his eyes. "I have to talk to my supervisor, Dr Talbot, about this whole situation. I'll let you know what he says. His decision is what I'll go with. I have to!"

Daniel went back to the cell block elated. He didn't care about the upsetting letter from Sonia any more. He had a whole lot of other things to spend his hours thinking and dreaming about now.

It's a gray afternoon. There's a light drizzle falling as I pull into the ominous-looking fortress. The concrete wall that serves as a fence is thirty feet high and very thick. There are gun-turrets at intervals along the top of this wall. I'm trembling as I go inside the prison and the series of steel doors clang closed behind me.

The visiting-room is packed full of women and children of all ages, and men in green clothing with numbers on the pocket. Most of the people in the room are black. It's very noisy. I feel scared and very self-conscious. Greenhaven Penitentiary. I haven't seen Daniel since Dr Talbot agreed that I should stop counselling him, but we have been writing. "Whatever you want to do with your personal life is your choice," Dr Talbot said. "But your professional relationship with him needs to terminate."

As I wait, I wonder if my hair looks all right and if my make-up is OK. I really just want to leave because the waiting is so painful. I feel like half the room is staring at me. Just as I'm about to get up and ask a guard where the toilet is, I see Daniel walking towards me in his green prison uniform. He looks pale and thin. He's shaking as he sits down across from me and takes my hands in his. I'm embarrassed and feel shy. My cheeks are getting flushed.

"It's great to see you, Genelle."

I can see how scared he is too. My heart goes out to him. "Were you waiting long?" he asks. "Sometimes they take forever to send the notice up that someone has a visit."

"I feel kind of shaky, Daniel. I mean – well, I guess I'm just pretty uncomfortable here."

"I'm kind of nervous myself. This place is a trip, isn't it?" His eyes do a fast scan of the visiting-room. "I mean it's some kind of zoo, don't you think?" He looks at me again and gives my hands a squeeze. "I'm real glad you came. I needed to see your face. Your hair looks beautiful. Gee, you look great!"

It's hard for me to look him in the eyes. He looks so vulnerable. The inmate and his mother who have been sitting next to us get up and walk to the back of the room where there's a coffee-machine.

"Could I kiss you, Genelle?" Daniel asks hopefully.

I've seen various couples locked in passionate embraces as I've been waiting for him to come down and watched some of the guards snickering at the contortions that inmates and their women went through so that the visitor kept the required "one foot on the floor" and the inmate stayed on his side of the metal table. I've never kissed Daniel or even touched him before. I feel uptight in this big room with a huge high ceiling and glaring flourescent lights.

"Just a little kiss, Genelle. It would mean a lot to me."

I close my eyes as I sit on the steel bench and lean towards him. His lips are soft and lovely. What a gentle, inviting kiss he gives me. When I open my eyes I'm smiling. He looks like a little kid who's feeling good about himself. His shaking has stopped. "Lots more where that came from, baby. Can't wait to show you."

I see Daniel once more at Greenhaven. I've convinced myself that even though I'm attracted to him and have feelings for him, I need to keep my distance until he gets settled.

His first night out. We're in a borrowed apartment. So much for my plans to keep a safe distance. Daniel takes out a little bag of hash he'd picked up to celebrate his release. He finishes rolling a joint and reaches over to stroke my leg.

"Wow. Stockings. God, they feel great. Stand up in front of me for a moment, honey."

As I stroke his hair, he closes his eyes and lets his hands travel over my calves and up under my slip to caress my thighs. He starts trembling as he undoes my skirt. I move my hands to try and help him.

"No, baby. Please let me undress you. Let me go slow and enjoy every moment of it."

I only have my black slip on when I climb in between the sheets. "Hurry up and join me, Daniel. It's cold in this bed." He's smiling at me and taking off his shirt. Even in the dimly lit room, I can see the tattoo on his arm and his leg, and the long scar he has on his stomach. Before I have time to ask about them, his lips have found my mouth.

Soft. Sensuous. His hands sliding, stroking, skimming over the surface of my body like silk slipping and slithering over polished ivory. He makes me purr in every cell of my being. "Yes," I sigh. "Yes," I laugh. "Yes," I breathe out heavily with a rush of ecstacy. Please don't wake me till it's over and don't let it be over yet. I must be dreaming but, oh, don't let it stop, ever. I want to come and come and come. Then come some more. Which one of us has been in prison anyway? Which one of us is coming now? Oh God, I love him. *Ooooh, yeah.*

"That was beautiful, honey. Really beautiful," he whispers

softly as he relaxes his body and eases his weight over a little to make sure I'm comfortable.

I kiss his shoulder and cheek softly. Giving him a hug with my legs, I laugh lightly.

He raises himself up on his elbow and smiles at me, stroking my neck. "I'm glad you're happy. This is just the beginning, honey. I've got a lot of loving to catch up on."

❖ ❖ ❖ ❖

I've seen the needle and the damage done, go on baby and have your fun, every junkie's like a setting sun to me . . .

Loving wasn't the only thing Daniel wanted to catch up on. Inside of nine months he had gotten his heroin habit back. By the time Genelle realized that he was shooting up again they were living together. At first her kids loved his easy-going ways but as he got strung out on the dope they got disgusted with him.

He got back on the methadone programme. Genelle was drinking daily and smoking hash with Daniel on the weekends. Her job was in jeopardy. She was struggling to hold things together. Fights were flaring almost every day between her and Lela. Daniel would show up to wait for her to get off work in the clinic. He'd end up nodding out in the lobby where drug-abuse clients were waiting to see their counsellors. Genelle started drinking on the job. She'd buy short ones. Little bottles of beer to have with her sandwich for lunch. She was fired two days before Daniel got arrested for his third felony. Forgery.

By now Lela had run away, escaped to live with a friend of the family. She was fourteen the summer she left. Ismet was twelve. He lay on the living-room floor in their little house on

255

Springtown road in New Paltz. He looked at his mother crying on the sofa. A police car had just left after arresting Daniel.

Ismet was quiet. Never spoke much. His sister did all the talking. He looked at his Mother that night and spoke as if in a dream. Quietly. Calmly. But it shattered Genelle's world completely.

"Mom, I don't have any respect for you. You drink all the time and smoke. You have men in the house and you sleep with them."

"Ismet, what are you saying. You liked Will, didn't you? And I thought you liked Daniel."

"Will never stayed around. And Daniel's disgusting. He's a drug-addict, Mom. How can you stand to be around him?"

"But I love him."

"Yeah," the young boy said. He looked at her not with hatred, but with deep disappoinment in his eyes. Then he got up off the floor and went to his room.

It wasn't the worst time in Genelle's life. Nobody was kicking her down the street or beating her. But her son's words stung like no physical blow could. Daniel got sent to a drug rehab as an alternative to prison. If he didn't remain in treatment it was three to five years in the penitentiary.

Genelle went into the Alcoholics Anonymous and got sober.

❖ ❖ ❖ ❖

Two weeks. Two weeks of walking down the lane at twilight.

Walking the dog down the quiet tree-lined street in West Albany, New York, holding Daniel's hand. Two weeks of lovemaking. Of holding his body close to mine knowing that soon he would be gone for years. Of looking into those eyes that I love so much and seeing the fear, the sadness, the

256

momentary joy and the relishing of each taste and touch of freedom. I'm in Albany to be close to him and he's leaving. It's not his fault. I know it's not. Up to a few months ago when they took him from the Treatment Center to have an emergency gall-bladder operation, he had been making progress. But in the hospital he had to go back on the morphine both during and after the surgery and he's been back to the races ever since. We know that tomorrow in court the judge will send him to prison because he's been thrown out of the rehab.

My son is in school. Daniel's getting dressed to go into downtown Albany. I know he's going to cop some heroin. I don't want him to leave me. I feel so shaky. I'm afraid I may drink, or take some painkillers that I relapsed on four months ago. I haven't had a drink in seven months, but I've relapsed once already on the tablets. I had thrown them in the garbage like my AA friend had suggested. But when she was gone I had gone into the garbage and picked them out, wiped them clean, and put them in an envelope just in case. In case . . . Today's the "in case". I want to get high on them.

"Please Daniel," I say taking him by the arm. "Please don't go downtown today. I'm really feeling shaky. I need to be with you. Take me with you or stay here with me. I want to get high. I'm scared."

"Genelle, baby – listen. I got to do what I have to do today and it isn't a place where I want you to be seen. It wouldn't be good for you. You're doing so good in AA. Isn't there a meeting you can go to this afternoon? Some people you can call?"

"Yes, honey. But, it's you I want to be with. I'm not going to see you after tomorrow." Panic was setting in. I hate separations so bad. I'm afraid something horrible is going to happen to Daniel or to me and I'll never see him again, ever.

It's the fear of a very little girl. A powerless little girl. I know I need help. And I know Daniel's got to get his drug. I know there's no way he can face leaving us and going inside the penitentiary without getting some dope. He isn't in any twelve-step progamme, but he's proud of me and how I'm trying to stay clean and sober.

"Come on, Genelle. Get your AA book and see where there's a meeting. I'm heading out on the bus downtown and I'll be back by three. See if you can get a lunchtime meeting somewhere and tell them how you're feeling." He gathers me in his arms and holds me tight. I'm choked up with tears. "Love you, babe. Got to go. Promise me you'll go to your meeting now. Come on, promise me."

Sitting in the Women's meeting, I'm overcome with sadness and fear. I want to take the pills and at the same time I don't want to. I felt crazy inside. It's a huge meeting. Must be forty women here. Where have they all come from? Everybody is sharing and I'm sitting on the floor wanting to hide. Just before the meeting is over, the chairperson says "Is there anyone here feeling like drinking that needs to share?"

I raise my hand in spite of myself. I share with the group that I have some painkillers at home that I had pulled out of the garbage several months ago and I have been wanting to take them all day. "My boyfriend is downtown copping heroin right now. He's getting sent away to prison tomorrow for a long time, and I want to get high real bad. He told me to go to a meeting. He said he couldn't help me today. So here I am. I don't feel like drinking, but I feel like taking a handful of painkillers and getting out of my head."

At the end of the meeting, lots of women come over to me and give me a hug and say they'll pray for me. I feel grateful and embarrassed. I sit down on a chair cause my legs are shaking. Three women come and stand before me. Strangers.

258

I start to cry as one of them speaks to me about throwing out the pills.

"You've got to wrap them in toilet paper and flush them away," she said to me gently. "If you wrap them in toilet paper they'll go down in a flash and you won't be able to scoop a floater out. Forget about tossing them in the trash. You've proven that doesn't work. Flush them."

They aren't pointing a finger at me, judging me or making fun of me. They seem to genuinely care. It touches me. My mind is racing however. What if Daniel is there or comes home while they are there? What if I really need to get high later and don't have anything? I mention to the women my worry about Daniel.

"Oh, we'll come with you and you can just tell him we came over for some coffee. We'll probably be gone before he comes home, anyway."

When we get to the door, I'm relieved to find Daniel isn't back yet. One of the women busies herself making coffee in my kitchen, while the other two make themselves comfortable on the sofa. I go up the stairs to wrap the pills and flush them. If I have any trouble, I'm to give the women a holler.

I go into the linen closet and dig out my cosmetic bag. Underneath all the make-up is a folded envelope with six Darvons in it. I look at them in the palm of my hand for a long time. One of the women calls up the stairs, "Everything all right, Genelle? Need any help?"

"No, no," I reply. "Everything's fine. I'll be down in a minute."

I tear off some toilet paper from the roll and place all six of the tablets in it, neatly wrapping them up. Then I drop the bundle into the toilet bowl and immediately push the flush handle. I stand there watching the swirling water scouring the sides of the bowl and pulling the bit of tissue forcefully down the hole to the waiting pipe and sewer below. My body is overcome with a weird powerful urge to stick my right hand down into the toilet, to force it down into the pipe and extend it elastically till it reaches all the way down to the sewer and grabs that bundle of tissue and pulls those pills back out. My arm actually aches all the way up to my shoulder, and the inside of my hand feels like it has a magnet in it. The opposite force of that magnet is in that bundle of pills. My palm is alternately itching and aching. On some psychic level it is following those pills all the way down the sewer pipes to their final destination. I stand in that little bathoom looking at the toilet bowl filling back up and I blink in shock at myself and the feelings I'm having. "You're an addict, Genelle," I say quietly to myself. "You're a flippin' addict."

When I go downstairs, I tell the women what I experienced and none of them seem surprised. My hand still feels like it has a magnet in its palm that is feeling a strong pull towards some unknown distant place.

The women are just leaving as Daniel walks in. "Who were they?" he asks as he gets a soda out of the fridge.

I tell him what has just happened.

"You had Darvons here and you didn't tell me? You were holding out on me, huh!" He's being gentle with me, joking, even though there's a sarcastic edge to his voice. "Well, if you're really going to get honest and do the right thing, why don't you flush the pills you've got stashed in that little tin Chinese box in the bottom of your dresser."

I'm busted. Addiction is so cunning, so insidious. I have even forgotten about that stash that I had hidden over a year ago. We laugh together over it and he helps me flush them, too.

That night in bed, Daniel doesn't want to lay down. He's in bits and so am I. We sit on the edge of the bed and cry together. No promises can be made. He won't ask me to wait. "Three to five years" seems like forever.

Too long for promises.

Bushmills

One-horse town. Barren. Poverty-stricken. Even the oil had got up and gone. Left the farmers high and dry with big ugly holes dug in the middle of their fields where iron monsters, like dark dinosaurs, dunked their heads ceaselessly day and night to see if there was anything down under the hardpacked clay knowing the answer would still come up "no".

Bushmills, Oklahoma. Halfway between a rock and a hard place. Flat land. Open-sky country. Trees scattered like an afterthought of God to dot the plateau filled with sagebrush, alfalfa, and maize. Sun so hot it melted the horizon into wavy lines of simmering vapour. 110 degrees in the shade. No wonder the river dried up. The Cimmaron was only forty foot wide by Bushmills, but from June to September it was empty except for a foot-wide vein of water washing through the centre of the caked clay river-bed.

Strange country. Jimson weed and tamarack trees. Hard-packed clay or dry sandy spots where rattlers could slither faster than a six-gun could shoot. Underground rivers in this part of Oklahoma could surface without a warning. Sun so hot it baked the hard earth into splitting, cracking and opening so the water would surge up from under the earth where it was hiding, flooding acres over night, covering trees – fifteen-foot-high trees. That's how deep the water could get in low-lying areas. Over in Drummond Flats down by Coyote Creek sixty acres had been underwater one year.

Weird weather too. Tornado territory. In 1957, when Genelle was just fourteen and living in Pennsylvania on the Mainline, Aunt Doreen phoned from Bushmills to say that it had rained twenty-one inches in one day. Turtle Creek had flooded and Uncle Dirk had only been able to get one wagonload of hay out that year before it all was flooded out and ruined.

For Genelle, Bushmills was a land she had visited in her dreams since childhood. Images that melted in her mouth like ripe strawberries hot from the sun picked out of Granpaw's hand. The warm metal seat of the tractor to her own little hand as she patted it playfully, waiting for Granpaw to come on and make it go. She hated a shadow being cast over it. Hated the silhouette of a man that stabbed the safety of her dreamworld and threatened to turn it into a nightmare.

She refused to tarnish the memory of the only one who didn't go away, the only one who loved her. Loved? What was the truth? Truth turned itself inside out and stuck out its tongue in the mirror if she tried to find out the answer. She couldn't. He couldn't have, could he? She could have. She could have killed him with her four-year-old careless selfishness to leave him lonely, unloved in a chair staring into space where no one was home after working the fields, mending the fences, doing what – what was he doing the day that his heart stopped? She didn't know. She only knew she wasn't there. Guilty, she was. He couldn't be. She should have saved him. He couldn't have violated her. Adult mind, child mind couldn't combine to make sense of it even sober. She needed to go back to Bushmills. She refused. Daniel was in prison and she was standing by her man. She'd go nowhere.

Camp Adirondack. Minimum-security prison. Two years, a month and two days of counting time. It's Sunday. I drive up early in the morning through the rain to spend the day with Daniel. Valentine's visit. February 18, 1982. Freakish weather for upstate New York. It's been in the sixties all week. Even though it's raining, we're determined to cook barbecued chicken on the open grill outside of the visiting-room. Between rain-showers, we get the fire going again and keep turning the foil-covered chicken.

There aren't many people here this weekend and we have been able to get a small table in a corner of the visiting-room that gives us a little privacy and coziness.

We try to relax.

Daniel glares at the guard. He hates the control they have over him, over us. His eyes move to mine, soften and begin to caress my face as if to commit every curve, every line to memory.

"I wish we weren't here, Genelle. I wish I could really give you all the love I have for you this moment." His eyes are watery and have suddenly gone all pink. It's the way Daniel cries.

"It's all right, honey. I know you love me. And we're going to have a lot of years together once you get out of this place. I just wish you could get into being clean and sober. Patsy, you remember her, she just died from an OD. It really threw me. I don't want anything to happen to you."

"It's not going to, baby. Quit your worrying. Everything is going to be fine. Nothing's going to happen to me. I promise. I got a good feeling about the future."

"Daniel, I've got a great idea. Why don't we give each other a gift right now, a symbolic gift for Valentine's Day?"

"I know what gift I want to give you right now, but these guards wouldn't even let me get started," he says smiling and stroking my face. His kiss is so soft, so gentle, so coaxingly sweet.

"No, honey. I mean something that we could plant in each other's hearts that would grow and grow."

"That's what I'm talking about, Genelle and it's growing right now. Wish you could put your hand down and feel it," he says with a grin.

"Come on, Daniel," I say smiling. "I'm serious. Take a minute and think. If you could give me a symbolic present, something that would be long-lasting, what would it be? Let's give each other something that no guard can take away."

We both sit in silence for a moment. I feel full of love for him as I look into his eyes. They are so clear and bright today. Sparkling.

I pick up an imaginary seed and pray for its fulfilment as I touch the centre of his chest with my hand.

"I plant inside you today the seed of love. May it grow and flourish until all doubt is removed and you are sure and fully filled with the knowledge that you are loved, completely loved." He holds my hand on his chest and presses it against his heart. He gazes in earnest at me and I feel a blush come on my cheeks.

He gently kisses my hand and lays it in my lap. "And what shall I give my lady fair?" He slowly lifts his hand to my heart and strokes my breast-bone lightly as he speaks. "I place in your heart today the seed of trust. I pray that it will grow into a strong tree that fills your whole body. Trust in me, trust in yourself, in love, and in God. As this tree grows strong, I pray that it drives out all fear and gives you peace."

The guards, the prison, the uncomfortable metal chairs and table all melt away for a few moments. I'm with the man I love and he's so beautiful.

Bushmills. First time Genelle saw that name on a liquor bottle she had to have it. She knew it was for her. Since she was a kid, the name Bushmills had meant Oklahoma, home, love, something that was always there waiting for her when she needed to know that she was connected, had some roots, belonged to this earth. She discovered Bushmills whiskey as a college sophomore. She loved its smell, how it tickled her nose with its sweet biting aroma. She loved the color. Lovely amber like the gems harvested on the shores of Lithuania. That warm golden liquid grew familiar to her tongue and turned to pure deal-me-another-hand-quick-this-is-too-good-to-be-true glow in the belly. It was the feeling-fine-on-time elixir in 1962. She kept the square softly contoured half-bottle tucked inside her college-dorm headboard, right next to the chocolate-chip cookies. Best way to study, to read philosophy, to learn biology. Whiskey and cookies. Then take a nice long shot as a nighty-night-tuck-me-in-good way to go to sleep.

Years later, a double-shot of Bushmills had brought back calmness to her shaking body in New Paltz after Mesut had assaulted her again. Will had kept a bottle of the whiskey above the kitchen sink in the house on James Street to help them cope with two kids, frayed nerves, and the need to escape from the incessant monotonous flow of dirty dishes.

Now, the winter of 1984, almost four years without a drink, Genelle sat staring at the familiar golden liquid in the glass Daniel held. It looked so good to her. Daniel was listening to the music the little jazz group was playing in the downtown Albany bar where they sat, but Genelle was locked in a one-way conversation with the whiskey in his hand.

He was out of prison three months now. Genelle had tried

everything she could to get him to stop drinking and stop smoking pot. It was to no avail. He had come to AA meetings with her. They had just been to a meeting together that night. Only thing he had agreed to was to not bring alcohol into her house and to not get high in front of her. She kept telling herself she could handle it. She'd be okay. She wasn't. Tonight the Bushmills was talking to her loud and clear saying "You can't lick him, may as well join him".

She knew it was coming to a showdown. She knew it before she fell down the front steps trying to get him to turn around and not go back down to the bar. She knew it when she was kissing him and tasting the marijuana on his lips and in the juice of his mouth. How she wanted more and more, sucking his tongue, his saliva, his soft fleshy lips. She was wound tight as a top that was ready to spin off the table and go crashing to the floor in bits.

Genelle looked at herself from a place on her own shoulder, next to the monkey that was back and knew if she didn't make a stand she'd be dead in the water.

Daniel left and went down to New York City to live. She wouldn't let him stay with her any more. He was shooting up again. He had to go. They both knew it.

Within a month he was back on methadone, boosting, lying, struggling to stay alive in the Big Apple. Accepted him but let him go. Entrusted him into God's care. She knew she couldn't save him and if she kept trying she'd kill herself in the effort.

She kept on loving him though. Loved him when he showed up to spend the weekend with her and Ismet and he was stoned and staggering. Loved him while she told him he'd have to get right back on the bus and go back down to the City because she couldn't be around him when he was high like that. Loved him when he got into a methadone residential rehab and his liver blew out. He was so weak they put him under quarantine and she couldn't see him. Loved him while she learned to let go of the rage inside her that wanted to blow up every methadone clinic in America. And kept trying to trust. Trying to trust God to somehow bring everything around right.

Daniel got stronger and came out of quarantine. Eventually, Genelle was able to see him. He still had quite a bit of excess fluid on him. He had to get new clothes to fit his altered body. She loved him anyway. She didn't fight with him any more about the methadone.

By the end of the summer he could come upstate for a visit. The following week they went to see his family in Princeton, NJ. He was doing much better, still on the methadone and in treatment but starting to look for work outside of the rehab.

Two weeks after the trip to Princeton Daniel took a drink of beer. It was a brutally hot August day in Manhattan. Some friend on a street corner passed him a cold quart of beer in a brown-paper bag. He took a sip.

Next day he went out of the rehab to look for work and scored some Valium on the street instead. In a few days, he was thrown out of the rehab for shooting up again.

They found him on the bowery a few weeks later, two steps up from the gutter in a tiny room with no window. The ambulance carried him to Mother Cabrini's hospital.

His liver had failed. His kidneys had failed. Thirty-five years old. No hope left.

❖ ❖ ❖ ❖

The hospital is nice and clean. I've brought a shirt down for Daniel that I just finished embroidering for him and a little

267

music-box with an inverted glass top – the kind that if you turn it upside-down and then right-side up snowflakes fall on a little ice-skating figurine inside the dome.

His eyes are closed. His hair looks clean and his face is shaved. They must have bathed him that morning. He looks so peaceful. I don't want to disturb him.

I watch him for a while, then touch his shoulder lightly.

"Daniel?" I say softly.

He opens his eyes slowly as if from a deep dream and smiles at me. "Hi, baby. I'm so glad to see you." His voice is soft and weak. It's an effort for him to speak.

"How are you feeling?" I ask.

"I feel okay, baby. Just so tired. I feel like I could sleep forever."

"Are you in pain?"

"No, honey. And they're not even giving me anything. Can you figure that?" He speaks slowly, faltering a little. "They say my system's flooded, whatever that means. So I'm clean." He gives me that beautiful Adonis smile. "You got your wish, baby. I'm drug-free. Give me a kiss, Genelle. I've missed you so."

I kiss the mouth that I know so well. He barely has the strength to kiss me back. When I lift my head, his eyes are closed again. I watch the IV dripping slowly into his arm. Great sadness wells up. I can't deny it any more. He's dying.

"Daniel, I want to stay here with you. It's too hard being all the way upstate with you down here."

"No. You got to work. You have your son to look after," he says opening his eyes. "The nurses will take good care of me. You'd end up just sitting here watching me sleep. That's all I do. I'm too tired to even watch the TV. No, baby – you just phone me. We'll visit that way. Can you give me a drink of water, my mouth is awful dry."

As he sips the water I show him the shirt I finished for him. He loves it. I help him to open the music-box I had wrapped. He grins from ear to ear as he watches the snow falling inside the glass dome.

"Play it for me, baby."

I wind it up and sit beside him as he dozes off listening to the music. I hold his hand. I'm here and I still can't save him, can't change it. Can't make it all better, no matter how much I love him.

He sleeps for a while. When he reopens his eyes and sees me still there he gives my hand a weak squeeze.

I see Granpaw in his eyes. I see him slipping away and I don't want to let him go. I see water gathering at the outside edges of his eyelids. He struggles to speak again. "More than anything, I want you to be happy, Genelle," he says very softly. He opens his eyes wide and looks at me. "It's funny, baby. I always thought I would love you forever."

I kiss his forehead. "I know, Daniel. I know. It's okay. It's okay, sweetheart. It's okay now, just rest."

✠ ⌘ ✠ ⌘

9:00 PM, December 14, 1985. Genelle sat in an AA meeting in the basement of Sojourner Truth Church in Albany. Upstairs a Gospel choir was giving a concert for the neighborhood. The basement meeting continued while clapping and songs rang out in the background. An old spiritual began to be sung. It was one Genelle loved to play on the piano when she was young *"Swing low, sweet chariot, coming for to carry me home . . . "*

Daniel's father looked at his watch in the hospital room. 9:00 PM. A moment later, Daniel began to cough and gasp and choke. "Dad, help me. I'm hot all over . . . can't seem to get any air . . . "

269

Mr Falcone pushed the button for the nurse and cried out frantically for help, but he didn't leave his son's side. He gathered him up in his arms and held him tightly as he called out again for the nurse.

Blacktime. Dreamtime. Night-time can seem so long. Granpaw's eyes, Daniel's smile, Granpaw's hands, Daniel's eyes. Silhouettes. Shadows. Wake up, startled into crying. Too much dying for one living. Too much losing, wrenching, not knowing and even knowing not able to change it or make it fit. Put the pieces back together. Can't. Something's always missing.

Anxiously, I try to piece together the last nightmarish dream. Bushmills. Sleeping in Granpaw's arms. Wrapping little legs in comfort and safety. Then the hat, head, torso silhouette appears and I writhe in fear, tears choking me awake. But I remember something else. Somewhere else. I'm lying in a bed in a room by myself. It's a big bed for my little body. It's dark in the room but the door is open and there's light in the hallway. I feel safe and warm under the sheet and light coverlet. Must be summertime. Where am I? Doesn't matter cause my little hand brings me home by reaching up under my nightie and finding my fanny. Little fingers, almost four-year-old fingers, resting on my happy place feeling like I'm home and good and safe now to go to sleep even though Granpaw isn't here. Man's silhouette in the doorway. Daddy-come-lately? Must be. Into the room he comes to say "Goodnight, Ellie" and bend down to kiss my forehead. My hand in happy place has no need to move. I feel nice and cozy. Man's voice changes – is cross and nasty.

"What are you doing?" He throws covers off me and grabs my little arm. "Naughty girl. Bad girl. Don't do that. Don't touch yourself there." He hurts my arm, holding it so tightly makes me cry. "Shame on you, Ellie. I catch you doing that again and I'll spank you hard. You keep your hands on top of the covers from now on, hear me!"

Scares me. Trembling. Can't sleep. Can't touch. Can't. Is it real or another bad dream? Some day I'll go back there and find out. Some day. I try to shake the images off. Waiting for the night to pass. Tomorrow is Daniel's funeral. Try to sleep tonight.

Nothing to knock me out. No drink to numb the feelings. No pill to get rid of these nightmares. Stone-cold sober all night to think about Daniel. My life. The pain. The confusion. To remember.

"You're so beautiful to me, baby. So sexy. I love it when you put on make-up for me and wear those sexy clothes."

"But I feel like a whore, Daniel, wearing this short skirt and eye make-up."

"You could never be a whore, Genelle. You're not made that way. Being a whore doesn't have to do with what you wear or how you look. It's about how you look at the world. It's an inside job. A whore is being on the take in life. That's not you, baby. You give. You give from the heart. You love."

Closed coffin. Daniel's family want it that way. I have to see him. I tell his father, "You can't put him in the ground without me seeing him one more time". I won't be shut out. This isn't Bushmills and I'm not five-and-a-half. Special arrangements at the funeral parlor. The undertaker will open the coffin for me two hours before the funeral. Just for me. Doors will be locked and I will be alone with Daniel to say my goodbyes.

He looks so peaceful. He's wearing the shirt I embroidered for him. His hair looks so beautiful. Dark chestnut-brown with a trace of silver just starting to show at the temples. I stroke his fine soft hair as I have done so many times. I love his high forehead.

Little Ellie tried to climb inside and lay down one more time with Granpaw. I know I can't. I'm big enough to know better now. I just stand beside the coffin and talk to Daniel. Stroke his forehead, touch his beautiful hands as they lay folded over his chest. I bend to kiss his forehead and think I see his eyelashes flutter. I wait for those soft fawn-colored eyes to open. They don't. I don't sob or weep at all. I just love and feel the throbbing ache of my heart. I don't cry until the undertaker leads me insistently out of the room. "Others will be arriving soon. We have to close the coffin. The family's orders. They must have told you. Sorry."

Sorry. "Sorry" echoing down empty corridors of nobody-cares methadone clinics, prisons, jails. "Sorry." I never got to say it. Let it go. Too much letting go. Too much to ask.

✠ ✿ ♰ ❈

Doreen wiped the red Oklahoma dust off the decorative dishes hanging on the wall in the parlour. Mementos of the different States she'd lived in. Widowed now and back in Bushmills, back in the family's house. Mother, father, and sister Winona dead and buried. Clinton lived in Oklahoma City. Was a big-time businessman who never came home. Rather forget his roots. Brother Dirk still lived on the outskirts of Bushmills. Farmed a bit. Tinkered some. His wife had run off with the fellow who brought around the Sears & Roebuck catelogues and sold vacuum cleaners.

Doreen was comfortable back in Bushmills. Retired. Settled in among old photos, furniture and memorabilia resulting from almost a century of her family's southwest prairie living. She was glad Genelle was coming home to help her after she came out of the hospital. She was doing some last-minute tidying before she went in for the operation. Hip-replacement surgery was sure to slow her down for a while. Her children had children of their own and were scattered too far and were too successful in their careers to take much time out to be nursemaids. Genelle was on her own now and living somewhere in upstate New York. Farm country, she said. Doreen didn't know New York had any of that, but Genelle swore there were cows and plenty of fields of corn there. Ismet was away at college and Lela was married and still not speaking to her mother. Doreen had been trying to get Genelle back to Bushmills for years, but she just wouldn't come for a visit. Now, there was a reason she couldn't refuse. She'd take her vacation time from work and come out west for two weeks after Doreen got home from the hospital. After that, Doreen should be getting around good enough for the neighbors and Dirk to take over.

It was three years since Daniel had passed on. Genelle felt the jolt of the plane's tires touching down on the tarmac. Oklahoma City Airport. People would be talking funny. They'd have that twang that made everything sound like a Hank Williams song. Genelle hated country-western music – its sloppy sentimentality and red-neck views. And here she was out in America's heartland where those songs originated and where people drove around pickup trucks with full gun-racks, rifles loaded and ready to shoot at anything that was wild or had hair that was too long.

She was putting the luggage on her little portable trolley when a suntanned arm reached around her shoulders from behind her and held her for a tense moment in a vice-like grip. She turned around in shock, only to see Uncle Dirk grinning at her.

"Surprise," he said.

"You startled me! I wasn't expecting to see you! Thought I was supposed to take a bus out of here and phone you from Laughton."

"Couldn't let you do that. Not my little Ellie."

"I'm hardly little any more. I'm about as tall as you these days, Uncle Dirk. Do you think you could call me Genelle while I'm here? That's what everyone calls me now."

"Come on now, we'll get you home in no time. You sure are a sight for sore eyes."

"You know my kids still remember going out to feed the cattle with you . . . "

Dirk had borrowed Doreen's air-conditioned car. The trip from the airport was smooth and cool. Genelle stared at the flat open country. She felt mesmerized. Great flocks of small black birds swarmed up and around in the sky like dark confetti with a mind of its own. They landed on a stretch of telephone wire looking like hundreds of clothes-pegs left on a drying line. Then swirling across the horizon came another flock that settled down in a maize field like pepper shaken out on the corn. Genelle had forgotten how wide open spaces felt. No hills to break the horizon, just scrub brush and flat land that went on forever. They drove in silence. Fields of full-grown love-grass waved in the breeze like a young girl's hair flowing back from her face as she ran to meet her beau. Genelle had forgotten how much she loved this part of the world.

"Have to stop in town and get some five-gallon jugs filled up with filtered water over at the police station," her uncle said as they entered the town of Bushmills. "Don't know if Doreen told you that our water has gone bad. They say it's the run-off from over-fertilizing year after year and too many cattle. But I think it's from all them pigs out the south side of town. Some big outfit's come in and is raising hogs over there. Smells something awful if the wind comes up from the south and blows cross town. Water went bad the year after they started up that business."

274

The police barracks was the gas-station-cum-convenience-store that had one back room where a fat middle-aged man in a gray uniform sat with his feet up on a metal desk smoking a cigarette and talking on the phone. He looked mighty tired. His police car was parked out the back of the convenience store. He pointed to the closet where the water-filtration system was housed when he saw Genelle and Dirk come in with the jugs, and just kept talking on the phone. Didn't sound like police business. Something about what movie did Pearl Anne want to see that night.

Doreen was thrilled to see Genelle. She gave her a big hug, then filled her in on the surgery and her recuperation so far. Her spirits were high. The visiting nurse was set up to come in once a day to see how she was getting on. Doreen was in her early seventies with plenty of vim and vigor left in her. She was anxious to get caught up on all the latest in her niece's life.

Genelle settled into the extra bedroom. There were old photos on the wall of the room she was sleeping in. Pictures much older than the ones she remembered on the wall of her Grandmother's basement apartment on the Mainline. Pictures of her grandfather when he was young and of his brother Caleb and his father. The Butler boys both had startlingly beautiful blue eyes. She could see from the old photos where they got them from. Jason Butler's eyes had a dangerous sparkle in them. They were pale as glass with a dark edge around the outside of the iris. But Genelle couldn't stop staring at her grandfather's photo. How handsome he was with all that black hair!

Then the hats caught her attention. In photo after photo there were men in all sorts of hats. Stetsons, Bowlers, straw ones, felt ones, Lone Stars, Brushpoppers, even Fedoras. As many different hats as there were different kinds of moustaches.

Her grandfather's photo drew her back every time. She wanted to climb inside it to try and know the man behind those eyes.

Genelle cooked the meals, got the groceries and water, did the laundry and kept her aunt company. While Doreen napped, Genelle would take long walks around the town. Memories came back. Fuzzy but almost retrievable. But the images in her mind didn't seem to fit the geography she was walking through. In her images she was seeing trees and a barn. Cows staring out from behind scrub-bushes like giants hiding in the shadows, quiet and still, only their ears moving. Puzzled, she asked her aunt about the images.

"Oh, you're probably thinking of the summer place outside of town. The ole homestead. Yes. That would have been where you were when you were a baby. Outside of town. That's where the original 160 acres were claimed by your granpaw. Well, he just got part of that when he married Mama. Dirk still works that land. I'll ask him to take you out there next week and show you around. I don't want you to take my car when you go out to the west place. It'll get all muddy and the road is kind of rough out there. Dirk can take you in his ole pickup truck," she said, changing the channel on the television with the remote control.

Genelle and her aunt watched the weather station together in silence. Tornado warnings covered half the state. Severe thunderstorms and hail from the Panhandle all the way over to Tulsa. Genelle slept with the window and door open in case the big one hit during the night. Why would anyone want to live here all their life she wondered? In less than a week she would return to the safety of her little home in the Catskill mountains of New York State where you could drink the water and you knew when you went to sleep at night your house wouldn't be torn up or moved into a pasture two miles away by morning.

✥ ✤ ✥ ✤

It's late afternoon when I climb into my Uncle Dirk's pickup truck.
He grins and gives the brim of his baseball cap a tug. We head out
of town. When we turn off onto a dirt road just west of Bushmills
he chuckles and speaks for the first time. "Shucks, I forgot to
pick up a six-pack of Black Label. You like that, don't you?"

"I don't drink any more, Uncle Dirk. I haven't had a drink
for over seven years now."

"Oh, one little-ole beer wouldn't hurt you. We could have
some fun on the way out to the ole place. Party. We could
have partied. That's what you call it, don'tcha?"

I feel uncomfortable and a bit edgy. I look out of the truck
window at the metal monster in somebody's maize field. Snap a
photo of it. The road is real muddy with deep tire-ruts from
tractors and pickups making their way back and forth since the
heavy rains last week. We travel on in silence. No houses, no
barns. Dirt roads criss-crossing each other seem to go nowhere.
I'm excited and a bit nervous at the same time. Uncle Dirk takes
his weatherworn leathery-looking hand off the gear-shift and
raises it up high as the dash-board and lets it hang suspended
for a dramatic moment and then brings it down on my left
thigh. He gives my leg a squeeze, holding it for a moment. I'm
real uncomfortable now. I cast an uneasy look at him and his
eyes are fixed on the road ahead. He lifts his hand up off my leg
now and places it back on the gear-shift. I'm confused. What's
going on here? Lean and lanky like Granpaw, Uncle Dirk is
silent like him too. Don't know what he's thinking.

Trees appear around a curve. Not just one or two but a
stand of trees. "We're coming to the ole place now. Charlie
Tucker's farming a bit of it and living out there so you can't go
into the old house. But I'm sure he won't mind if you take a

look around. Take some photos if you want. I got to talk to him about a few things anyway. Then we'll go out the west eighty where I've got my cattle and grow my alfalfa."

He introduces me to Charlie, an old bachelor, and they start talking. Charlie is chewing on tobacco and spitting. I take my camera and walk around the house.

Yes. There's the hand-pump. Still there. I look in through one of the windows and see the old wallpaper peeling off the walls. A shudder goes through me as I see the screened-in back porch. The room inside looks so small. There's a dry sink in it. I don't remember that. The floor is sloped steeply toward the back of the porch. Was it always like that?

I see the barn out beyond a clump of cottonwood trees. Instinctively I move towards it. Almost want to run. Maybe. Maybe . . . of course not. Granpaw's not baling hay. Grandpaw's gone.

I go to the open barn door. Familiar smell. It's dark inside. I step a few feet into it. I freeze. Terror grips me. Something's wrong. Someone's in here. I'm scared something's going to hurt me. I turn and rush out into the sunlight. I see Uncle Dirk and Charlie by the truck. They wave to me. I'm feeling real uneasy. I want to leave. I go to the truck, climb up inside and wait for them to finish talking. I snap a picture of the barn from the truck, and take one of the old house too. It looks different than I remember it. Different but familiar.

As we go back down the clay road that's just a truck-width wide, Uncle Dirk points out the field to the left of us.

"That's my alfalfa field. Good crop this year."

We turn again. Travel a mile or so further into the back country. Wooded area. Come to a gate. It's a swinging metal farm gate but I can see the chain and lock from the truck.

"We'll leave the pickup here and walk on the rest of the way," Uncle Dirk says as he finds the key for the padlock.

I walk along the side of the truck and look at the meadow to the right. Lots of young trees in it. A flash of color surrounds me. Orange, fluttering orange, swirling around me. Monarchs. A swarm of monarch butterflies land on the pokeweed and scrub-brush in front of me. I've never seen so many butterflies in one place. I bend to look more closely and one lands on the back of my right hand. It moves its wings ever so slowly. I hold my breath, not wanting to stir the air in the slightest. I see its fine antennae moving tentatively. So gentle. So vulnerable. Waiting. Then it flutters away to join the others in the brush. Some are even around the puddle of red muddy water to the right of my foot. I look up. Uncle's standing with a hand on his hip, waiting.

"Well, anytime now, Miss Genelle, would be fine."

I laugh and ask him about the butterflies. He locks the gate behind us. Why?

"You'd be surprised. Even with my pickup parked there, people could steer some cattle in here and they'd disappear into the woods and be grazing and I'd never even know it. Got to keep it locked."

I don't understand what he's talking about.

We walk a little ways on in silence. The ground has become white and sandy. He puts his arm around me. Big hand grasping my shoulder tightly, then he moves his hand down to my waist. I pull away. I don't know this man. The only memory I even have of this man is when he picked me up at the airport with his wife when I was eighteen and I came out to meet my family at Grammaw's.

I'm starting to feel scared. I don't even know where we are going. Something stirs in the trees and startles me. I peek through the foliage and see the outline of a few steers. I jump. He laughs.

279

"They're all over here. They won't hurt you none. Let's cut across to the left there up through those tamaracks."

"Are there rattlesnakes out here?"

"Oh, maybe. Better stick close to me so you don't get bit."

I turn my face to look at him and he's wearing a big grin. I don't know if he's teasing me or telling the truth. He's sticks out his left hand towards me to grab my hand. I don't respond. I don't want to touch him. I pick up my pace.

"Knew I should've brought a blanket with me and some beer," he says as he walks behind me. I feel fear surge through me. I'm far away from people out here. If I scream probably nobody would even hear me. In that moment I make up my mind. If he lays a hand on me I'll kick him in the balls. I don't care if he is my uncle or not. I don't care. I don't want him touching me. I don't. I'll kick him as hard as I can and run. I can climb over that fence. I can find my way back to it. And I will.

The path opens up into a barren area, a small plateau. It's surrounded by woods. I never knew there were so many trees anywhere near Bushmills.

"This is where I feed the cattle," he says. "I come in with the pickup with big bales of hay on the back and just honk the truck's horn to call 'em. We took the short-cut up the path. I drive the truck in from beyond that ridge over there."

I feel very vulnerable. I keep questioning myself. Why am I feeling so afraid?

Uncle Dirk takes off his cap and mops his forehead and neck, then looks at me intently. He's bald like Granpaw, but he doesn't have Granpaw's eyes. He takes his glasses off and sticks them in his pocket and licks his lips. He stares at me. Then turns his head still looking at me out of the corner of his eye.

"Nobody else around 'ceptin' you and me, is there?"

I don't answer.

He turns towards me. He takes a step closer to me. Then another. He's close enough to grab a hold of me.

God help him if he does.

He looks at me. "Nobody even knows where we are for sure," he says.

A cold shiver goes down my spine but I don't move. I stand still. There's a quiet "No" happening deep inside of me. It's in my belly and it's solid like the "No" that I said the last time Mesut came towards me to strike me. Even though we were divorced it hadn't mattered to him. He still came at me to beat me again. As he crossed the floor and I could see the blow coming I didn't move. I stood stock still.

"No. You can't do that to me any more, Mesut," I said with conviction in my eyes. The truth of it couldn't be mistaken and he stopped midway across the room. Never hit me.

Uncle Dirk scans the treeline.

I don't open my mouth. I'm trembling. I don't know what's going on here.

He steps back. Rubs his hands on the sides of his jeans. Are they sweaty or dirty? He looks at me and laughs a bit nervously, then turns and heads back for the gate.

"What you need is a few beers. You're bound up tight as a drum."

I don't talk the whole way into town.

When he drops me at Aunt Doreen's house, he says "I was just kiddin' you 'bout the beers. I don't even drink myself. I was just jokin'."

Inside I'm still trembling. What has just happened? Is it the place? Is it that he looks like Granpaw?

"Was Uncle Dirk around when I was living in Bushmills as a little girl?" I ask my aunt over our meal that night.

"Oh, sure. He used to help your granpaw out on the farm up until he married."

"Did he always wear that baseball cap?"

"Dirk always had a hat on. He balded early like your Granpaw. No, it's only in the last fifteen years he's taken to those baseball caps. Used to wear a straw hat or felt one like Daddy."

"Daddy?"

"Like your granpaw."

Sleeping dream. Waking nightmare. I keep stepping into the barn. I'm so little. I have to piddle. I'm looking into the cool darkness. Thin shafts of light through the rafters. I've been napping. Woke up wanting Granpaw. Nobody in the house. Go to the barn.

"Granpaw?" Silence. "Granpaw?"

Turn to go. Something rustles. I spin around.

"BOO!"

I jump. Wet my panties a little. A figure jumps in front of me laughing.

I'm grumpy. "Got to piddle."

"Make a puddle, like me," he says going out in the sunshine. "Watch this, little missie."

He takes a piddle on the ground. Splashing yellow puddle forms.

"You can do it too. Take off your panties and squat down and make a puddle. We won't tell. It'll be our little secret."

Panties off. I lift my summer frock up under my little arms and bend my legs like he shows me, squatting. My piddle's warm and runs between my feet. I giggle and look up. The bright sun shines in my eyes over his right shoulder. Blinding. I see hat against sky. I slip backwards onto my bum, my back. Lying down. Squinting at the sunlight in my eyes . . . everything is spinning round like a pinwheel in a fresh wind,

282

colors blurring, whirring. Who is he? Whose hat? Whose hand? What finger? Which man?

None of this is true. Can't be true. Too little. Too old. Too big. I can never know. Never know. Must all be lies. But where'd the silhouette in my mind come from? Why the dream? Why the terror yesterday in the pokeweeds and the crib pasture? I don't know. Can never know. Won't ever ask the one who remains. Too terrifying to tell the truth from a lie. Why does it matter? What's the difference? What's done is done.

Staring. Sweating. Silently screaming into the pillow not to wake Aunt Doreen. Pummelling the bed with my fists, bed next to the wall hung with old photos of men in hats. On my knees I tear at the sheets. I want it to be over. Sitting on the floor watching the dawn's light illumine the curtains. Sitting there on the floor under the gaze of the Butler men's eyes, I grab my pillow and hold it to my belly. Rocking. Rocking. Feed the baby. Nurse the baby. Don't leave her. Don't abandon her. Don't leave her with these men. Aunt stirs in her bedroom. Bedside lamp goes on.

"You all right, Aunt Doreen?" I call out to her room across the hall.

"Yes, I'm fine. Just fine."

Dry wind billows the curtains for a moment. Old wooden screen-door in the kitchen *rat-tat-taps* to the sudden gusts of hot air.

"Fraid it's gonna be another scorcher today, Ellie."

Silence.

"Ellie? Do you hear me, Ellie?"

Stop dancing with the ghosts, Genelle. Stop trying to make all the pieces fit. Just answer her.

Go on, Genelle. Just answer.

Epilogue

" . . . When I was a child, I spoke as a child, I understood as a child, I thought as a child; but when I grew up, I put away childish things. For now we see in a mirror, dimly, but then face to face. Now I know in part, but then I shall know just as I also am known . . . "

Promises.

" . . . You will intuitively know how to handle things that used to baffle you. Fear of people . . . will leave you. You will not regret the past or wish to close the door on it . . . "

Memories fly skywards like balloons filled with helium.

"Trust, baby. Just trust."

Bright-green moss grows on a dead tree-stump.

" . . . And now abide faith, hope and love, these three; but the greatest of these is . . . "

. . . Eenie, meanie, minie, mo. Catch a tiger by the toe. If he hollers let him go. Eenie, meanie, minie, mo. My mother told me to pick the very best one and the very best one is . . .